HEART'S PREY

NATALINA REIS

To all—men and women, young and old—who stand up to bigotry
and prejudice. You're my heroes.
Never give up hope!

Chapter One

OUTBREAK

Jia

The growling still rang in her ears. Low. Ominous. Terrifying. Giant fangs covered in blood so close to her, she could smell it. Fast! She must move fast and quietly. Away from the beasts. Far from the carnage and the stench of death.

The streets were empty, but she didn't dare stop. With the sun low on the horizon and the faded stars beginning to dot the darkening skies, the sense of urgency grew deeper in her soul. Jia needed to find shelter. Quick. Like a faulty faucet, her knees dripped blood into the cracked asphalt, breadcrumb-like drops for the predators. Those damned rocks, blades slashing against her exposed skin and flesh as she crawled and climbed her way out of the basin where the city was built.

Don't think about it. Move on. Don't look back.

She couldn't allow thoughts of those left behind to invade her mind. There was nothing she could have done for them, and only fools cry over what cannot be undone. She scanned the length of the deserted street, out of breath and dizzy. It was getting increasingly harder to walk. She had lost her shoes somewhere along the way, and her knees burned and buckled with every step. At this rate she wouldn't last much longer.

On the edge of her vision, far too distant to discern details, she saw the promise of a shelter. Her pace quickening, Jia limped her way toward it, her heavy gas mask slamming against her left leg too loud for her own liking. This time of the day anything could attract them, even the faint sound of metal clanking against flesh.

Her sight blurring slightly, she stumbled, and her right knee hit the hard road. Like a coiled spring, she bounced to her feet, ignoring the blood that ran even more profusely down her leg. She needed to hide.

Darkness had fallen by the time she reached it. Her eyes and her keen senses had not deceived her. This would be a good hiding place for the night. The heavy concrete door led her to a crumbling staircase, spiraling steeply down into a dank basement and another door. The door was heavy, and after she had forced it open, it wouldn't close behind her. She leaned her whole body weight against it until the concrete slab grudgingly moved. With a sigh of relief, she heard the telling click of the lock fastening, and she finally allowed herself to slide all the way to the floor and sit. The dim emergency lights lining the bottom and the top of every wall lent the space an almost spooky aura.

This is a good place.

Not only was the room deep in the ground, protected by the two heavy doors, but it smelled of sewage and mold, two odors the Predators stayed away from at all costs. She was more than willing to sleep in muck if it would keep her safe from them.

She hardly recognized her own legs, stretched in front of her; the skin on her knees and shins had long been scraped off to reveal a mess of blood and torn flesh underneath. Now that she was not in immediate danger, the sharp burning pain intensified in a crescendo that demanded her attention. She was going to have to do something about it or the wounds would end up septic like everything around her in that bunker. She scanned the room in search of something she could use to clean the wounds.

Whatever had possessed her that morning to wear her uniform skirt to work? There had been rumors of attacks in other cities around the world. Mysterious massacres that no one seemed to be able to explain or confirm. Central was adamant that the stories were fictional, rebellious propaganda, but the populace was wary. People had been whispering around corners and at home in the evenings. Still, pressured by the ever-growing fears, Central decided to prepare its people. Children and adults were trained to expect an attack and to survive it. She was no exception. Except for the idiotic idea of wearing a totally impractical outfit to work that day.

Stupid. So stupid.

Impressing her work mates did not seem so important now, sitting on a dirty floor, bleeding to a possible death. At least, she had packed her required gas mask and gun. The food and water she had carried had been left behind in the panic that followed the attack in the city basin. Her choice had been painfully clear—leave her things behind or die along with everybody else.

A tear surprised her as it rolled down her cheek. She licked it and took a morbid pleasure in its saltiness, knowing she had nothing to quench her thirst. Summoning strength long depleted, Jia got up on her feet, cringing as the pain dug deeper into her body and soul. She walked gingerly around the massive bunker, trying to ignore the reek of waste, the stink of rot. There was not much to be seen: piles of ubiquitous metal containers mostly empty and lying on their sides, a broken chair in a corner, some unidentifiable shapeless objects lying in a puddle of something viscous.

Her eyes darted to the left as she spied movement from the corner of her eye.

She pulled the gun out, tucked in the waistband of her short skirt, a sudden flash of metal in the dimness of the room. "Who's there?" Her voice sounded stronger than she felt. Inside, her body was raked by tremors both from fear and weakness. With the gun pointed in front of her, elbows solidly braced on her sides, Jia advanced cautiously toward the corner where she had seen a ghost of a movement. "Get out now while you have a chance," she yelled, arms steadier than her insides. "I won't hesitate to shoot."

It wasn't a Predator, that much she knew. The pungent smell would not allow the creatures to set foot in the bunker. But there were other dangers out there, and she was not about to take any risks. After a few seconds, a slim shadow emerged from behind a pile of metal barrels stacked up ten feet high. It was human. Both her eyes and her senses told her that, even though in the semi-darkness it was hard to tell what species. Not all species of humans were friendly, she'd been taught.

"Who are you?" she asked, shaking the gun at the figure.

The human, hands raised in surrender, walked into the light. Her breath caught in her throat as she met the telltale azure of his eyes. A *Zuiver*. Her surprise quickly turned into fascination. She had never seen one. They were creatures of legend that lived mostly in self-contained communes out in remote areas. Stretching way above six feet, the *Zuiver* tilted his head slightly and locked eyes with her. Jia stumbled back as the stranger's powerful glance hit her with all its strength, the blue of his irises made ever so more intense by the wide black stripe that crossed his face from one side to the other, covering his eyes like a mask.

"My name is Cees." A low, melodic voice escaped his lips. "I won't harm you. I'm not armed."

"I don't believe you," she yelled back at him. Everybody was armed. Under the pressure of the local governments, Central had made sure that every human had at least a chance to defend themselves from attacks. A gun and a gas mask were distributed far and wide to adults and children alike.

"I'm a *Zuiver*," he explained unnecessarily. "We're not allowed to carry weapons."

He was telling the truth; she remembered it now. The blue-eyed *Zuivers* were believed to be a sub-human species and have some kind of powers. People, with their fears and superstitions, had immediately assumed that, given the chance and the right weaponry, the *Zuiver* population would rise against all other humans and destroy them. Weapons were outlawed for them, even as everyone on Earth was fighting for their lives.

"Please, put the gun down," he asked, his hands coming to hover in front of him. "I won't hurt you."

Jia was not about to back down. "What are you doing here?"

"The same as you, I'm sure," he replied. "Survival. I found this place two days ago after I fled my commune. We were attacked during the night. I fear there were not many survivors."

"I thought you had special powers." She waved the gun at him.

"Myths," he said simply. "We have no more powers than you. Please, put that gun down."

Hesitantly, she complied. He didn't seem too dangerous. He was tall and broad-shouldered, but she had a gun. She could take him down if needed.

"I have water." He pointed behind him. "Would you like some?"

Jia was very thirsty, but still not sure about the wisdom of sharing anything with a *Zuiver*. "I'm Jia. My city was attacked last night. I managed to escape."

His piercing eyes scanned her body and came to rest on her legs. "You're hurt. Come. I will clean your wound before it gets septic." He stretched his hand toward her invitingly. She hesitated. "If the Predators don't find you, that wound will surely kill you."

Exhausted, she decided to put her fears aside, at least for now, and trust the stranger. He guided her into a corner, a wide spot on the floor where all the sewage and dirt had been wiped away. A backpack was leaning on the wall and a blanket stretched out on the floor. Jia sat on it, her back against the wall, her legs clumsily stretched in front of her. Once again, she cursed herself for the bad choice of clothing and wished she had something more sensible to change into.

"I have a change of clothes," he offered as if reading her mind. Cees was busy taking some items from the backpack. She recognized a roll of gauze and a bottle of something she guessed was a disinfectant of sorts. "My people had to become self-sufficient. We learned how to make medicine off what nature offers."

Knees on the blanket beside her, he ministered to her wounds with surprisingly expert care. She flinched from his touch at first, still wary about being touched by a *Zuiver*, but exhaustion and a relentless urge to let go won over her doubts. By the time he was finished, the wound, though still angry, was not bleeding or hurting as much as before. "Normally I would leave it uncovered, but there is a lot of airborne bacteria in this room." He gently put a big piece of gauze on each of her knees and held them there for a few seconds. Then, he ripped off a long piece of his own shirt and tied it around the gauze to hold it in place.

"Thank you." She touched the bandage with the tips of her fingers. "I'm sorry I mistrusted you."

"I don't blame you." He offered her water to drink. "These are trying times for all of us. It's hard to know who to trust. We might as well rest for the night."

Jia went behind a container and changed into the pair of soft, loose jeans the *Zuiver* had offered her. They were way too big for her, so she rolled the hems several times and threaded her own belt through the waist loops to keep them from sliding down her narrow hips. Less than a day before, she wouldn't have been caught dead wearing that get-up, but now she was grateful she had something warmer and more protective to wear.

With a sigh of relief, she joined Cees on the blanket. The floor was cold and hard, but the blanket offered some measure of warmth and comfort. She curled up on her side with her back to the generous stranger and closed her eyes, willing herself to sleep. But as soon as slumber threatened to take her, the images of the slaughter she had witnessed came out to haunt her—men, women and children herded like animals for the kill, bodies collecting in every corner of every street as she ran aimlessly, only one thought in her head. Survival. Even if those caught in the carnage that followed the attack included her neighbors, her friends.

A sob escaped her lips. Cees, still alert, must have heard it. "I know it hurts like hell," he whispered just behind her.

"How do you know what I'm thinking?" she asked, embarrassed to be caught in a moment of weakness. Her mother had taught her to always be tough. "Can you read my mind or something?" Maybe *Zuivers* did have strange powers after all.

"You made the same kind of noise I've made before falling asleep for the past few days." His voice was soothing despite of her irritation. "I recognize the pain and desperation in it."

He reached out for her and tried to draw her into a warm embrace, but she shrugged his hands away. Jia felt rather than saw him back up a little and settle on the blanket behind her, close but not touching.

"You're not alone, *liefje*." His whisper reached her ears like a caress. Her instincts told her to push him further away while her need for human contact begged her to trust him. "Sweetheart," he had whispered. "You are not alone anymore."

Chapter Two

BEFORE

Lieven

Hell hath no fury like a woman scorned... or a pissed off artist. Lieven ducked ever so slightly under the icy glare of his friend and dropped the rags to the floor.

"Shit, Liev." The dark haired young man waved his right hand and splashed the area around him with big globs of blue paint. "I told you to take those rags out of here before they stained the canvas. And now look at it!"

Lieven chanced a quick glance at the canvas. He honestly couldn't see anything out of the ordinary. With his non-artistic eyes, all he could see was an expanse of whiteness.

"It's stained. Big areas of pinkish hue." Lieven still couldn't see anything but white. "I will have to either throw the canvas away or prep it again."

"I'm sorry, Cees," the young man said, bending down to retrieve the offensive rags. He had forgotten to remove them from the top of the canvas as it rested for the night. The instructions had been, hang the canvas on the easel and wash the rags for reuse. Lieven was not always very good at following directions. Especially around his best friend, Cees, who blinded him with his dark looks and amazing talent. "I just forgot, but I can't see the stain. I really can't."

Cees brushed a hand over his face and sighed. "For all that is sacred, Liev. How can you say that? It's obviously ruined."

Another quick glance showed him the exact same thing he had already seen—whiteness. As he was opening his mouth to tell Cees just that, he thought better of it. "Should I go get the gesso?" he asked, knowing all too well that would be the best way to appease his irate friend. "I will help you prep." He may not be an artist, but he knew how to prep a canvas.

As quickly as his anger had surfaced, it went away. A smile spread across Cees's lips, wrinkling the corners of his blue eyes. "Sorry Liev, I shouldn't have yelled at you. Not a big deal. Sure, get rid of those rags and come help me with the gesso."

Lieven cherished the time they spent together. It didn't matter what they were doing, as long as they were doing it together. They had been friends since they were ankle biters, running around the village and the woods that surrounded it, playing hide-and-seek or getting themselves in trouble with some of the Elders. As they grew, it was obvious they had very different interests. Cees was the artist, always buried ankle-deep in some kind of art project while Lieven was the more athletic, albeit accident-prone, of the two. By the time they were out of school, in their late teens, Lieven had been noticed by the Elders and hand-picked for military training.

Different or not, they were still best friends now that their teen years were a thing of the past and they had entered the adult world. Theirs was a friendship that ran deeper than most. Especially where Lieven was concerned.

The canvas didn't take too long to prep—considering the so-called stains were invisible to anyone's eyes but Cees'. By the time they were finished, the canvas was back to its immaculate, pristine whiteness, and his friend was happy.

"Are you staying while I paint?" Cees asked him while mixing up the cool blue oils with a tad of turpentine to thin it. The strong odor of the solvent assailed Lieven's nostrils and he sneezed, prompting a familiar chuckle from his friend. "Sorry. I don't even notice it any more."

Lieven looked up at him, beginning to collect the rags again. "I got to go. I have a drill in a couple hours and I have to get ready."

"Where is it this time?" His fingers worked fast and methodically, mixing up the paints in the palette.

"Not sure," Lieven said, admiring his friend from a distance, his focus already into the act of creating his art. "Something about attacks up north and that we must be ready. I heard rumors they are taking us to the border today."

That caught his friend's attention. Cees' head snapped up to look at him. "The border? That's a first."

"Yeah, something is really worrying them, and they want to secure the perimeter of our commune." Lieven combed his unruly long hair with his fingers. "The *Zuivers* cannot be too careful," he said, echoing what his trainers had always told him.

"Well, be careful and do your soldiering thing," Cees said, laughing softly at his own joke. "And come back in one piece!"

Lieven waved and turned to go. As he passed the mirror by the door, he caught a glimpse of his friend pulling his shirt over his head. Lieven sighed. Cees might be an artist, but he had the body of a warrior, tall with a strong chest and shoulders, the scars of his childhood still stretching over his back like the branches of a ghostly tree. The bitter taste of regret soured his mouth. He often wished things were different—that the world was a different place.

With a last glance in the mirror, Lieven left to go join his squad.

Cees

The beautiful blue of the oils covered most of the canvas now. He had been working at it since dawn. For most, it didn't look like he had accomplished much, but to his expert eye, he had finally reached near perfection.

Cees took a step back from the easel to have another look. Yes, it was just right. He had caught what he imagined to be the essence of the oceans in that square of white. Happy with the result, he dunked the brushes in the cleaning pot, wiped his hands on a towel and slipped his shirt on. It was warm today. A little too warm. Beads of sweat gathered across his forehead and neck. Maybe he could go for a bath in the public house, but he didn't feel like enduring the looks of disapproval from the other patrons. Too bad he did not have the luxury of a bath at home. Then again, orphans like him were lucky to have a roof over their heads and food to eat. All things considered, he hadn't done too bad in life. He had a nice home, a good job that provided him with enough money to eat well and frequently. And he had the best friend a man could ever ask for. Yes, he had been very fortunate indeed.

Maybe he would just go for a swim in the lake. At this time of the day, with the soldiers gone, there wouldn't be too many people there. The children were still in school and everyone else at their jobs. It was the perfect time to enjoy a bit of solitude. Cees was not like most males in town. Though he enjoyed company as much as anybody else, a little alone time was always welcomed. Lieven seemed to always crave company—which, of course, he got easily. With his blond good looks, he had a semi-permanent entourage of marriage-age girls that followed him everywhere he went. Cees, on the other hand, didn't welcome any advances from the rare women who had tried to approach him. Being a Tainted One did not endear him to many women. He didn't care. It was not that he didn't like female companionship. If he was being honest with himself, he not only enjoyed it but craved it often. His childhood, though, had not made him too receptive to love or affection. It was hard for him to trust people, to allow himself to be vulnerable with anyone. Except with Lieven. He was more than a friend. For all intents and purposes, except blood-ties, Lieven was his brother.

Cees walked the short distance to the lake at a fast pace. Happy to see there was no one there, he quickly stripped off his clothes and dove into the cool water. A pleasant shiver went through him as his warm body met the chill of the water, and he allowed himself to stay under the liquid shelter a little while longer. When his lungs started burning from the lack of oxygen, he pumped his feet and broke the surface with a big splash.

After a few laps around the small lake, he felt refreshed and ready to go to his job at the community cantina. Not bothering to dry off, he slipped his clothes on, shook the strands of his hair like a wet dog, and began the short walk to work.

His job at the cantina was not ideal. It was boring and lacked any opportunity for creativity, but it paid the rent. The best part about it was it gave him time to focus on his true passion—painting. Everybody knew who he was but nobody *really* knew him at all.

As usual, the morning moved sluggishly by, one customer at a time. Cees often blacked out at work. It was as if he became an automaton, all mechanics and no brain. His mind was occupied elsewhere. By the time his shift ended, he normally couldn't remember what he had done for the past four hours. Today, the ocean-blue canvas called him. His mind kept wandering off to swim in the painted waves, to lose himself in its sea of calm. To be somewhere else. Maybe even be someone else.

Being the only one with no family, he had been quickly put in charge of closing. After everybody left to join those they loved, he always stayed behind cleaning, turning off lights, making sure the ovens were off, the food refrigerated and the doors locked. But today, he was covering the earlier shift of a co-worker who had fallen ill. Instead of closing, his shift was done before four. He packed his backpack with the usual fare. One of the perks of this job was the ability to take leftover foods home. He always packed extra so he could feed the stray cats and dogs that roamed the neighborhood at night. As he packed, he realized he still had a spare set of clothing in his bag. He had packed it a couple of days before when he spent the weekend at Lieven's house. He hadn't spent much time there since he got his own place, and his friend had insisted. Cees was glad he did. For once, it was nice to have the company of someone he loved, and who truly cared for him.

He lived in an isolated part of town, not far from the *cantina*. While the rest of the population followed the streets that led them to the heart of the village, he went the opposite way. His social status hadn't allowed him a more central location, so he lived in semi-isolation in the woods that edged the town. He didn't mind. His artistic soul enjoyed the solitude and silence it provided.

The walk home was a quiet one, but as he was nearing his house, a clutter of voices joined by sounds of falling—or maybe thrown—objects assailed his ears. He paused, trying to make out what the voices were saying. With a start, he realized there were no words, only screams of sheer terror.

A shiver ran through his body, shaking him to the core with its intensity. Tightening his hold on the backpack, he walked around the small house, hidden by a copse of tall trees, and cautiously glanced through a small gap in the greenery into the village. His blood ran cold.

Every corner of the village was swarmed with people running in all directions, their arms flailing about them like wind socks in a storm. The air was thick with the stench of fear, and the screams—like sharp knives—lacerated his eardrums. Chasing the villagers were creatures he had heard about but never seen. Empty white eyes and gigantic sharp fangs dominated their wolfish features, their gray, spiked furry bodies towering way over the people they hunted. The villagers were no match for the Predators. In the space of just a few seconds, most had fallen under the sharp claws of the beasts and were torn to pieces by their strong, fanged jaws.

Cees averted his eyes, his stomach threatening to empty from disgust and fear. Then, he made himself look once more. His brain, frozen for a moment, started functioning again as he began planning his escape.

He had the advantage of being in a semi-hidden part of town. For once, being a poor and ostracized orphaned man worked in his favor. He had food and supplies in his backpack. All he had to do was reach the edges of the commune undetected. Easier said than done.

Keeping as close to the ground as his tall frame allowed, Cees began his progress through the green woods, moving from one bush to another, hiding behind trees and controlling the overwhelming urge to run for his life. He raised his eyes to the sky and muttered a prayer of thanks to the Guardians, grateful now for the many and often boring "soldiering" lessons his friend Lieven had made him sit through.

Lieven! The thought of his best friend at the mercy of those monsters made him gag. Telling himself that Lieven had weapons and was with a company of other armed men and women didn't make him feel any better. The Predators moved faster than lightening, and their claws trumped any weapon the *Zuiver* had available to them. He squeezed his eyes closed for a few seconds and asked the gods to be merciful and protect Lieven, the gentle soldier, his only friend. His only family.

From a distance he could still hear the odd scream of pain, but these were rare and farther apart. Cees shuddered at the meaning of that growing silence and pressed on. Hesitation could be fatal.

By dusk, Cees was outside the boundaries of the commune and breathing a little easier. He knew not to be too cocky about his relative safety. The Predators could pick up human scents at great distances, or so the books said. Thankfully, the wind was on his side, blowing whatever scent he exuded away from the village and the beasts.

Lieven would have known what to do. Ever the practical one, his friend would have come up with a plan right away. A memory of a conversation came alive in Cees' mind.

"We were scouting today," Lieven had said that bright summer day. "We came across this abandoned city. Concrete, tall buildings, and asphalted roads."

"Who lived there?" he had asked, mildly curious but distracted by his friend's aura. A misty wave of wispy blues and purples encircled his head like a halo. Cees' fingers itched to paint it on canvas.

"Who knows?" Liven's blond hair whipped the aura to shreds as he moved. "Those who came before us, I guess."

"Anything interesting?" He was thinking of artifacts or maybe some ancient art. Now, that would be worth something.

"Strange rooms underground," Lieven said. "Almost every building had one, the doors marked with a red sign. These rooms had no windows, the doors were reinforced with metal and locked only from the inside... We all wondered what they were for."

Cees had lost interest. Ugly, functional rooms were useful but not at all interesting. He uttered a sound as if acknowledging he was paying attention, his focus shifting instead to the gorgeous color of the maple tree behind Lieven. The leaves were purplish, making the tree stick out from all the other greenery.

"The funniest thing," he heard his friend say. "There was a large supply of a chemical in each of these rooms. A foul-smelling material that made the whole place reek like a sewer. Very strange."

Lieven, fascinated as he was by all things from the past, had drawn him a map of the ghost town's location. Cees had memorized it. Not because he was interested or hoped to use this information someday. He couldn't help it. He had a gift for committing visual information to memory. Maybe it had something to do with his artistic talent, or maybe that's why he was an artist. Every color nuance, every subtle curve or angle were stuck forever in his memory. Painting was his way of freeing that knowledge, using it to make room for more.

That memory could save his life now. Searching for directions in the map in his mind, Cees laboriously made his way through the forest until it finally poured out into a vast clearing where only wild blond grasses grew. He knew he would be able to see the tall buildings of the concrete jungle, and he was not disappointed. Giant towers stretched all the way to the skies like hands in prayer, seeming to defy the basic laws of gravity. Cees stopped and stared in awe. Never had he seen such architecture. Bits and pieces of the towers glistened in the dying sunlight, diamonds sparkling in the horizon.

Making himself snap out of his trance, Cees took off at great speed toward the city, hoping he would not be spotted in the expanse of the clearing. It was not far, but the run there was riddled with anxiety. Here, there were no trees, no bushes, nothing to hide behind. In his dark clothes, he stuck out like a sore thumb.

Sweat was running down his back and the sides of his face by the time he arrived within the perimeter of the abandoned city. Recalling what Lieven had told him, he didn't waste any time. As soon as he cleared around the block, he ducked into the first door he saw marked with the telltale red sign. The door was heavy, and it took all his strength to push it open and then close it behind him. As he did, the space was suddenly illuminated by a sickly white light coming from small light fixtures installed low along the walls, leading down a staircase into the dark bowels of the building.

The smell was overpowering, making his eyes water and his nose itch. What was that? It smelled as if he had walked into a latrine and buried himself in human waste. It didn't matter. They had all learned in school that Predators didn't care for the smell any more than he did. In fact, the books claimed they wouldn't go anywhere near a stench like that. Something about it interfering with their keen sense of smell and direction. Cees could live with the smell if it meant staying alive and out of the Predators' jaws.

Downstairs, another heavy door opened up to a large, damp room. In a far corner, he dropped his backpack and allowed himself a moment to rest. His legs' muscles hurt from hours on the run, and his back and shoulders were sore from carrying the heavy backpack. His thoughts wandered off to Lieven again, hoping he was alive and well. But his exhausted body didn't allow him too much time to dwell on what may have happened to his best friend. Soon, his eyes grew heavy, and he slipped into a heavy sleep.

Chapter Three

SHELTER

Jia

The acrid smell reached her nostrils and exploded in her brain, waking her up from her slumber. Her head was lying on a rhythmically moving surface, both soft and hard underneath her. Her foggy brain transported her to her mother's arms and the times she had comforted Jia as a child. Jia recalled her mother's chest moving up and down as she hid her teary eyes within the folds of her mom's sweet-scented blouse. Those days were long gone. She had lost her mother to the Big Freeze, almost five years ago. A small mercy, perhaps. Anything was better than falling into the hands of the Predators.

Wait! Why was her head lying on a moving surface? Pouncing to her feet like a feral cat, Jia took two steps back and assumed a fighting stance. The young *Zuiver* didn't seem too startled by the sudden movement. With his bright blue eyes trained on her, he stretched lazily, his mouth curving slightly at the corner.

"You got great reflexes, I'll give you that." He sounded amused. "But it's only me, and I have no intention of attacking you."

Her shoulders relaxed visibly, but her eyes were still fixed on him, weary and alert. There was a strange ease to his posture considering their situation. "How can you just lay there as if you don't have a care in the world?"

"Would it help anyone if I fidget a bit?" he asked, sitting up in a single, fluid move. "Or should I pace the floors? Maybe that will solve the world's problems?"

Irritated with his sarcasm, Jia let a low growling sound escape her lips. "Funny. It just seems strange that you lost everything and still find time and motivation to relax."

A dark cloud blew over his deep-set eyes. "If I could bring them all back with a panic attack, I would be running around in circles, screaming like a banshee."

She bit her tongue, well aware of who *them* were: their families, their friends, their neighbors... the gods-only-knew who were still alive and who had perished at the hands of the monstrosities known as Predators.

"I'm sorry," she whispered, her shoulders slumped forward and her chin dropping an inch or two. "I know we all have lost loved ones. I shouldn't have said that."

Cees jumped to his feet and took a step toward her. "It's not easy." He reached out for her shoulders. "But we must keep calm. Panic means certain death."

Normally, she would slap his hands off her, but there was something about him; his touch was like a soothing lullaby at the end of a hard day. From the spot where his hand touched her, a wave of warmth radiated to the rest of her body, like the effects of a hot tea. Maybe the myths were right after all; maybe the *Zuivers* had special powers.

"I don't like doing nothing," she protested feebly.

"We hunker down for a few more days," he said, dropping his arms and walking toward a crate behind them. "The Predators will only linger in the area until the food supply runs out."

Jia shivered at his words. Her city was not large. With their voracious appetite, the Predators would soon move on to another location. *Solstad* on the coast, most likely. She wondered if they had any idea of what was coming their way. "We must warn them." Urgency filled her with the bitter taste of fear again.

"Even if we could stay ahead of them, it's a good two days' walk for us," Cees said as he searched through a variety of objects on the crate. "They will get there first."

There was truth in his words. The creatures moved with the speed of motorized vehicles and the stealth of drones. The monsters could cover great distances in a fraction of the time it would take for humans.

"We'll focus on heading the opposite way," he said, holding a metal container in his hands. "If we can, we'll radio the cities in their path to warn them."

With her back to the wall, Jia slid all the way to the floor. "What's the point? We may as well kill each other and spare ourselves from being torn to shreds by their jaws. There's no way out."

Cees approached and handed her the container. It had food unlike anything she had ever seen. "Grains from my village. Not tasty, but healthy," he explained when she shook her head. "There is a way out."

Taking another dubious look at the orange rations, she wrinkled her nose and looked up at him. "How exactly are we ever going to get out of this alive? The whole freaking planet is doomed."

Without waiting for an invitation, Cees scooped a portion of the starchy orange grains with his fingers and took it to his mouth. "Water," he said simply.

"What?"

"Bodies of water," he clarified, rolling the food in his mouth and swallowing it whole. "They can't swim or even float. Water will stop their progress. Then, we just have to wait it out."

"Wait what out?" She tasted the food. It had no taste at all. Ignoring her revulsion for the texture, she swallowed a mouthful.

"Wait until they turn on each other and eradicate their species." He was so matter-of-fact, Jia burst out laughing.

"So, we're talking a few years." Her words escaped between chuckles.

"Have you noticed how fast they devour their food?" She didn't want to think about it. What she had witnessed on the way there could not be unseen and would forever haunt her. But Cees was right; the Predators devoured their food faster than anything she had ever seen. They would run out of their food supply quickly. It still gave her the chills.

Cees was munching happily on the strange grains, but Jia's stomach was doing flips inside of her. Just thinking about the Predators eating their way through their world made her queasy. She put the container down and sat on the floor.

"How's your leg?" Cees asked, replacing the lid and putting the container away on the makeshift shelf.

Funny how she had forgotten about her injuries. She rolled up the loose pants to her knees to check them. The improvised bandages were blood-soaked all the way through, but the burning had subsided. The young *Zuiver* knelt beside her and began unraveling the bandages to reveal her ravaged knees. With gentle but deft fingers, Cees examined the wounds. She started at his touch, more from surprise than pain.

"Did I hurt you?" He raised his eyes to hers. She shook her head, and he continued his examination. "It's healing. I'm going to disinfect it again and wrap it in clean bandages."

From a bag, he pulled out a piece of clothing that he quickly shredded into long strips to wrap around her injured knees.

"At this rate, you won't have any clothing left." Jia studied the back of his head. Cees' dark hair fell in waves around his face as he bent over her legs. He had a single tattoo on the back of his neck, but she couldn't make out what it was.

"What's your tattoo?" she asked, allowing her curiosity to get the best of her. His head snapped up. "I noticed you have a tattoo. What is it?"

With his hand, he swept the hair off his neck and lowered his head so that she could take a good look at it. Along the length of his neck, spreading toward one of the sides, there was a single angel wing and a word: *geloven*.

"What does it mean?" Jia asked, tracing the edges of the letters with the tip of her fingers.

"Believe..." He shivered under her touch. "You must always believe."

Retracting her fingers, Jia stared at him curiously. "Believe in what?"

"In a greater power, in yourself, in others...." A small smile appeared in the corner of Cees' lips.

The black stripe across his face made his ice-blue eyes shine like jewels in black velvet. A shadow of stubble darkened his chin and his upper lip, giving him an aura of rugged handsomeness. Jia was suddenly reminded of her intentions to impress her boss at work the day of the attack. She had been so shallow, wearing her skimpy uniform skirt, exposing her legs to attract Aart, the wealthy man who ran her department. No thought for "greater powers" or beliefs in anything else other than being invited for the weekend party at the community center. Maybe Aart would take a shine to her and ask her to be his wife sometime down the road. Maybe Aart would rescue her from her own life. All of that seemed like a lifetime ago instead of just a couple days.

"Where were you when they attacked?" he asked, finishing up with the bandages.

Her stomach flipped again. "At work." Her voice dropped to a whisper. "I had just got to work."

"Why were you wearing those clothes if you were going to work?" He tied up the ends of the improvised bandages. With his teeth, he ripped the longer edges away, and she felt his warm breath caress her skin.

"That's one of my uniforms," she explained. "Females must wear short skirts unless the boss says otherwise."

Finished with his nursing, Cees stretched his long legs in front of him and leaned against the wall, frowning. "Really? What do you do?"

"Global Affairs." She hesitated, feeling a little exposed suddenly, as if he wanted to know more than what she was willing to reveal. "I started working there the last year of school. Do *Zuivers* go to school?"

A hand behind his neck, cushioning his head against the hard wall, Cees smiled. "We go to school to learn our letters and our numbers and a few other things, nothing else. There aren't many teachers available to my people. Central wants to keep us ignorant and docile."

Not sure whether he was being serious, she watched him with curiosity. "How do you learn your trade or craft?"

"Sponsorship… On-the-job type of thing." His eyes grew suddenly icy and hard. "But *Zuivers* like me are only allowed enough schooling for the basics."

"*Zuivers* like you?" she asked, even though his eyes were telling her not to.

"Tainted *Zuivers*." He didn't offer any further explanation, and she thought it wiser to let it go.

But curiosity gnawed at her insides. What did he mean by *tainted*? What had he done to deserve such a label? Was she locked in that bunker with a criminal of some kind? The thought made her shiver. Cees looked so... not quite harmless, for his dark hair and tanned skin gave him a certain aura of danger and mystery. *Pure* was the word she would have chosen to describe him. He had an aura of purity as if whatever had happened to him did not mar his soul, his outlook on life. Or maybe the noxious fumes in that place were making her delirious.

Jia studied him from beneath half-closed eyelids. The black stripe over his eyes. Did it have any special significance? She didn't know much about the *Zuivers*. They were considered a lower race, an ethnic group with low standing in the social hierarchy of *Wêreld*. They were believed to be weak in academic skills and emotionally unstable due to their rather primal instincts. Because of this, *Zuivers* were not given sophisticated weapons to defend themselves or much technology at all. They also had not been offered the gas masks that were supposed to protect people from the toxic gases Central had promised would annihilate the Predators. The whole group had been relocated to a commune far away from all other cities. Out of sight, out of mind, she remembered people whisper.

There were rumors, though. Whisperings of special gifts, special talents that rendered them even more unstable, more dangerous. Cees didn't strike her as unstable in any way. In fact, he looked perfectly capable and in full control of all his senses. Had she met him in *Wêreld*, she would most likely pursue him the same way she pursued Aart. There was a wild beauty to him that attracted her like a magnet.

Are you crazy? You know nothing about this man, this Zuiver. But he had taken care of her wounded knees and kept her warm through the night, more than what other men had done for her before.

"What's it like?" Cees asked out of nowhere. He stared at her with those unsettling blue eyes.

"What?"

"Being a *Gezegenden*?" At first, she didn't understand him. Then she realized he was using an Old World word for 'blessed'.

"I'm not sure what you mean." Jia's cheeks flushed. How do you explain to someone from an inferior race what it is like to be one of the upper echelon of *Wêreld*?

"What does it feel like to feel superior to all other humans?" His words were like shards of glass. "To feel like you're better than every other creature in the world and be perfectly happy knowing you have privileges that most don't even dare dream about?" Bitterness dripped from his words, like blood from an open wound. "How does it feel to create a world where you are judged by your circumstances and not by your deeds or skills?"

"You obviously know everything about us, the Blessed. So why even ask?" She could play this game of accusations and sharp barbs.

"The *Gezegenden* are given advanced weapons and protective gear while we, the dirty *Zuiver*, must survive on our street smarts," he continued.

"A lot of good those weapons did for us when the Predators came." Jia matched his bitterness with her own.

Cees looked properly chided. His icy eyes thawed and spoke of sorrow and sympathy. "I'm sorry." His voice grew soft. "I shouldn't judge you and your people. You have suffered great losses just as the *Zuiver* have. In the end, we are all just humans."

Jia's anger was replaced by a nagging sense of regret and shame. Here she was, in the same exact position as this young *Zuiver* who had not hesitated to help her, and she was still measuring him by the social rule that had divided them in the first place. What did that say about her as a human being? Had she grown so jaded that her bouts of rebellion as a teenager were nothing but memories? Had she really changed so much, she had lost sight of what she felt and believed in her heart?

"I'm sorry too," she said, apologizing for so much more than just their fiery exchange. "I'm eternally grateful to you. If it wasn't for you, I would be hungry, thirsty, and alone. I owe you big."

A tiny smile lifted the corner of his lips. She wondered whether he realized how handsome he was. "I didn't do anything that I wouldn't do for anyone else," he said, springing to his feet in a graceful move. He walked up to her and offered his hand in peace. "Friends?"

Jia looked up, her neck complaining—he was very tall—and accepted his hand in hers. "Friends," she said, his warm skin sending waves of shivering pleasure up her arm. "Now, where's the bathroom?"

Lieven

The squad had barely set up camp by the borders when they heard it over the radio — the red alert their people were to send out should something dire happen while they were gone. Through the tiny, archaic one-way radio they heard the alarm, quickly followed by the sound of screaming and then the silence of death. The word "Predators" hung in the air as a palpable object of terror. So, the rumors were true—the dreaded and almost mythical Predators were on the prowl. For months now, whisperings of attacks had reached their commune, but with no details, no proof, it was hard to believe that such creatures of legend—characters made up to scare children into obedience—were actually walking their world. The words were heard clearly through the static of the old radio, "Predators are attacking us. Help!"

Some wanted to run back home in hopes of fighting the beasts; others thought it better to take a more defensive stance. Lieven couldn't think straight. Cees was in the commune, alone and defenseless. Lieven's heart hurt. His stomach was tied in such tight knots he folded in two with the pain. *No, not Cees. Please, Guardians, not Cees.*

"Move it, Lieven! This is not the time." It was the squad leader, staring and yelling at him.

On his knees, his head bent all the way to the floor, Lieven shook like a leaf. He just couldn't wrap his head around the idea of losing his friend, his heart, his soul mate. He looked up at his fellow soldier, horror and disbelief in his eyes. "It can't be true Alfons, it can't.".

"Put yourself together, soldier." Alfons' voice was hard but his eyes soft. "You won't do anyone any favors by losing control right now. We all left people behind."

Knowing that didn't help with the pain, the fear. "Do you think they're all—?" He couldn't bring himself to say the words.

"We must expect the worst but hope for the best." Alfons pulled him up to his feet. "Right now, we need to get to safety, regroup, and decide on what to do next."

After a brief discussion, they all agreed to lift up camp as quickly as they could muster and head south to the big concrete jungle they had discovered some weeks back. The profusion of smelly bunkers in the city would provide them with some protection for a while.

Lieven threw himself at the task of putting down tents and gathering materials with gusto. While his body was busy, his mind didn't have time to think about things he'd just as soon forget. Unshed tears stung his eyes as he covered his body and clothes in animal waste for protection against the Predators. With his laden heart beating madly inside his chest, he trudged through the woods with his companions, careful to stay hidden and alert to any change around him. They all knew that their weapons were no match for the monsters. Old and inaccurate, they would, at best, provide a mild annoyance for the beasts. The squad's only chance was to stay out of their way and find somewhere to hide.

Lieven moved with the squad through the forest, his heart the only sound he could hear. He knew they were all hurting, burdened with the enormity of what had just happened to their loved ones. No one had ever seen a Predator, but they all knew stories, seen illustrations in old science books. Science had failed humanity this time. In their hunger for stronger and more effective weapons, the military had engaged scientists in a quest for genetic enhancements. The Predators were their biggest fail—too strong and too out of control. Now, they were all paying for it.

With luck, they would be at the concrete city in two days and be ahead of the beasts. Only instinct and his military training kept Lieven moving, barely aware of what he was doing, his mind too busy with thoughts of Cees and what may have happened to him. At night, when they stopped to rest for a while, he felt numb, detached from his own body as if he was walking in a dream. Sleep evaded him, though, and when Alfons woke the men up a few hours later to resume their march, he had been sitting against a tree, eyes wide open but unseeing. Something had yanked his beating heart out of his chest, and he would soon bleed to death.

In his mind, he recalled every conversation he had with his friend, and he was reminded of Cees' special talents and gifts. Cees was unusual among his people. His strange beginnings and hard life seemed to have activated dormant genes. Being a Tainted one had isolated him from the rest of the population in more ways than one. Lieven knew this because he had refused to treat him as an outcast, instead cultivating a friendship that had started in their childhood and lasted to this day. A friendship that had turned into so much more than Lieven ever thought possible.

When Lieven's father passed away over three years ago, Cees had been there with a generous shoulder to cry on, a sympathetic heart. Now it was only the two of them against the world. Lieven laughed softly as he made his way around a group of large trees. That had been their motto since they were kids, *the two of us against the world forever.* His chuckle changed into a sob. Gods, he hoped it was still the two of them. He prayed, with all the passion of his youth, that Cees was still alive and hidden somewhere. He would crawl through fire to rescue him if only he knew where Cees was. If only he knew whether Cees still was.

Time both dragged slowly by and rushed through with the speed of storm winds. Two days later they had arrived at the big city, unscathed against all odds. At least physically. No one had exchanged more than a couple words for the past two days, sadness and shock mingling together in their hearts and rendering them mechanical and numb.

"Men, spread out." Alfons' voice sounded strange after such long silence. "There are twenty of us. We will need a couple bunkers at least.

Check them, make sure they still have a stench and that the lock on the door is working. Meet here for report."

In groups of four or five, they began their search for viable hiding places. Most bunkers they examined were perfectly functional, strange as it was after these many years. One of the patrols reported that they had found one locked from the inside.

"We knocked for a while, but the door held true," one of the soldiers said. "It is possible someone else has taken refuge there."

"Leave them be then." Alfons pointed at the buildings around them. "There are plenty others for us."

They spent the next few minutes strategizing their positions and deciding on when to come out of hiding. Alfons estimated that the Predators would be soon—if not already—in the next town over, the coastal *Solstad*. If that was the case, it would give them time to move in the opposite direction without attracting attention from the beasts.

"Give ourselves two more days," Alfons said. "After that, let's meet here. Make sure to collect a good sample of the chemical that causes that smell. It will be our armor."

Lieven and four other men took shelter in one of the bunkers and locked the door behind them. The smell was almost unbearable, but he knew that, as the hours went by, their noses would get used to it, and it wouldn't be as noticeable anymore. They set up camp with their meager supplies as far away from the chemical storage bins as they could and sat, each one in his corner, unspeaking, staring at the ground. Lieven was not sure he would be able to hold it together was he to see what he felt in someone else's eyes. It would make it all too real. He preferred to hold a little hope in his heart for as long as he could.

Cees

It made him irrationally nervous to have her out of his sight. Jia had gone to hide behind one of the big chemical containers to relieve herself, and he felt strangely alone.

"That's ridiculous," he said out loud. "I've been alone all my life. Why would that bother me now?"

"Did you say something?" Her voice came from the other side of the tall containers and echoed through the space. He had to be more careful. It was impossible to speak without being heard in that cavernous space.

Cees jumped to his feet and paced, feeling jittery and full of an energy he didn't know he had. His fingers itched to paint, but, of course, there was nothing there he could paint with. He remembered his backpack. He always carried a notebook and pencils with him. Just in case.

"Just in case what?" Lieven had asked him once. "In case the world can be saved with a pencil?" They had both laughed, and Cees had punched him playfully across the top of his arm.

Just in case his creative energy threatened to overwhelm him to the point of madness if he couldn't find a release. That was the reason. He wished he had told Lieven that instead. It hurt to know that he may never have the chance to do it now.

Jia came from behind the containers, and Cees stopped moving. Around her, wrapping her like a giant halo, was a bright red aura. It was the first time he had a glimpse of her aura, and it took him by storm. She was angry, very angry, but there was more to her feelings. They held a restless energy, a passion that gave him pause. He held his breath and watched her walk across the space toward him. Jia was a small woman, only reaching up to his chest. Slender and beautiful. Sure, it was not the first time he noticed, but her aura now beckoned him with an all-powerful pull.

Cees wanted to draw her so badly, his hands began shaking. He bent down to get his backpack and retrieve his pencils and notebook.

"What are you doing?" she asked curiously, her hand resting loosely on her waist.

He had slid down along the wall and was now sitting, his knees drawn up to support his notebook. "Drawing you." His eyes studied her from top to bottom.

Jia looked uncomfortable. "Why?"

Cees bit the top of his pencil. "That's what I do. You're very pretty, you know?"

Her face turned scarlet. Funny, she didn't seem the kind of girl who would be embarrassed by flattery.

"That's what you do for a living? You draw?" She sat crossed-legged across from him.

"No, I work in a cantina, shoveling food onto plates all day long." Bitterness climbed up his throat. "Art is my gift, my life-line."

"Are you good at it? The drawing?" She played with her gun as if it was a toy, twirling it in her fingers.

"Careful with that," he said, not stopping his sketching. "You will shoot something. Or someone."

Jia laughed, and the crystal-like sound she produced was like music to his ears. Cees noticed her aura subtly changing into a lighter red.

"The security is on," she said. "Besides, this is a smart-gun."

He looked up at her, tilting his head slightly. "Oh, guns have brains now, do they?"

"A smart-gun is connected to my implant." She seemed shocked he had never heard of it. "It only does what I want it to do."

He couldn't help being surprised. "Really? It reads your thoughts?"

Jia smiled, and the room got a little brighter. "In a way, I guess it does." She put the gun down. Her aura was much lighter now, almost a pink. "I'm surprised you've never seen or heard of one. They've been around for years."

His smile faded quickly, and he tasted bile. "I'm a *Zuiver*." His voice was almost a growl. "We don't get any new technology, remember? Way too volatile and unstable."

Her beautiful smile died on her lips. "Sorry, Cees." It was the first time she used his name, and he found that he liked the way she pronounced it, a little wrong, and yet so right. "I wasn't thinking."

Stealing a glance at her, he broke a smile. "Unlike your gun there."

She laughed, and her aura became a soft shade of pink. It made his heart flutter and his gut tighten.

"Why the short hair?" Jia had raven-black hair, shorter than his own, and gray-blue eyes that went from soft to hard at the slightest provocation.

"Why not?" she asked, shrugging. "Easier to take care of."

"*Zuiver* females normally wear their hair long." His fingers moved across the paper at the speed of light.

"More power to them." Jia's aura turned one shade darker. "But the Blessed like variety. Girls are free to wear their hair as they please. Some of us even go bald. Do all *Zuivers* wear long hair like yours?"

Her question made him smile. "No." He didn't offer any further explanation. He liked it when she looked a little annoyed. There was something very attractive about her pouting lips and darkening eyes. Not to mention her ever-changing aura.

"What about that face stripe?" she asked, surprising him. "Is that a male *Zuiver* thing?"

The pencil stopped as he looked her straight in the eyes. "It's a Tainted thing," he said, his voice low and barely audible. "A *Bedorven* thing."

Silence fell, Cees grappling with the anger and shame that word always carried for him. Jia seemed to be struggling with her feelings as well, her eyes very soft and her aura purplish now. As if coming to a decision, she stood up and came to sit next to him. Out of habit—Lieven was always trying to sneak peeks at his work in progress—he hid the drawing from her sight.

"I'm sorry." As she placed her hand on his arm, a jolt of energy went through him as if she had electrocuted him. "I don't know what being Tainted means, but it is obviously something painful. You don't have to talk about it if you don't want to."

Speaking of his social status among his people was not something he did except with Lieven, and even then, very rarely. His rank on the bottom of the barrel had caused him too much pain to be comfortable talking about it.

A loud banging echoed through the room. Jia automatically latched on to Cees arm and he dropped the notebook, body at the ready to flee.

"Oh gods!" Jia whispered, her face nestled in his arm. "They're here."

The banging sound echoed again, and Jia shivered and whimpered against him. "They can't go through that door," he said, not sure whom he was trying to convince; Jia or himself. He had, after all, neglected to lock the door the night Jia had found him. "It's too strong."

The nerve wrecking sound continued for a while, but eventually subsided. Jia was trembling as he wrapped his arms around her protectively. Lieven used to do the same to him when they were little after Cees had been whipped or publicly shamed. He remembered many occasions when the tears fell nonstop and his body shook so violently his muscles had spasmed and ached. The shelter of his friend's arms had been his only solace, and Cees would be forever grateful for that. He sighed, his fear of what may have happened to his dear friend renewed.

"They're gone," he whispered, his lips on her hair. In spite of the stench that surrounded them and the blood and sweat of the last few days, there was a sweetness to her scent that soothed his nerves. "It's okay."

"They'll be back," she said, her voice trembling like her body. "We're going to die, Cees. We're doomed."

Even though her words rang true, he refused to accept them. There had to be a way out of this mess. He could feel it in his bones. Jia had thought *Zuivers* had special gifts. There were a few who did, in a way. He was one of them. Ever since he could recall, he had a way of *feeling* things no-one else could. Not quite a premonition, but more of a gut-feeling that, more often than not, turned out to be right. Just like the way he could see people's auras when no one else could and know how they were feeling, be able to predict their next moves. It had saved him a lot of grief growing up to be able to remove himself from volatile situations before they were out of control. Of course, other than Lieven, nobody knew about this. He was already considered a freak, an outcast. Anything that set him further apart from his own people would make the situation even worse.

"We're not doomed." There was a certainty in his tone that belied the quivering of his muscles, the twitching of his eye. "We'll figure out a way. You'll see. I'm very good at figuring out puzzles." He was. His visual memory allowed him to solve puzzles and mysteries in ways that always astonished Lieven, who struggled with them to the point of frustration.

Jia lifted her head and looked at him with a tiny smile. "I don't think puzzles are going to help us with this." The usual bite was back in her voice.

Their eyes locked, and Cees felt a stirring he had not felt in a very long time. It was wrong to feel this way now, he knew. Lieven was out there, maybe dead. The whole population of his commune gone. Jia's own family and friends butchered. This was not the right time for these feelings to start—first in his gut and quickly spreading to his whole being.

Cees' breathing became shallow and quick as his gaze descended from her eyes to her full, pink lips. Her breathing had gone from irregular and spastic to fast and steady as she undertook her own eye-journey across his face. This magnetic field had appeared between and around them, powerful forces that pulled them together in spite of their resistance.

With a stretch, Jia reached out with her lips to cover his. His whole being was telling him to take them, to accept her offering, but he flinched instead. "We shouldn't," he said, his voice hoarse from need. "I'm a *Zuiver*, you're *Gezegenden*. It's forbidden."

Her eyebrows curved upwards. "Who's going to know?" Bitterness colored her voice. "They're all dead. We will be dead soon too. What does it matter? I want to feel one last time, to feel alive. Don't you?"

He had not felt alive for most of his life. As a Tainted one, he was not offered many chances to feel anything other than pain and sadness. No, that wasn't true either. He had been happy many times. Lieven and his family had made sure he had the opportunity to laugh, to feel loved, to love something—his art had fulfilled a hole in his life, as well.

His hesitation was replaced by a hunger he had never felt before. Yes, he wanted to feel alive. His mouth took hers this time. Jia opened her lips to his and allowed him to taste the full sweetness of her. For a moment, he forgot the Predators, his life as a Tainted one, Lieven. He lost himself in that desperate kiss, her hands frenzied underneath his shirt, searching, begging for more. Before long, Jia had straddled him and pulled on his shirt, trying to strip him of it. Frustrated that she couldn't, she pulled on her own shirt instead and threw it over her head to the side. Cees' breath caught for a moment. She wasn't wearing anything underneath. Her upper body was totally bare, her small breasts tantalizingly close to his mouth. He moaned and hesitated.

What was he doing? This was a *Gezegenden* he was getting ready to have sex with. Memories of stories he had been told as a child of his own parents and the reason he was to pay for their sins for the rest of his life burst in his mind, unwelcome and painful. He pushed her gently away from him.

"I want you," she protested, holding his hands in hers. He knew she didn't really want him. She wanted someone, anyone. He tried to pull away again, but she held firm. "No, please Cees." There was a distinct tone of sadness to her voice. "I need this. I need to forget for a few moments. Please."

As to emphasize her plea, she pulled on his hands and brought them to rest on her breasts. Cees shivered. He wanted her. He felt himself swell at the contact, but he was scared. The consequences to *wellust* were dire, and he wasn't in a position to endure any more punishment than what he had most of his life. He pulled away again, a bit more firmly this time.

"I can't," he said in a strangled voice. "I'm sorry Jia. It's *wellust* and I can't..."

Jia was not making it easy on him. Desperation gave way to anger in her beautiful grayish eyes as she slid her hand between them to touch him. Cees' whole body shook, and a heat wave exploded from where her hand caressed him over the thin fabric of his pants. Soon, he would lose all control.

Firmly, he held her by the waist, pulled her up off him and gently placed her beside him. "No! No, Jia. We can't."

"Why not? No-one will know."

Her exposed breasts were playing havoc with his senses, so he averted his eyes and retrieved her shirt from the floor. "Put this on. Please."

With fire shooting out of her eyes, Jia slipped into the shirt and walked away from him. Cees watched her as she curled up in the corner, a few yards away from him, her face turned to the wall. He took a deep breath and tried to focus on something else, anything. She had him so aroused, he felt he was in danger of exploding.

Years of learning how to keep his feelings and emotions under tight control had given him the strategies to calm himself down. After some deep breathing exercises and deliberate visualization, he felt himself come back to Earth. A quick glance toward Jia's lying figure told him she was crying. Her shoulders shook, and if he strained his ears he could hear the faint tale tell of sobbing.

Taking a deep breath, he stood up and went to her, not sure at first what to do. He summoned Lieven's image. He was the only point of reference Cees had ever had in terms of kindness and comfort. What would he have done if it was Cees on that floor crying his eyes out of fear, out of frustration and helplessness?

"Jia," he whispered, sitting down next to her and reaching for her shoulder. "I'm sorry. Don't be hurt. I was just scared."

The young woman didn't move or say anything. He stretched his long body next to hers and slid his arm over her, pulling her close to him. "My mom was a *Zuiver*. She fell in love with a *Gezegenden*." He felt her start in his arms, her quiet sobbing subsiding. "They dated in secret, but they were found. When it was established they were intimate with each other, they were arrested."

Jia turned around to face him. "What happened?"

Cees swallowed bile. He hadn't told this story to anyone ever. Not even to Lieven, who already knew it from his parents. "My father was returned to his people in disgrace, but my mother was pregnant. As the law demanded, they waited for her to give birth, and then she was charged with *wellust* and executed."

Shock spread across her face. "But in *Wêreld* the sentence is temporary shunning and loss of some privileges," she said, disbelief in her voice. "Execution? For breaking the caste law? That's barbaric."

A lock of her jet-black hair had fallen across her eyes. He reached out and gently brushed it away. "Not our law. Central's." Bitterness threatened to swallow him whole. "Another perk of being a *Zuiver*."

"Who took care of you?" she asked.

"I was Tainted, so I was to pay for my parents' sins," he explained, supporting his head on his bent arm. "I grew up in an institution for the children of criminals until Lieven and his family took me in—at great risk to themselves."

"Who's Lieven?"

"My best—my only friend. My brother really." His heart ached for Lieven. "He's probably dead now." Catching a sob before it escaped his lips, Cees lowered his eyes to the ground. He felt her hand on his head, her fingers burying themselves in his thick hair in a comforting caress.

"Sorry," she whispered, her fingers gently massaging his scalp.

He could feel her breath on his face, and he felt an overwhelming urge to kiss her again. It had been too long since he had any kind of romantic connection. His social status didn't quite endear him to women, and he was too poor to pay for sexual favors.

"We should sleep," he said, certain that if she kept with her absentminded stroking, he would have to once again take her in his arms. This time he was not so sure he would be able to stop. "We need to gather energy for what's coming." Whatever it was, it wouldn't be easy; they both knew it. With the Predators on their heels, nowhere was safe. No matter how far and how fast they ran, the beasts could run faster.

That night, they slept entangled in each other's arms, comforted by the contact, the reminder that they were not completely alone, even if the world as they knew it was coming to a violent and abrupt end.

Jia

The voice felt like a hammer against her aching head. She had too much to drink again last night. The night had been long, and the wine had flowed freely at Luce's house-warming party. How could she turn it down? Her bones were cold, and the wine warmed everything from the inside out.

"Jia! Wake up," the voice hammered again. Hell, what could be so important as to interrupt her much-needed rest? "Wake up. It's your mom."

She sprung to a sitting position a little too fast. Her head swam, and her stomach heaved. Automatically, her hands went to her forehead as if the simple contact would banish the pain. She blinked her eyes open and was able to discern a familiar figure standing by her bed.

"Luce, what's going on?" Her childhood friend was bent over her, a frown on her face.

Had Luce stayed over last night? A quick look around told her that she was the one who had stayed over at her friend's house. She realized she was lying on the couch in Luce's room. She must have been totally wasted the night before.

"Your mom." Her friend handed her a coat. "Come quick."

Still confused, Jia stood up on wobbly legs and slipped into the coat her friend was offering. It was not hers. Gods only knew where hers was. Luce insisted she wore a fur hat and a woolen scarf before leaving the house with her. Her muddled brain couldn't make much sense of what was happening, but there was a definite sense of urgency, a feeling of foreboding coming from her friend.

"What's wrong?" Her mind buzzed with scenarios of what-ifs as they stepped into the deep freeze outside. Nothing much had changed in the last few weeks. The snow still blew at blizzard-like speeds, covering the whole world in a blanket of ghostly mist. Long ropes had been stretched from one building to the next so that people could walk without getting lost in the whirlwind of icy whiteness. She held on to the rope, unsteady and afraid she would be blown away by the wind. "What happened to my mom?"

"We have to get you to the hospital." Luce's voice was muffled by the thick scarf covering half her face. "She's not doing well."

A few weeks ago, Jia's mother had become sick. First it was only the chills that precede the common cold, but as the days went by and the usual medicine didn't seem to be making a difference, Jia had persuaded her to visit a doctor. In his expert opinion, she had a strong case of a chest cold, nothing to worry too much about.

"Just go home, drink lots of fluids, and take the medicine I prescribed," he had said in that know-it-all tone some doctors like to adopt.

Except she was not getting better. With each passing day, her mom got sicker, her body ravaged by terrible chills and high temperatures, a cough that seemed to want to eject her lungs, and a growing weakness that worried Jia more than anything else. Mom had always been a strong woman. She had single-handedly brought her daughter up after her father had left to Central never to come back, and her energy was legendary amongst friends and family.

The snow blinded Jia, and she pulled the scarf a little higher to cover her freezing nose. "What did they tell you?"

Her friend couldn't hear her over the howling wind and the punishing whipping of the snow. Jia had to wait until they got to the hospital to find out. Transportation was at a standstill. Only very few emergency vehicles could drive through the storms. Thankfully, the hospital was not too far. On a fair day, they could walk there in under ten minutes, but with the storm the journey there would be a lot longer. The Big Freeze had turned her fair and mild Wêreld into a hellish realm, and there was no end in sight.

An eternity passed before they arrived at the warm lobby of the hospital. Only public buildings could offer much in terms of warmth these days. Even in the houses of the higher Blessed, the air temperatures were kept at a tepid level at best. Those like Luce, who were lucky enough to *have fireplaces in the houses, could still warm up their houses with the little wood they could scavenge from their own houses and surrounding areas. But everybody else had to be content with minimum heat and make sure to bundle up, even indoors.*

The elevators were out of commission to save energy. They climbed the service stairs to the third floor where her mom had taken residence for the last week. The climb was made that much harder because of the numbness that had taken over Jia's legs and arms. They felt heavy and clumsy, and she practically dragged herself up each step.

Once on the third floor, Luce interlaced her arm with her friend's, and they both walked down the hallway to room 354. The door was wide open, and as soon as Jia was able to peek inside, she knew; the news couldn't be any worse.

From the doorway, she could see her mother lying pallid as a ghost in the sterile hospital bed, her wires already removed and a dead monitor above her. She seemed peaceful—the most peaceful Jia had seen her in the last few weeks—but she had no life in her.

Jia let out a sob and stumbled. Luce held her tight and cooed in her ear as Jia looked around looking for her mom's life force. Maybe if she could see it, she could hold on to it and coax it back into the body of her mother again. It couldn't have gone too far.

"Where is it?" she yelled incoherently. "Do you see it, Luce? Her life force. We need to find it."

Luce held on to her arm tighter. "Honey, she's gone," she whispered. "She died over an hour ago. Her life force is gone beyond."

Jia shook her head violently and pushed her friend aside. "No, no she can't be gone." Her voice was hoarse from the cold and she refused to accept the inevitable. "She's all I have." She took a few steps into the room and threw herself on top of her mother's innate body, weeping. "Mom, don't leave me. Mom, please..."

Luce approached her and laid a hand on her shoulder blade. "I'm sorry, Jia. I loved her too." Her voice caught on a sob. "She's gone, Jia. She's gone."

Her head snapped up so violently it woke up Cees, who was sleeping next to her. Tears rolled down her cheeks, and the pain she had felt then still burned in her chest as vividly now. "Mom," she whispered between sobs.

Cees sat up and reached out to put his hand on her shoulder. "What's wrong, Jia?" he asked, his eyes wide open and alert. "Did you hear something?"

She shook her head and tried to wipe the tears without him seeing it, but it was too late. His eyes widened and then softened at the sight. "Just a dream," she said, trying to pull herself together and failing. "Just a bad dream."

Looking baffled, Cees cocked his head to get a better look at her. "Some dream it must have been," he said, wiping a tear from her face with his finger. "Are you sure you're okay?"

Jia jumped to her feet, not used to be on the receiving end of sympathy. She had been brought up tough by a mother who knew the world was not easy, and then becoming even tougher by circumstances. Long gone was the time she would take refuge in her mother's arms—or even Luce's—for comfort. She was a grown-up, and she couldn't let anything—especially a dream, a memory—affect her like that.

Faster than necessary, she walked around the containers into the place that she had been using as her private space, but instead of relieving herself, she indulged in a silent weeping. "Get it together, girl," she whispered to herself as tears kept mercilessly rolling down her cheeks.

"Are you all right?" Cees asked, concern in his voice. "You've been back there for an awful long time."

"I'm fine. Stay away!" Her voice was unnecessarily ornery, she realized. "I'll be out in a second."

That dream had not bothered her in a few years. *So why now?* Was it because her own life was at imminent risk of being no more? Was it because of the horrors she had witnessed as she escaped *Wêreld*? So many lives lost, and in such a violent way. Had their life forces escaped unscathed, or were their souls wandering the beyond just as scarred and bleeding as the bodies they had inhabited?

The young *Zuiver* was waiting for her, pacing the floor just beyond the canisters. "I'm fine," she said again, swiping a hand on her face to check for undried tears. "I had a bad dream, that's all. It's over and done."

He didn't look convinced but let it go. "We need to plan our next move." He walked side-by-side with her back to where they had set up camp. "I think we give it another day. If it was them out there banging on our door, they will be gone by then. There's no food here."

Jia nodded just as a shiver of apprehension went through her body. "Agreed. We still have a little bit of food and water. We can hold off for another day or so."

Like old friends, or maybe battle companions, they sat. Heads together, speaking in whispers as if afraid someone would overhear. Cees offered her more of the strange grains and a gulp of water, which she gladly accepted. They would both need their strength for the journey ahead.

"You have a gun that only works for you," Cees said out of the blue. Jia stared at him in surprise. Where was he going with this? "You've got to promise me that if we go head to head with the monsters, you will shoot me before you turn the gun on yourself."

His striking blue eyes were as pleading as those of a child. They were so transparent she could not only see but feel his fear, his terror at being caught by the Predators and shredded to pieces. Who could blame him? She had witnessed the terror with her own eyes, and she didn't cherish the thought of being caught by one of them. The thought of suicide had already crossed her mind a few times. Her survival instincts had won that battle, but she was certain she would not hesitate to use her gun on herself should she find herself at the losing end of a hunt.

"I promise." It was a mere whisper. The thought of taking someone else's life was not pleasant. It made Jia's stomach rumble and her heart clench in revolt. She had never as much as killed an animal. As a little girl she used to rescue small creatures, like frogs and lizards, from certain death at the hands of her mother who abhorred them. How would she ever be able to kill a human being?

Cees grasped her hand in his. "I would do the same for you if I could. A bullet is a much easier way to go than falling prey to them." She knew that. Despite her second—and third—thoughts, she would do it. It was the humane thing to do.

"I told you I would do it." The snappiness was back in her voice. "I keep my promises."

A shudder shook her body when Cees's face opened into a smile. It was like the sun had just risen in that dank room. His grin was contagious, and she felt her lips stretching into a matching smile. "Good. Do you mind if I draw you again? I haven't finished it yet."

Shrugging her shoulders, she leaned back against the wall and watched Cees as he busied himself with the notebook and pencil. His back was hunched and his head bent toward the paper, only coming up once in a while to look at her. Jia's cheeks burned every time he stared at her, studying her every shadow, every line, but he didn't seem to notice. The drawing had his full attention.

She took advantage of that to do her own staring. He was such a stunning specimen of a male. Unusual, the blue of his eyes brought into sharper focus because of the black stripe that crossed his face. Taller than most men she knew, but graceful in the way he moved. Strong. She had felt his hard muscles the night before and had seen him carry some of the heavy canisters around with such ease. Yet there was a vulnerability about him that made her want to protect him. She giggled at the thought, and he looked at her, a question in his eyes. She shook her head and he went back to his drawing. The idea of her protecting him was amusing. Cees towered over her and was possibly double her girth. But there was a tenderness to him, a gentleness that she lacked and desperately needed.

What was she thinking about? They would most likely not survive the week anyway. The world—and everything in it—was doomed. The Predators would win in the end. Period. She wouldn't go down without a fight, though.

Cees lifted his head and dropped the pencil inside the backpack. "Done." He bit his bottom lip in concentration.

"Can I see it?" Jia stood up and took a few steps in his direction. No-one had ever sketched her. In fact, she couldn't remember anyone who was artistic enough to do such thing. All her friends and relations were down-to-earth people who concerned themselves only with the practical, the now, the what-it-is not what-could-be.

Turning the notebook so she could see it, Cees wistfully looked at her. "What do you think?"

Her legs gave in underneath her, and she had to sit down. Was that what she really looked like or was it the way he saw her? Back in *Wēreld*, she had been in high demand. Men liked her looks, and she used them to try and make her life better, to secure some kind of a future for herself. Jia was well aware of her attractive figure, but this was something else. This drawing caught a side of her that she didn't know existed. There was a brightness to her eyes, a gentleness to her expression, and an aura of transcendent beauty. Overwhelmed, Jia remained silent.

"Did you know you have the most beautiful aura?" His eyes were intent on her face.

The heat resurfaced on her cheeks. "Aura? What do you mean?"

"Everyone has an aura," he explained. "You can tell a lot about a person and how they are feeling by its color."

Jia looked at him curiously. What was he going on about now? "Never heard about it."

"When someone is mad, the aura turns into an angry red." Cees' hands got busy with the corner of his shirt as if he was not sure of what to do with them. She wondered why he was uncomfortable talking about this. "When you're sad, you may have a purple aura. But each person's aura has its own hues, its own individual stamp. Yours is beautiful."

"You're messing with me." Jia laughed.

"No, it's true" Reaching out, he brushed a couple fingers across her burning cheeks. "Right now, it is a soft tone of pink that wavers around you like the wings of an angel." She stopped herself from leaning into his hand. "Maybe auras are a manifestation of our life forces."

"How come I can't see them?" She both loved and hated his touch and his words.

"I don't know," he admitted, a little hesitation in his eyes. "I've always been able to, but I was the only one I knew of. I never told anyone about it for fear of being branded an even bigger outcast."

Without warning, her heart reached out for him with such a strong pang of sympathy it made her gasp. "Is that why you have that stripe over your eyes? Because you were an outcast?"

The sorrow in his eyes was almost too much to bear. When he moved his hand away from her cheek, she grasped it in hers, not wanting to break the contact.

"Yes," he said, his eyes lowered to the floor. "The council of elders had the stripe permanently inked onto my face so everyone knew I was Tainted. I'm to carry the sins of my parents forever with me. They will never forgive me." Jia didn't know what to say and opted for holding his hand in silence instead. Eventually he lifted his eyes to her again. "It doesn't matter anymore. They're all dead, and the world will never be the same again."

The finality of the statement hit and weighed down on them like lead. There was nothing else to say.

CHAPTER FOUR

ESCAPE

Lieven

The haunted expression in everybody's eyes wasn't going away. They barely talked to each other and walked aimlessly around the enclosed space. Lieven was almost glad they would be leaving today. Anything—even facing the Predators—would be better than another day stuck with his traumatized squad. There was still the mystery of the locked bunker. Someone must be inside. What else would explain the door being locked from the inside? Maybe other survivors from the attack? He was anxious to go and find out. Having a goal would help distract him and the rest of the squad from the enormity of the situation.

He had spent most of the two days thinking about Cees, and it was eating him alive. Refusing to accept the obvious, Lieven chose to believe that his friend had somehow escaped the massacre and was waiting for him somewhere, safe and sound. The alternative was too painful to even contemplate.

Cees had been a wisp of a child when they had met for the first time. Lieven's father volunteered in a home for the children of criminals once a week, and that morning he had decided that it was time his own son faced the ugly reality of one of his society's worse features—the punishment of innocents for the sins of their parents. Lieven had reluctantly tagged along, moaning about the town's children's celebration he would miss. His father ignored him, and he had never been happier he did.

Shock didn't even begin to describe what he felt looking at the poor children in that place. There were infants and teenagers, all inked across the face and treated as if they had single-handedly committed crimes against their own people. As ten-year-old Lieven walked through the institution's hallways, half hidden behind his dad, he wished he could close his eyes and forget the misery he witnessed.

A door to the left suddenly opened up, and his eyes were drawn to what was happening inside. A young boy, about his own age, was tied to a post, shirtless and barefoot. Lieven stopped, unable to look away in spite of his young heart's fervent wish to do so. A tall, middle-aged man lifted a switch in his hand and lowered it with gusto onto the boy's back. Again and again. Blood gushed from the open wounds and splattered freely in the air like tinted rain. Lieven gasped, horrified.

The boy's blue eyes strayed to him, and the pain they reflected nearly killed him. How was it possible that such a young boy could hold so much heartache within him? He couldn't even imagine feeling that much pain. His back and his soul hurt as he watched the beating go on until the boy finally passed out, hanging from the ties around his wrists, his head lolling backwards as if he was dead. Lieven felt a wetness on his cheeks and realized he was crying. How could he ever look at life the same way when there were children being treated worse than common criminals?

That night, he had nagged his father until he finally gave in to his request; Lieven wanted to help the boy he saw being whipped within an inch of his life. Being only a child, he didn't know how but hoped his dad could figure out a way. His dad didn't disappoint. Shortly after that, his father managed to convince the Council of Elders to allow him partial guardianship of the young boy. Cees was to spend a few days in the institution—so he could be properly punished—and stay with Lieven's family the rest of the time. It was not ideal, but it was a hell of a lot better than what Cees had going for him at the time.

Lieven would never forget the day Cees first came to the house. His whole demeanor was more like that of a scared animal than a human, intense blue eyes fluttering in every direction, jerky motions, and lips always set into a frown. He wouldn't talk for weeks, and if accidentally touched, he would flinch as if in pain. Lieven had done everything he could think of to try and get Cees to open up to him: toy offerings, candy, even a pair of shoes once. Nothing seemed to coax him out of his protective cocoon until the day his father brought a set of coloring pencils home.

Cees' eyes opened so wide, Lieven thought his eyeballs would pop and his lips, always glued together, parted into a tiny smile. Lieven had grabbed the pencils out of his father's hands and offered them to the boy. From that moment on, he had lost a pet and won a best friend. Color and art called to Cees like athletic sports called out to Lieven—it was as if when drawing and coloring, all of Cees' pain and tribulations went away and were replaced by a sense of peace and well-being. They had inadvertently found Cees' life-line.

Now in that bunker, Lieven's heart clenched at the thought that his friend might be gone forever. Shaking such thoughts of his head, he took a glimpse at his watch. It was almost time to exit the bunker.

"Gather round, soldiers," he called out, more for something to keep him busy than real necessity.

For the next hour, the men busied themselves packing their gear, stretching their stiff muscles; for a little while, they forgot what had happened and focused instead on the immediate. When the door was unbolted and the sunlight shone through the opening, they all let out an involuntary gasp. Lieven inhaled a deep breath of the cool, cleaner air and took a step outside. Looking around him, he could see that several of his fellow soldiers were also emerging from the other hideaways. He gestured for them to be quiet and spread out. Until they were sure there were no Predators in the area, it was too risky to be totally visible.

Lieven and a couple of his men padded their way to the door that had been locked. Much to his surprise, as he approached, the door suddenly cracked open. The soldiers hid around a corner of a neighboring building to watch what emerged from the bunker without being seen. Whoever or whatever it was, was taking its time to come out, but eventually two figures stepped out into the light.

Lieven couldn't believe his eyes. "Cees!" he yelled out, forgetting where he was. His other men glanced at him in surprise, raising their guns at the sight of Cees' face stripe. "It's okay. He's my friend."

Cees had heard him too and was striding toward him, closely followed by a girl he didn't recognize. Lieven didn't wait. Taking off toward his friend, he threw himself at him with arms wide open and wrapped him in a tight embrace.

Cees laughed as he patted his back. "Gods! I can't believe you're alive."

Lieven had lost the power of speech. With his face buried in his friend's shoulder, he cried freely and unabashedly. His heart drummed a happy song, and he just couldn't let go.

"You're going to kill me, Liev," Cees joked, pushing him gently away. "I need to breathe."

Lieven released him and wiped the tears from his face. He couldn't believe this twist of fate. "I'm so happy you're alive. We thought everybody had died."

Cees' smile died on his lips. "It was a massacre. Thank the gods you were out with your squad."

With a side glance toward the girl, Lieven nodded his head. "But it looks like you both got out safely." His fellow soldiers had gathered around them and were watching the scene curiously, staring at the girl's unusual haircut.

"Lieven," his squad leader said suddenly. "She's *Gezegenden*." It was more of an accusation than a statement.

The girl took a step backwards and glanced at Cees, who stretched a hand toward her. "This is Jia. She's a survivor from *Wêreld* just like us."

The young woman accepted the hand Cees was offering her and tucked herself against his side. Lieven watched it, a slow-burning fire starting inside his chest. "But she is *Gezegenden*."

"That world is dead, Liev." His friend pulled Jia closer to him. "We're just all survivors."

Anger turned his vision scarlet. "I wonder if she would say the same about you if we were a *Gezegenden* squad." His eyes must have spoken volumes because Jia flinched.

His friend stretched a hand to touch his shoulder. "Stop it, Liev." Cees' voice was low but firm. "Things have changed. Her world—just like ours—has been destroyed. We have to put that behind us and help each other if we are to survive."

Jia took a small step forward, still holding on to Cees' hand and arm. "You have every right to be suspicious of me. I grew up thinking the *Zuiver* were lower humans, unstable, untrustworthy."

Lieven cringed at the words as if she had just slapped him. "But now, thanks to our unfriendly neighborhood monster, you realized how wrong you were." His voice dripped with sarcasm, and his lips twisted into a frown.

"I realized that I was not given the full scope about the *Zuiver*." Her silvery eyes honed on him. "I would be lying if I said I have now changed my mind completely, but I definitely see that there is a lot more to consider, a lot more to know."

"The *Gezegenden* treat us like animals." Lieven's tall frame—just slightly shorter than Cees—towered over her like a threat. "We are refused good weapons to defend ourselves, technology, education...not allowed beyond the borders of our commune."

"Enough!" Cees' voice echoed through the empty street. "If I was to think like that, Liev, I wouldn't want to be with the rest of your squad. My own people treated me like a criminal, isolated me, forbade me from aspiring to a good life." Lieven quieted down and avoided his friend's eyes. "You were the only one who did not agree with the system's decision to make me pay for my parents' mistakes. Can't you extend the same kindness to a fellow survivor now?"

Lieven scratched his head and licked his lips. Should he trust this girl, this *Gezegenden* who, in other circumstances, would look down on all of them? Cees seemed so sure that she was on their side, but that was what his friend did—believe. He was so willing to believe in the goodness of people, he had tattooed the word into his neck. In his heart, he knew that whatever higher power had created all of them was also inside each one of them, part of their life forces, their souls. Lieven wanted to believe that, but he had seen such cruelty among his own people; he was more of a skeptic.

Looking into his friend's deep blue eyes, Lieven gave up. Who was he kidding? Whatever Cees asked him to do, he would do it. No questions asked. He sometimes wondered whether Cees knew the power he had over him.

With a hand stretched to Jia in a gesture of peace offering, Lieven summoned a ghost of a smile to his lips. "If Cees vouches for you, I will accept his judgment."

Jia accepted his hand in hers and shook it. She had the soft hands of someone who never had to work hard one day in her life. Lieven swallowed bitter resentment. This was no way to start an alliance.

"What about your men?" Cees scanned the group now staring at them with blank faces. "Will they accept me, a Tainted one, within your ranks?"

Lieven turned to his squad leader with a question in his eyes. After a moment of hesitation, Alfons nodded in assent. "He's right. The world as we know has ended. We don't have the luxury of separating castes anymore. There aren't enough of us. We must unite against the common enemy if we want to survive."

It was the speech of a true leader, and every man in the squad listened, their heads bent down slightly and nodding as he spoke. They would follow him into battle with no hesitation, and this was no different. If Alfons thought this was the right strategy to keep them alive, so be it.

"Now that we got that out of the way," Alfons continued. "We must go on. The question remains, where to? Where can we have a chance of survival?"

"We head somewhere smelly," Cees suggested. "They will stay off our scent that way."

"Right, but we don't know of any other place like this." Alfons pointed at the area around them. "*Zuivers* are only allowed up to a certain distance from the commune. This is as far as we have been able to explore."

As by common agreement, they all turned their eyes to Jia, who did a double take, her eyes widening. "What? I don't know about any stinky place."

Cees, still holding onto her hand, pulled her around to look at him. "Think.You went to school for a long time. You must remember some place—from geography or history—that has a strong smell or is close to somewhere with a bad stench."

Jia closed her eyes tight. Lieven noticed her hand squeezing Cees' and his heart lurched. What had happened between the two of them while in the bunker?

"I got it!" she suddenly yelled, her eyes popping open. "I remember reading about a swamp, not too far from *Wêreld*—a two-days walk, maybe. The scientists frequently took trips there to study the chemicals in the water that made it smell so bad. They were hoping to figure out some kind of product to—" Her voice died down as they all realized what the scientists had been trying to produce—a Predator repellent.

"They knew this was coming." Lieven's outrage was hard to contain. "They knew we were all in danger and said nothing."

"No, that's not possible." Jia's eyes flittered between Cees and his friend. "They would have warned the populace. They would have tried to protect the Blessed."

Bitterness crawled back into Lieven's heart. "How does that make you feel, little *Gezegenden*? To be treated as if you are nothing? Now you know how we feel."

Cees threw him a warning look. "This swamp. How far is it from here?" he asked, trying to deflect his friend's anger.

Jia's eyes hardened. "I've sort of lost my bearings trying to escape the beasts." A subtle hint of anger emerged in her voice. "It is west of *Wêreld*."

"This is west of *Wêreld*, as well." Cees looked at his friend whose lips were set into a frown. "Which means we should be about a day off. A little less if we're lucky."

Alfons took command. "All right, men. We will march west, and hopefully we will come upon this swamp before nightfall. In the meantime, rub your body and clothes with the chemical we collected in the bunkers."

Lieven watched the girl as she gingerly—but with determination—rubbed a generous amount of the odorous material on herself. "What if this is toxic?"

"I'd rather die of poisoning than be those animals' chew toy," Lieven said. No one argued with him.

Soon they were on their way, in a two-men file, armed soldiers in front and on the back. Lieven took his place right behind his friend and swallowed hard when he realized Jia was still holding on to Cees as for dear life.

She's lost everything. She's just grateful to him. Let it go, Liev. Let it go.

Cees

The forest was thick and luscious. Another time, Cees would have enjoyed exploring it—touching the cool, velvety leaves of the overgrown bushes, smelling the fresh scent of the evergreens. But this was no time to admire nature. There was terror and urgency in all their hearts. All they cared about was quickly getting to safety.

Lieven walked ahead of them, his step sure and confident, his whole demeanor that of a soldier trained to take charge in a time of crisis. If he hadn't known Lieven so well, Cees would have never guessed the gentleness his friend carried in his soul. A smile crept onto his lips. The relief that washed over him when he saw Lieven just outside that bunker was indescribable. Lieven was his only family, his only connection with the world at large. Losing him would have meant losing everything.

By his side, Jia walked silently, her hand periodically seeking his as to make sure she was not alone. Cees wondered whether her seeming toughness was but a facade, a mask she used to protect herself from others. What secrets was she keeping? Were her nightmares about the Predators or something else? He watched her from the corner of his eye as she made her way through the thick covering of the forest floor, her gun tucked in the pants he had given her and her face glistening with sweat. Her short black hair suited her outward toughness, but her orange aura discredited it—the color told him she had the fire and thirst of the very young, a certain warmth of spirit.

"We will stop for a few minutes," Lieven said, raising his hand. "Eat and rest for a while. Make sure to rub some more of the *stank* on yourselves." The men had named the mysterious reeking chemical right after they had left the concrete city.

Lieven walked a few steps back toward Cees. Jia paced restless. "Maybe we should keep on moving," she said.

"We're not machines." Lieven dropped to a tree stump and opened his backpack. "We need to rest and recharge. Sit down." His tone of voice left no room for discussion. Cees watched, amused as the girl obeyed with no further argument.

They all shared a piece of bread Lieven had in his bag. It was hard and stale, but it was food. Cees spotted some bright red berries on a nearby bush and stood up to go gather them.

"Those are probably poisonous," Lieven said. "Red berries often are."

Cees sat back down, his hands brimming with the brightly colored berries. "Not these," he said, popping a few in his mouth. "They have a yellow aura. Perfectly safe." He offered his friends some.

At first eying the fruit suspiciously, Jia hesitated. "I will wait to see if you die before I eat it." She frowned.

Lieven burst out laughing, spitting out some of the berries he was chewing. "Nice friend you got there, Cees. Looking out for you."

With a grin, Cees popped some more berries in his mouth. "More for me, Jia. These are deliciously juicy." Some of the red juice was dripping down his chin. Lieven reached out and wiped it off with his fingers. "Okay, Mom. I can wipe my own mouth."

Jia looked at him and his friend, a question in her eyes. "You guys are weird." Then, she took another look at the berries and, giving in to hunger, popped them all into her mouth. "These *are* good."

The short rest soon came to an end and they resumed their walking. Cees had hoped they would reach the swamp before nighttime, but considering they had a very sketchy idea as to where they were heading he feared they probably wouldn't. If they had to make camp before reaching their destination, they would be vulnerable to an attack. The Predators had eyes tailored to see in the dark unlike their own. If *Zuiver* soldiers had been provided with night-vision goggles, they could have kept going without the need to stop. Since *Zuivers* were not allowed any of the cutting-edge technology available to Central and the *Gezegenden,* their very human, normal eyesight was all they had to rely on.

"What do we do once we get there?" Jia asked him in a whisper, tucking herself against his side.

His arm went automatically around her shoulders, as if they had been doing this all their lives. "We rest and regroup. We need to gather as much information about these monsters as possible so we can come up with a plan."

Her head was resting against his chest, just under his shoulder and Cees had to slow down his pace. "How are we going to do that? No computers, no libraries..."

Cees sighed a little, enjoying the warmth of another human being against him. "We may be able to find a library somewhere along the way. But what's a computer?"

Her head jerked up to stare at him. "You're kidding, right?" Her mouth fell open slightly. He looked at her and shrugged. "Oh gods! They really have deprived your people from a lot, haven't they?"

"If by *they* you mean the *Gezegenden*, then yes. They have." His voice hardened, his smile dying on his lips.

"The rules are not coming from the common Blessed Ones," she protested weakly. "Central comes up with all those rules."

"Which you don't fight." Cees glowered at her. "If you questioned those laws, fought them even, the *Zuiver* wouldn't be so isolated."

Jia pushed herself away from him and stopped, letting him go ahead a few steps. Cees looked back, took a deep breath, and stretched out a hand to her. "Come on, don't be stupid. We can't get mad at each other. We must stick together."

After a moment of hesitation, she took his hand and sped up to keep pace with him.

"I'm sorry." Jia had been silent for a long while. "I'm sorry for the injustices done to your people, and I wish I could go back in time and change things. But I can't. My only excuse is I didn't know any better."

"I know." Cees pulled her against him, planting a gentle kiss on the top of her head. "I'm sorry, too. I shouldn't blame you for the sins of those in charge."

"Will you two stop schmoozing and keep going?" Lieven didn't look happy, staring at them from a few steps away.

"We are moving." Cees frowned at his friend, puzzled. "What's your problem?"

Lieven stopped walking and waited for them to catch up with him. His usually generous smile was turned into a hard line. "My problem is that you are too busy with each other to focus on the task at hand."

Cees was surprised by his friend's attitude. He and Jia had not stopped yet and even though he had slowed down at times to allow the girl's shorter legs to catch up, nothing had kept them distracted from their march. To Cees' utter confusion, Lieven seemed angry, as if he had done something terribly wrong. What exactly was going on?

Before Cees could ask any question, Lieven turned around and resumed his quick march.

"What was that all about?" Cees asked out loud to no one in particular. "He's acting really weird."

Jia resumed her walking, prodding him along. "Give him a break. He just lost everything. Didn't he have a family? A girlfriend?"

Moving a branch out of their way with his hand, Cees shook his head. "No, he lost his dad a few years back to sickness. And he doesn't date much. Or at all, now that I think about it. At least, he does not talk about it."

"He's very handsome." Jia giggled.

His head jerked in her direction. "What?"

She smiled, amused by his reaction. "You heard me," she said. "I would date him."

A growing irritation flared in his chest. "Are you kidding me? We're running away from monsters, and you are thinking about sex?"

A strong tug pulled him backwards as Jia abruptly stopped, her eyes clouding in anger. "I just made a harmless comment about your friend. He's cute. Do you want me to say he's ugly as sin?"

Her aura turned a furious red, and his own annoyance grew to match it. "I just find it weird that we are running from danger, and you can't keep your mind off sex." Even as he said it, he knew he was being irrational. But his mouth was not getting the message. "What's the problem? Since I didn't give it to you in the bunker, you need to get it elsewhere, *Gezegenden hoer*?"

Her hand rose up in the air and descended, fast as lightening, across his cheek. His head turned with the shock of the slap, and he grabbed her hand before it came down again on him.

"Bastard! Filthy *Zuiver*." Anger choked her voice. "How dare you?"

Lieven and a few of the other soldiers had stopped to watch the scene. "What the hell are you guys doing?" He took a step back toward them. "One minute you are all lovey-dovey, the next you're beating each other up."

Still holding her wrist in his hand, Cees stared at her light gray eyes. Was she tearing up? Guilt quickly replaced his anger, and he softened his hold on her. "Sorry, Lieven." He threw his friend a quick glance. "We're okay."

Jia's heavy breathing belied his words, but Lieven seemed to accept it and resumed his walk.

"Sorry." Cees had whispered so softly, he wasn't sure Jia could hear him. He searched her eyes again, but she was hiding. A purplish aura rose around her. "I'm sorry I hurt you. That was uncalled for. I was..." Was he jealous? How could he be jealous? They had just met, and they couldn't be from more different worlds if she was from another planet. And there was the whole matter of running the danger of being eaten by monsters. It was madness.

With a jerk, she pulled her arm off his hand and began walking forward, chin on her chest, hands stuffed in her pockets. Cees knew he shouldn't push it and, giving up on any pretense, just followed her in silence. He could see her hunched back as she tucked her chin in and her aura following her like a purple ghost. How could he have called her a whore? Used to being the tormented—not the tormentor—Cees felt guilt drowning him, suffocating him with its weight and stench.

"Wait!" Cees' hand shot forward to her. With a gentle pull, he turned her around to face him. Her face was wet, tears rolling down her cheeks and hanging precariously on her chin. "Gods, what have I done? I'm sorry Jia. I didn't mean it." He searched for her eyes, hidden underneath her dark lashes. "Please, say you forgive me. I don't know what came over me."

Her eyes rose to meet his, and a powerful current of energy went through him, electrifying every inch of his body. "I didn't mean it either," she whispered, wiping her tears with the back of her hand. He narrowed his eyes, eyebrows knitted together. "When I called you filthy *Zuiver*. I don't think that at all. I was mad, that's all."

Hell, his heart was going to burst. He pulled her closer to him in a hug. "Are we okay?" he whispered in her ear. She nodded. "We better get moving. I'm getting dirty looks from Lieven."

She giggled against his chest and pulled away. "You may have snot on your shirt," she said, turning around beside him. "It serves you right calling me a *hoer*."

"Will the two of you quit this lover's quarrel and get a move on?" Lieven yelled out, making both of them laugh. Lieven threw his arms up in the air and walked on.

Jia

We're not going to make it.

Darkness was quickly enfolding them, and there was no sight of the swamp yet. They would be exposed and vulnerable not only to the Predators but any other wild animal in the forest. Fire would protect them, but it would also flag them for the enemy. Jia looked at Cees who was just a few inches away from her. His brow was knitted together in worry, but he doggedly marched forward without any sign of slowing down. Her own legs were painfully complaining about the all-day walk, but she was not going to let the others know that. The *Zuiver* soldiers already thought her to be a privileged weakling. She didn't want to reinforce their assumptions. Jia would keep on walking until her legs wouldn't hold her anymore.

"Ahead!" Alfons, ahead of the convoy, was excitedly waving at them. Everyone hurried to see what he was waving about.

The density of the tree covering had suddenly thinned out and, stretched in front of them, was a large swampy area. The air was thick with a strong, rotten odor, and they could see gases rising from the viscous water like long, ghostly fingers in the dusk.

"We've made it." Jia could hear the relief in Cees' voice. He looked at her and smiled. "We made it," he said, a little louder this time.

Jia smiled. His joy was contagious. "Yes, we have," she said, nodding.

After a short survey of the area, Alfons announced there was a dry area they could use for camping out for the night. They all gingerly made their way over the slippery rocks until they reached a piece of land that strongly resembled an island. Surrounded by the murky, smelly waters of the swamp, it made for the perfect hideout. The soldiers immediately erected shelters and prepared for nightfall. Jia and Cees were the only ones without a tent or a sleeping bag.

"Cees can share my tent," Lieven said when she brought it up. "You can share the tent with one of the girls."

There were three females in the squad. Jia had barely noticed them, hidden as they were by their beige uniform. But now, as they removed their hats, Jia was in awe of their long hairs, falling freely over their shoulders. Not many Blessed women wore their hair long. It was inconvenient and hard to keep up. Like Jia, most of them had adopted a short, cropped look. The *Zuiver* females, despite being soldiers, all had thick hair they apparently tied into large buns under their military hats.

"You can bunk with me," one of them offered, stepping closer. "I'm Aleid."

Jia shook her hand. Aleid was a tall, dark-haired woman with big brown eyes. "Nice meeting you," Jia said, a bit intimidated by her height. With Jia's five-foot-three stature, Aleid looked like a giant to her.

Huddled together to protect themselves from the cold, they ate what meager supplies they had left. The temperature had dropped substantially since they had first arrived. Jia shivered as memories of the Big Freeze assailed her mind. Cees, sitting next to her, protectively draped his arm around her shoulders and pulled her closer to him. "We'll be warmer this way." He shrugged.

Jia didn't mind. In fact, she welcomed his body heat. Who was she kidding? She welcomed his body. Period. Even though they had known each other for such a short time, she felt as if she had known Cees all her life. He felt comfortable, he felt like home to her. In her long list of past boyfriends there was not a single one who had made her feel that way. It was a bit unnerving to think a stranger, a *Zuiver*, could make her feel all warm and fuzzy inside. She settled against him, her eyes drooping with exhaustion.

"You better go to bed," he whispered. "You're tired, and we don't know what's waiting for us tomorrow."

"I am tired." Her voice slurred with the weight of sleep. "Stay with me." Jia was not sure where that had come from, but she didn't regret it. She was safe with him.

Cees was quiet for a moment. Then he pulled her even closer and kissed the top of her head, the heat of his lips sending a tingling wave through her skull. "It may look...inappropriate."

"Who cares?" Hard to be outraged mollified by her fatigue as she was. "I want you by my side, Cees. Please…"

The movement beside her told her Cees was on the move. Not that she could see it because her eyes had closed, heavy with sleep. Jia felt herself being lifted in the air by strong—but gentle—arms and carried away. She could feel hard muscle against her side as she wrapped an arm around his neck for a better hold.

"Thank you," Jia whispered against his shirt before the world faded into soothing blackness.

She woke up sometime during the night to find herself enveloped in Cees' warm arms. Wiggling a little, she adjusted herself to fit perfectly with his curved body and fell asleep again.

In the morning, her eyes slowly opened to dim light, as if even the sun did not want to venture into such reeking air. Instinctively, she reached behind her to touch Cees, but there was no-one there. With a flip, she turned around and was shocked to find Aleid sleeping a mere few inches away from her. Where was Cees? Why was Aleid there instead of him?

Jia stretched her arms above her head and sat up slowly, not wanting to wake up the other woman. Thankfully, she wouldn't have to climb over her to leave the tent. On all fours, she crawled out into the sunlight and looked around. A few men were already up, huddled in a tight circle speaking in whispers. Cees was among them, sitting by Lieven, their heads leaning close in an easy, familiar way. Cautious not to step in the many muddy puddles that covered a large portion of the "island", Jia approached them a bit apprehensive.

"Good morning." Several heads turned to her. Cees smiled and her heart felt lighter immediately.

"Hi, sunshine," he said. "Come and sit by us." He patted the ground between him and Lieven. For a minute she was hesitant to accept the invitation. Lieven didn't look too excited about the idea. "Come on, Jia. What are you waiting for?" She sat down as Lieven and Cees scooted apart to make room for her.

"Did you sleep well?" Lieven had moved his gaze to the ground in front of him and his voice came out strained.

"I did, thank you." She turned to Cees who was scribbling in the dirt with a stick. "Where did you go?" she asked him.

Lieven answered for him. "We don't have enough tents and I couldn't share with Aleid. So, after you fell asleep, Cees moved to my tent."

Cees shrugged and offered her a sheepish smile. "You looked so peaceful," he said. "I didn't want to wake you up to tell you. Want something to eat?"

They partook of a thin ration of mushy grains and a piece of stale bread. While they were eating and talking softly, the rest of the squad woke up and joined them. Soon the informal, friendly gathering became a more official planning meeting. The soldiers, led by Alfons, exchanged ideas on what to do next. Jia listened in silence, feeling she had nothing of value to contribute. She had lived all her life in a party-haze. Being one of the Blessed, and attractive, she had been able to hide behind the fuss of social interactions. Unwilling to share her true feelings, her hurts, Jia had adopted the life of a socialite with gusto. No one knew what she held inside, and that had always been okay with her. Showing what went on in her heart was not something she relished doing. It was a sign of weakness, of admitting she needed somebody else. Her mom had taught her that.

"You must rely *only* on yourself," her mother always said. "That way, you won't ever be disappointed or hurt." While she may have not been disappointed, Jia had been hurt plenty of times.

"What do you think?" Jia realized with a jolt that Cees was addressing her. What did she think? He really wanted to know? "We stay here a few days and plan our next move, or we move right away?"

Her usual tough shell crumbled under the scrutiny of all those eyes. What could she say? "I'm not sure," she mumbled, her cheeks burning. "I'm not a soldier or an explorer."

Cees slipped his hand in hers until their fingers were entwined. "You've learned things we haven't." His voice was gentle and encouraging. "Try to remember; what's beyond this swamp? Is it far?"

Jia, once again, dug into the depths of her memories in search of a kernel of knowledge that may be helpful. She wished she had taken those geography classes more seriously now. At the time, they were just what was required, and once they were done, she had no wish to recall any of the information learned. Not much came to mind, and anger at herself erupted inside her chest.

"I'm useless!" she cried. "I am absolutely useless." She stood up and stomped away from the group, feeling tears of frustration burning in her eyes.

"Don't say that." Cees was standing behind her, his hand on her shoulder. "You're not useless. You got us to this safe haven. Without you, we would still be wandering around like lost life forces. We would probably be dead."

She turned around reluctantly and looked at him with moist eyes. "I lived a life of no purpose, no import. Even the little I learned does not come easy to me because I didn't take anything seriously. Ever."

Cees drew her to him and held her against his chest. "Don't put yourself down like this," he whispered, his lips resting on the top of her head. "We need you. *I* need you."

The beating of his heart underneath her ear was like a soothing song; it calmed her, it lulled her into peace. She lifted her face up to his. "You need me?"

"I've always been alone. Lieven was my only friend." His eyes were soft. "When his father was alive, he was also there for me. But other than the two of them I have been alone all my life. Trapped on an island surrounded by people who do not see me, who do not care whether I am alive."

"But I'm Blessed. Why would you need me?"

"What does it matter who you are or where you come from?" Cees dismissed the notion with a shrug. "I feel a connection with you. Simple as that."

Jia smiled. True or not, his words made her feel whole inside. She lifted her hand and brushed her fingers across his face, tracing the outline of the black stripe across his temples and eyes. The ink made the blue of his eyes pop out, inadvertently enhancing the beauty of his face. Ironic that a symbol of hate would be thwarted by the purity of his life force.

Cees bent down slightly, and his face came inches away from hers. For a moment Jia thought he was going to kiss her. She wanted him to. Unconsciously, she tilted her face up, ready to welcome his lips, but they never came. Instead, the *Zuiver* planted a warm kiss on her forehead. His lips left a moist burning sensation on her skin, and an alarmingly familiar yearning filled her heart. She had felt it in the bunker when they were alone and thought they were going to die. At the time, she thought it had been desperation, but how could she justify it this time? The flames in her core were quickly devouring her whole. Her breathing became rugged and fast. If he didn't move away from her, she was going to lose control and show him—and everybody else—how she felt.

As if sensing her thoughts, Cees took a step back, letting her go. "Let's join the others?" Was she imagining it, or was he breathing a bit too fast, as well? He rubbed his hands on his pants as if they were wet, and his gaze bounced between her and the others. She didn't reply. "Jia? Are you okay?"

Jia nodded, not trusting herself to speak. She pointed towards the others and stepped forward on shaky legs, her face burning as fiercely as her chest. This was no time or place for these kinds of feelings. The focus was on survival.

"Are you done with the love-fest?" Lieven's face was set in a grimace.

Cees slapped him gently across the back of his head. "Will you stop that, Liev?" he said, dropping to the ground beside him. "Stop teasing her. And me."

Lieven let out a dry chuckle. "Then focus, damn it! Focus on what is important."

Her heart felt ripe with so many overwhelming feelings, Jia just couldn't sit next to Cees. She opted for an open spot on the other side of Lieven, who looked up at her with a frown. "Have you thought of anything helpful to share?" Sarcasm colored his voice.

"There is a small city, south of here," she said, surprising herself. Where was this information coming from? The dismissive stare Lieven had given her seemed to have triggered a memory. "Less than a day's walk. They should have resources. It's a town of the Blessed."

"A town of the *Gerechtigd,* the Entitled," one of the soldiers said, and they all laughed.

All except Cees, who had turned an angry shade of red. "She's trying to help us, and you have nothing better to say than making fun of her people?" he growled. "You should be ashamed of yourselves. I'm disappointed in you, Liev. I thought you were better than this."

Silence fell, heavy and oppressive. The soldiers all stared at each other as if searching for validation. Lieven licked his lips and looked at Cees, a stricken expression in his eyes. "I'm sorry, my friend. I don't know what came over me. "

Cees shook his head. "It's not me you have to apologize to." His eyes turned to Jia.

Lieven twisted around to face her. "I'm sorry, Jia." He offered his hand in peace. "We were wrong to say that. You have been a great help."

They shook hands as Jia's lips stretched into a smile. Cees' friend grinned in return. But Jia was not smiling for him. Her gaze overshot Lieven's blond head to dive into his friend's ocean blue eyes, the two azure orbs that soothed her nerves and electrified her heart. The only eyes that mattered to her.

Lieven

The decision had been made to leave the reeking island in the morning and try to reach the small town Jia had mentioned. They were all hoping and praying the vapors from the swamp were strong and the town close enough to protect them. They didn't have much choice. The food supplies were quickly dwindling; soon it would be a matter of either dying at the hands of the monsters or of starvation.

After a long conversation with Cees, Jia had retired to Aleid's tent, and his friend was now sitting by his side. Cees' dark, wavy hair was tousled the way it always seemed to be when the young artist was worried or stressed about something. Ever since his teens, Cees had this habit of raking his fingers through his hair obsessively until the hair was sticking every which way. It used to make him laugh when they were kids, but as they grew into adults, it became an endearing quirk that made Lieven's heart beat just a little faster.

"I'm going to bed," Cees yawned loudly. Darkness had descended upon the swamp, and the gases that escaped from the mire created a ghostly fluorescent mist all around them.

Lieven stood up. "I'm coming too." There was nothing else to do, and all the other men had gone to sleep already.

They both crawled into the small tent. Cees wiggled around like a dog looking for the perfect position to sleep. Lieven laughed softly.

"What's so funny?" Cees asked, turning half way around to look at his friend who, lying with his arms behind his head, laughed in earnest.

"The way you just burrow into your sleeping space," he said, chuckles punctuating his speech.

Cees looked surprised. "I do not!"

"You do too," Lieven protested, sighing deeply. "You've always done that. I used to think, who needs a dog when I have Cees who does the same thing?"

A quick rise of the eyebrows was all the warning Lieven had of the attack. Cees pivoted around and playfully punched him on the shoulder, which led to a tactical defensive move from his friend. Soon they were rough-housing like they had done since they were kids. Except, Lieven's feelings for Cees had changed radically in the last few years. What started as their usual friendly game was now making his heart race at full speed, and that too-familiar feeling of yearning erupted inside of him. Lieven abruptly stopped and looked in the wintry night eyes of his friend, feeling an overwhelming urge to kiss him. What would happen if he did? Would Cees go with it? Would their friendship—and his heart—forever fracture?

For a moment, he allowed himself the fantasy. He could feel Cees' warm lips welcoming his in a kiss that eclipsed everything else: the mire they had been stuck in for the past couple days, the stench rising from the swamp, the Predators even. All he could think and feel was that long-yearned-for kiss and how it made every part of him tingle and glitter, how it made him come alive.

"Shit, Liev! You weigh a ton," Cees said, breaking the spell. Lieven was still pinning his friend down, Cees's face mere inches away from his—yet it may as well be planets apart. He quickly flipped to the side, freeing Cees from the weight of his body and the temptation to go through with his fantasy.

Both winded for different reasons, the two friends lay on their backs. Cees laughed softly. "That brought back memories." It had brought back so much more than memories to Lieven.

"Cees?" Lieven's voice was but a whisper. "What's going on with you and the *Gezegenden* girl?"

"What do you mean?" Cees turned his face to look at his friend, his eyebrow arched all the way up.

"You look very...close." Lieven was at a loss for words. "Are you and her... You know?"

Cees's eyes opened wide in sudden comprehension. "No, we haven't... No, we're not." The stuttering was more telling than anything else he may have said. They may have not slept together yet, but it was obvious there were feelings between them.

"You like her?" Lieven already knew the answer. He could have sworn he saw Cees blush even in the semi-darkness of the tent.

"So what if I do?" Cees said, reverting to the childhood tone he used whenever Lieven would challenge him with a hard question. "Is that a problem?"

His heart was bleeding, but Lieven could not find fault in his friend's interest in another human being. He had been alone for so long, even among his people. Rarely looked at with more than despise, Cees deserved to be loved and love fully in return. Lieven couldn't—wouldn't begrudge him that. He just wished he was the object of that love. "No problem. Just wondering..."

Soon, Lieven could hear his friend's breathing slowing down, and he knew he was asleep. Lieven allowed the sigh he had been holding in to finally escape. Turning on his side, his back turned to Cees, Lieven closed his eyes and willed himself to sleep even when his body was still alive with desire and frustration.

CHAPTER FIVE
WALLS

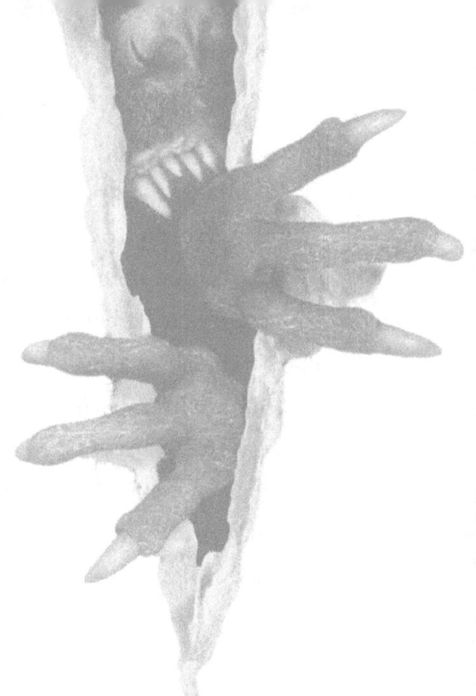

Cees

The journey was shorter than they had expected. The small town appeared on the horizon a few hours before nightfall. Silence permeated the air, thick and ominous. Even animals seemed to have vanished. As they walked through the lonely streets, it quickly became obvious that the town had already been raided by the Predators. Blood stained the sidewalks, and every so often, they came across human bones picked clean. The good news was that since the beasts had already been there, they wouldn't be coming back any time soon. For a while at least, they could breathe easily.

Alfons sent them in separate groups to scout the town in search of locations where they could possibly gather some information on the creatures. Jia had mentioned computers, but none of them had ever seen one, so she had to describe them in great detail before they went searching for them.

When Alfons paired Cees with Jia, Lieven had glowered at her as if she had committed a crime against humanity. Cees was having trouble understanding his friend's reaction to Jia. Lieven had always been so understanding, so compassionate toward anybody who was out-casted. However, that was not the case with the young *Gezegenden*. His good friend seemed to harbor some strange animosity for the girl that he couldn't comprehend.

The small town had been inhabited by *Gezegenden* of humbler resources than those in *Wêreld*, where the buildings were tall and sumptuous. Cees and Lieven had once snuck into the outskirts of town despite the danger of disciplinary action. He was as curious as Cees to see what the world of the *Gezegenden* looked like. They had been both stricken by the luxury of the city where Jia once lived. People drove rather than walked, and they wore such a variety of clothes that both friends were dizzied and confused by the kaleidoscope of colors parading before them. In the *Zuiver* commune, clothing was mostly monochromatic, either black, brown, or drab green. Lieven's uniform was made of beige linen that could only be described as nondescript. Colorful clothes were rare and reserved only for celebrations.

Jia had taken the lead since she was a lot more familiar with the cities of the *Gezegenden*. "We should look for schools or a library," she said. "If the servers are still functioning, we could also look in offices."

Cees had no idea what a server was or why it was important they were functioning, but he was willing to follow her lead. She seemed to know what she was doing. "Should we go inside the buildings?" he asked.

"As soon as we find the right one." They were both walking in the middle of the road where the blood splattering was fainter and less frequent. It just felt wrong to walk over the spilled blood of others.

"Did you sleep well last night?" Cees had dreamed about her all night. Wonderful, yet unsettling dreams that made him shake and crave her presence. "Was Aleid a good bed companion?"

Jia laughed, throwing her head backwards. "You make it sound like Aleid and I just had sex or something."

Cees felt his face burn. "I didn't mean it that way," he mumbled, annoyed that she was laughing at him. "It was not *that* funny."

With a great show of surprise, Jia stopped and stared at him. "Yes, it is. And yes, Aleid was an awesome companion."

Cees hung his head, embarrassed. The heat of her hand in his arm made him look up again. Jia was standing in front of him, her eyes no longer mocking but soft and warm.

"But I wish you were there instead," she whispered, so low he was not sure he had heard her correctly.

She took a step closer to him and he quivered. "Why?" he asked.

"What do you mean why?" She took another step toward him. Her body was now almost flush with his. "Isn't it obvious? Don't you feel it?"

Cees' body vibrated with a mixture of fear and excitement. He could feel her body heat and every pore, every inch of his skin came alive with electricity. "Feel what?"

"Don't be thick, Cees." Jia's hand landed flat on his chest, over his crazed heart. "You know what I mean. We have this connection, this attraction for each other that won't be denied."

Despite the lack of washing and the layer of dust and sweat that covered them both, her scent reached his nose as sweet as if she had bathed in perfume. She was so close. "Jia...the others," he stuttered, searching for an excuse not to do what he was dying to do.

"The others are in a different block." She tilted her face up to his. "We're alone."

Hesitantly, Cees lowered his face to hers until their lips touched. He was not ready for the jolt of energy that ran through him at the contact. His arms, still hanging beside his body, were twitching to hold and crush her against him, but she didn't give him the chance. With a small jump, Jia wrapped both legs around him and locked her arms behind his neck. He stumbled backwards, surprised by the sudden weight, but regained his balance almost immediately. Cees anchored Jia against him, his arms underneath her as his lips explored hers.

His heart thumped like a wild rabbit sensing danger and his whole body, more alive than ever before, was electrified. He felt himself respond to her so intensely, it scared him. Not once had he ever felt like this. Being Tainted meant very little human contact. Dating was out completely. He had trained himself as soon as he was old enough to feel the normal stirrings not to look, not to want, not to feel... Now, he wanted Jia so badly, it made it hard for him to breathe. Her tongue had found its way to his, and they were dancing together as if the outside world didn't exist. As if they were not running away from and surrounded by the stench of death.

"Jia..." he whispered. It took a lot of self-control to pull his mouth away from hers even for just a moment. "We have to stop. We have a job to do, and it's getting late."

Jia, still hanging from his neck and waist, looked him in the eye. "Do you ever relax?" she asked, her gaze dropping to his lips. Cees' stomach muscles clenched.

"Not the time right now." He hated that he had to be the voice of wisdom. When had that happened? Lieven was always the one to bring him down from the clouds. "Night will be here soon. We have to do this. You know that."

If she did indeed know the urgency behind their search, she didn't care. Her lips followed her eyes and she gently nibbled at his lips. He groaned. "I know that," she breathed over his mouth. "But I want you so bad!"

Cees' body was pulsing with desire. Gently but firmly, he lowered her to the ground, unknotting her legs from around his waist. "I know...."

Jia held on to his neck, forcing him to look at her. "Say it!" Her breathing was fast and choppy. "I want to hear you say you want me too."

Her gray eyes shone in the dimming light. Why was it so important to her to be wanted by him? With her looks, he was certain there were plenty of men who wanted her. Maybe too many. The truth was he did want her. Badly. "I do," he admitted, kissing the tip of her nose. "I want you. Gods, I want you so bad it hurts. But we have to go."

A smile stretched across her pink lips. "Promise me you will do everything in your power to share your sleeping quarters with me tonight." She was serious.

Despite the hunger inside of him, he laughed. "Lieven may have other ideas."

"Screw Lieven." There was fire in her voice. "He's a big boy. Unless, of course, you prefer him to me." Her eyebrows arched up.

"He's my best friend, my brother," Cees said, confused. "I can't compare both of you or pit you against each other."

Jia let go of his neck, bringing one of her hands down to his crotch. He flinched. "Your body tells me otherwise." A wicked smile crept to her lips.

"You use sex as a weapon." He was angry now. Did she do this to every man she met? Was he just the one available right now? "Why? You just need me to fuck you? Is that all this is?"

Cees noticed her flinch at his harsh words and felt guilty. Her body suddenly stiffened as she stepped away from him. "I don't use sex as a weapon."

Mollified by his guilt, Cees lowered his voice to a gentler tone. "Then why me? Why are you so intent in having sex with me?"

Her face twisted into an angry frown. "You stupid *Zuiver*." Spit flew out of her mouth. "Why do you think? Because I like you. Because we connected. Because we are both lonely and scared."

She looked very young all of a sudden, standing in front of him, her lower lip trembling and her eyes suspiciously shiny. He couldn't stand it. Opening his arms wide, Cees drew her in for a hug. "Sorry. I don't know what's wrong with me. I'm always saying the wrong thing."

But he did know what was making him act that way. Jia had very quickly become part of his world. In the last few days she had turned from a total stranger to someone who lived in his heart. If there was something he had learned from being a Tainted *Zuiver*, it was that carrying people in your heart only led to pain. He was scared to death Jia would hurt him. That she would yank his heart out of his chest and stomp on it mercilessly. Cees was not sure he could handle that. Not even all the walls he had built around his heart would prevent him from bleeding to death.

"I'll try to convince Lieven to let me share your quarters tonight," he said, surprising himself. "But it is still *wellust...* punishable by death."

Jia looked up at him, her neck bent backwards at an odd angle. "Cees, they are all dead. There is no more *wellust*. We can make our own rules from now on."

Cees realized she was right. As far as he knew, the squad and him were the only survivors from the commune. Whatever rules the *Zuiver* Elders had imposed on their people out of necessity or prejudice were no longer in effect. Despite the horror that had caused it to happen, a new era—hopefully a more merciful and tolerant one—was afoot.

Whoever survived would build from scratch, from the ashes of the old world.

Darkness was already falling when they found a school where the computers—these nondescript rectangular glass boxes that blinked and came alive at the touch of a button—were still in working conditions. Cees and Jia mapped the place and rejoined the others in the market square of the town to report their findings. Everybody was already there, and they were greeted by a metal-melting stare from Lieven.

"What the hell were you guys doing for so long?" Lieven snatched the piece of paper from Cees' hands. He looked at the notes his friend had written. "This is not too far from here, but we probably should rest for the night. We don't want to turn on too many lights and alert the monsters."

The rest of the squad agreed and Alfons busied himself giving his men instructions on what to do next. Lieven stayed close to Cees and Jia, his usually warm eyes, hard and unyielding. "You can bunk with Aleid and the other women again, Jia," he said, waving distractedly toward the others. "You're free to pick any of the residences around this block."

Jia was about to protest when Cees jumped in. "She'll stay with me tonight." His voice was a lot firmer than how he felt. He was not sure why his friend seemed so set against his relationship with the *Gezegenden* girl, but he didn't like going against his adopted brother.

Lieven's eyes opened wide, whether in surprise or anger he couldn't tell. "Beware, my friend," he said, lowering his voice so only the three of them could hear it. "You are skirting a thin line."

"Liev, what line?" Cees combed his fingers through his already tousled hair. "The line is gone. The Predators destroyed it and, for once, that may not be such a bad thing after all."

Softness came back to the young soldier's eyes. Cees knew those so-called lines were not something Lieven agreed with. "You're right. They are gone. Just be careful. Change does not happen overnight, especially in the hearts of people."

Why did Lieven sound hurt? They were all hurting inside from the terrible loss of life, but there was something else bothering his friend.

"Are you okay, Liev?" Cees placed a hand on Lieven's shoulder. "You're welcome to bunk with us if you want."

A sad, strange chuckle escaped Lieven's lips. "No, thanks. I'm not too fond of pain."

He walked away, leaving Cees confused by his strange choice of words. Jia was staring at him, studying his every move. "What did he mean by that?" he asked her, waving in his friend's direction. "What's gotten into him lately?"

Jia sighed loudly and took a step closer to him. "You really don't know?"

"No, I have no clue." Cees dropped his hands alongside his body. "Do you?"

She nodded and took yet another step closer. "I can't believe you don't know. It's so obvious."

"What? What's so obvious?" He was getting frustrated now. How was it possible that Jia who barely knew Lieven seemed to know things he did not?

"Cees," she said, her voice very quiet so no-one else could hear. "He's in love with you."

Jia

From the corner of her eye, Jia watched him. Cees was restless, pacing from one end of the small room to the other. At times, he would mumble to himself while mussing his hair into what her mom would have called a rat's nest. He hadn't said a word to her since she had told him about Lieven's obvious feelings for him. They had walked in silence across the market place and taken residence in a second floor apartment above what used to be a restaurant. While she changed the sheets of the made-up bed—too creepy to sleep on sheets people who were now dead slept in—and searching through the still-working refrigerator for food, he had been quiet, slowly digesting the information she had given him. As hard as it was to believe, he really hadn't known about his friend's infatuation. To be fair, it was obvious it was much more than infatuation. Lieven's love for Cees danced in his eyes every time he looked at him or his lips spoke his name. It made her a little jealous. Deep down, Jia had always wanted to be loved like that.

"Cees, will you stop pacing around? You're making me dizzy." Jia had finished the beds and sat down at the bottom edge, watching the handsome *Zuiver* cover the floor in wide circles.

Cees looked up at her, surprise in his eyes as if noticing her for the first time. "What?"

Jia sighed and patted the bed beside her. "Come and sit down. There is some food in the kitchen. We should eat."

Once he was sitting, Jia fetched the food she had found and brought it to him in a plate. "Here, there was some bread and veggie spread in the fridge. I tried it. It's still good."

Cees accepted the plate and the glass of water she was offering him. "Are you sure?"

"Yes, I tasted it. It's good." She sat next to him with another small plate.

"No, I mean about Lieven." He looked up at her and put the plate down on the floor by his feet. "Are you sure?"

"I think everybody knows." Following his lead, she also set the plate on the floor. "Except you…"

Cees rubbed his eyes furiously. "He's my brother, my friend…I just never thought…"

Jia caught his hand to stop his frantic rubbing. "He isn't blood-related, Cees." She held his hand in hers. "And you can't control how you feel or who you love. It's not for you to decide. Your heart makes that decision."

"But what do I do now?" he asked, looking at her with wild eyes. "How do I act around him? I love him, but like a brother."

"Don't beat yourself up. There's nothing you can do or say. Just act like you always did."

As she said it, she knew it wasn't possible. There were things that, once revealed, changed everything. She wondered now whether maybe she should have kept it to herself. Did she tell him because of how annoyed she was with Lieven's attitude toward her? Gods, she hoped she wasn't that petty.

"He doesn't think that I—does he?" His eyes, buried in the black stripe, were panicked and confused. "I don't want to hurt him."

"You would only hurt him if you lied to him," she said, sliding off her boots. "And you've never done that. He knows you see him as a friend, a brother. Nothing else. That's why he has never told you."

Cees threw himself across the bed, his legs hanging off the edge, and crossed his arms over his chest. "I hate this. I wish—shit! I don't even know what I wish. Maybe if I had never been born..."

Jia slid over the bed on her stomach until she was beside him. "Don't be daft. I, for one, am very happy you were born."

He turned his face to her with confusion still shadowing his blue eyes. "Why? I serve no purpose but to make people miserable. First, I made myself miserable for years, then I put both my friend and his family at risk of being ostracized, and now I am making my best friend—my only friend—unhappy because I allowed him to fall in love with me, knowing all too well I couldn't reciprocate."

"You didn't *allow* him to do anything," she said, her hand coming to rest on his chest. "No one can make someone love him. It just happens. Trust me. I know."

Cees blinked a couple times. "How would you know? Were you in love before?" He turned his body toward her and rested his head on his arm.

"Never been in love before." Jia lowered her eyes to his lips. A now-familiar stirring erupted inside of her. "Have you?"

He laughed, Lieven forgotten for the moment. "Gods, no. Who would I fall in love with? Nobody even talks to me unless is to call me names or give me orders."

The import of that hit her full-force. What would it be like to live all your life knowing no-one would ever be there for you? Not that she had a lot of so-called friends. Jia had expertly shut most everybody out of her life after her mother died. But she did have a few casual friendships, and she certainly was not called names or stared at in public places or parties. She had also had plenty of male attention, too much actually. Nothing serious, nothing romantic. Just sex. Empty sex. She wanted something more. There was a part of her missing, as if she had lost it somewhere between birth and her adult years. An empty space that she longed to see filled but didn't know how. Strangely enough for the past week or so, since this mammoth catastrophe has befallen her world, she had felt as if that emptiness was shrinking. She suspected Cees had a lot to do with it. It both scared and elated her.

"Do you want to?" she asked him in a whisper. His blue diamond eyes shone in the dim light, and she reached out to touch his face.

Smile gone from his lips, Cees swallowed hard, his Adam's apple jerking up and down in his throat. "I don't know. I think so. How would I know how it feels?"

Jia slipped a hand under his shirt and felt the ridges of his well-formed muscles alongside his abs and ribs. She felt him shiver at the touch.

"I'm not sure." Her fingers found their way to his chest. "Maybe a little like this?" Her hand, flattened against his pec, told her his heart was beating fast and furious. Emboldened by his reaction, Jia pulled his shirt over his head, half-expecting him to fight her. But he didn't. Obligingly, he allowed her to slide the shirt off him and explore his strong, scarred chest with her hands. There were so many scars!

"How could they do this to you?" she said, more to herself than to him. She raised herself on an arm and brought her lips down to kiss each scar. He quivered under her touch, and tears welled up in her eyes. *Why are you crying, stupid?* Tears rolled down her cheeks and fell onto his skin.

"Are you crying?" he asked, lifting her face to look at her. "Why? What's wrong?"

With tears still rolling down her face, Jia let out a sob. "I think I'm happy and sad all at once." She sat up next to him. "Sad because of all that's happening, but happy that I'm with you."

Cees sat up and studied her face with probing eyes. "I feel the same." Reaching out to her, he pulled up the tank top she was wearing. She felt a sudden gust of cold air caress her breasts, and a shock-wave of yearning went through her. Cees lowered his eyes to her naked torso and then up again. "You are beautiful, Jia. And your aura…"

Still crying, Jia asked, "What about my aura?"

He smiled. "Pink. Soft, sensual pink." He kissed her, laying her back on the bed and leaning over her. His lips found their way to the crown of her head. "Here, you're purple—you may think you're tough and have no use for love, but this part of your life force tells a different story."

With her lips aching to touch his again, she stared, curious nevertheless. "What do you mean?"

He brushed his hand along the middle of her torso from the throat to her navel. She moaned. "We all have these centers, points that connect with our life forces, our souls. Each one tells a story about you," he said, his eyes half-closed, drinking her in.

"What's my story?" She rubbed her hand up and down his strong bicep. He scooted a little closer.

"Here, your aura turns indigo, dark blue," he continued, touching his lips in a maddening soft kiss to her forehead. "This is why you will save all of us."

Jia was so surprised by the statement, her head jerked up almost hitting him. She was no hero. "What do you mean, I'm going to save all of you?"

Cees laughed softly and continued the tantalizing feathery track of his hand, up and down her chest. "You have a big imagination, creativity." He lowered his lips to her forehead again. "Your ideas will help us find a way out of this."

Jia felt herself relax, lulled by his voice and sweet caresses. Cees moved to her throat, bending down to fit his mouth over the nook on her neck, and kissed her. "Your blue is like that of a summer sky. Yes, you will be our savior," he whispered against her skin.

Her whole being seemed to be enveloped in a cloud of pleasure and peace. As much as she wanted—she felt she should—argue with him and this crazy idea of her saving the world, she couldn't make herself do it. Being in his arms felt so good.

Cees scooped down and was now working his magic over her heart, his lips and tongue flickering between her breasts. "Green like the meadows on a spring day or the needles of an evergreen." His warm breath was teasing and soothing all at once. "The color of hope, of life..."

While he lingered close to her small breasts, Jia dug her fingers in his thick hair with a moan of pleasure. Her chest rose and fell with the quickening of her breath and the drumming of her heart. She felt Cees swell against her leg and an insane sense of happiness flooded her. What was happening to her? She was not exactly a blushing virgin having sex for the time. But maybe, in a way, she was. All the other times meant nothing outside the moment, the sensual pleasure. This time, there was more. Jia was not sure of what exactly, but there was definitely something more.

The beautiful *Zuiver* dragged his warm lips lower still to just underneath her ribs. He lingered there, brushing small circles with his fingers over her sensitive skin, making her shiver and squirm. "Yellow, the color of the sun," he said in his singsong voice. "Your energy is intoxicating, it brightens up everything around you."

Cees kept going down. When his mouth met her navel he stopped and, using his tongue to draw a circle around it, he caressed her whole middle with his hand. "Orange. Sweet, juicy," he whispered, a slight amusement in his tone. "Desire..." A fire was consuming her. She wanted him inside of her, she wanted their bodies to be connected and unified, she wanted to be one with him. She wiggled under his touch, her hand tracing the muscles of his strong, hairless chest. He was beautiful, olive skinned and smooth like velvet.

Jia was not expecting it. When he suddenly moved even lower and, sliding her pants slightly down her hips, transferred his focus to the base of her belly, she yelped. Cees laughed against her skin. "Red. Gods, your red is exquisite. And sweet." His lips were moving on her, each word a caress interspersed with kisses. "But there is also fear here; fire and fear. What are you afraid of Jia? You look so tough, yet you're scared."

Her body stiffened at the words. She was not scared. Driessen women were not scared of anything; her mom had made sure she knew that. As a child she had learned to face spiders, snakes, all sorts of scary animals. Later she trained herself not to be scared of the burly guys that got handsy on the transports to school or at the local clubs. The men that sought her out and forced themselves on her. The Driessen women were not scared of anything or anybody.

"I'm not scared!" She sprang up to a sitting position, barely missing Cees' head who, surprised by the reaction, sat back to watch her. "I don't know what makes you think that, but I am not afraid of anything."

"Not even the Predators?" he asked quietly, his hand still lying on her belly.

Maybe she was afraid of the beasts, if she was being honest with herself. Who wouldn't? She had seen firsthand what horrors they brought down on her people. Of course, she was afraid of them, terrified even. Her stubbornness wouldn't permit her to admit it to Cees though. It would be just like admitting weakness. Driessen women did not do that.

Jia shook her head in vehement denial. "I'm not scared of death," she said, her voice trembling a little, aware she was not quite answering his question. "Not scared of dying."

"Beautiful Jia," Cees spoke in a quiet voice. His eyes displayed the same softness, a tenderness Jia was not used to, a type of caring she was not equipped to deal with. "You've built that wall so high."

Resentful of the implication in his words, Jia jumped off the bed and grabbed her shirt from the floor. "I have built no wall." She slid the shirt over her head. "And even if I did, who says I would let you climb it?"

Feeling like a child having a tantrum, Jia left the room and went to sit in the darkness of the living area, her arms crossed and her heart thumping in her chest. Gods, why did she have to be so...? She didn't even have a word for it. Unwilling to open up to others, reluctant to let people in, loath to be vulnerable. Her whole being was begging her to go back in that room and lose herself in Cees' arms and sweet caresses. The yearning was so strong she felt physical pain across her stomach and chest. Jia folded herself in two, her head resting on her knees, and cried. Why couldn't she just let go?

Lieven

Winter was coming. The morning breeze held an icy chill that was not there just a few days before. The mood among the men was also cold. Lieven couldn't understand why. Nothing had happened or was said that would justify it. Not that he was aware of anyway. Even Cees seemed cold and distant, and Jia had removed herself from any human company, choosing to sit by herself when they met and barely looked at his friend. They had seemed so friendly with each other the night before. Too friendly for Lieven's comfort, but he was not sure this coldness was any better. They must work together if they were to have any chance at survival, and that kind of attitude didn't bode well for any of them.

The soldiers had been gathering supplies from the abandoned buildings. The attack on this city must have not taken place too long ago because the food supplies were still reasonably fresh. Even the milk they found in most stores and refrigerators was still usable. They had also managed to gather some arsenal—better weapons than what they had, but a lot of the guns they found were the same type Jia had, DNA-connected, and therefore useless to any of them. They knew better than to stay there for very long, but there was still information they were hoping to gather from the computers and other resources around town. None of them had any experience with the technology, so they relied heavily on this *Gezegenden* girl who now seemed less than willing to help them.

"What's going on?" he asked, crouching next to Jia. They were having their late morning meal inside a restaurant, and Jia chose to sit on the floor instead of on the available comfortable chairs.

The dark-haired woman looked up at him and offered no smile. "Why don't you ask your bestie?" she replied, an unfriendly glower in her eyes.

Lieven knew when not to push. Jumping to his feet, he decided to approach his friend instead. Cees had barely graced him with a second look this morning. Granted, the artist in him often had sulking spells, but Lieven had never seen him so quiet, so distant. It brought painful memories of a time when Cees didn't trust him yet. Couldn't trust him.

"What's wrong, Cees?" he asked, pulling and straddling a chair next to his friend. He rested his arms on the high back of the chair and studied the young artist's face.

"Nothing's wrong," Cees answered, not lifting his eyes. A spoonful of oatmeal hung suspended between the bowl and his mouth.

Lieven brushed a hand over his face. He was getting frustrated. Alfons had told him earlier that whatever was going on needed to be resolved. Quickly. "Will you stop sulking and look me in the eye?" he said, trying to keep calm.

Cees did look up at him then, but he was not prepared for what he read in his eyes; sorrow and shame. Sorrow he could understand, but shame?

"I'm sorry Liev." He dropped the spoon back into the bowl. "Just not in the mood for talking."

"What the hell happened last night?" Lieven swept his fingers over his hair. "You went to bed happy and woke up cranky and weird."

"Jia and I had a fight." His blue eyes skirted around Lieven, never quite making eye contact. "It's nothing. We'll be okay."

Lieven grasped his friend's shoulder. "No, you may well have had a fight with the *Gezegenden* girl, but you're not even looking me in the eye. What's happening? Did I say something wrong?"

"Leave it be, Liev. Please," Cees said, his gaze finally resting on his friend's eyes. "I don't want to talk about it. Not now."

As much as he hated the feeling of not knowing what was causing Cees' awkwardness and distance, Lieven could not refuse him the space and time to work out whatever was bothering him. "Okay, I won't press it anymore." He gave Cees' shoulder a friendly squeeze and smiled. "You should eat that oatmeal. It's starting to look like glue."

Lieven had been paired with Aleid while they conducted forays into the town's official buildings. The plan was to meet in the evening and share their findings. Nobody was really sure of what exactly they were hoping to find, but maybe there was some kernel of information that would help them devise a plan to not only escape but vanquish the Predators. It was a long, frustrating day, and by the time they all gathered in the lobby of what used to be a hotel, Lieven was none the wiser as to what the Predators were and how to fight them. He hoped that some of the others had had better luck.

Jia sat slightly to the side, apart from the others as if she was afraid they had some contagious disease. She kept her face stubbornly lowered to the floor while they all sat in a big circle on couches and chairs.

"Anyone find anything of any value to us?" Alfons settled himself in a large armchair. The soldiers looked at each other, and it was obvious nothing of major import had been found. "Nothing?" Alfons repeated, an air of despondence in his expression.

"I found something." Jia surprised everybody. Every head turned in her direction. She had gone off with Cees like everybody else, but their animosity was so obvious no one thought they had actually uncovered anything. "I worked on the computers in the school and was able to find some files on these creatures."

Alfons scooted to the edge of his chair, ears at the ready. Lieven looked at her, curious. "What did you find out?" Alfons asked. Nobody had much information about the Predators. Nobody ever thought they were real monsters, flesh and bone like everybody else.

Jia bit the corner of her lip and lifted her eyes, conspicuously avoiding Cees. "They are the product of an experiment," she explained, uncrossing her legs only to cross them again the other way. "Central sponsored a group of scientists to genetically enhance certain animals of prey in an attempt to create a super-soldier of sorts. The experiment went awry. The animals became too strong and unpredictable. They ate through the staff in the lab and escaped the facility a year or so ago."

Looks were exchanged. "A year ago?" Lieven asked. "What have they been doing all this time? They obviously have a voracious appetite."

Cees was the one who answered. "The lab was in a sort of isolated camp." He looked briefly at Jia, who had lowered her eyes to the floor again. "We knew these creatures can't survive water—meaning they can't swim, and because of their muscle weight they can't float either. Once inside a deep enough body of water, they sink like rocks to the bottom. The lab was on a small island. They had no way out."

A collective gasp left everybody's lungs. "So, how did they leave the island?"

Jia's face contorted into a scowl. "The idiots at Central sent ships to collect their super-soldiers." Her voice was soaked in anger. "They thought they could tame them. The scientists had come up with a very strong tranquilizer, a chemical gas of some kind, which was lethal to humans but believed to work on the beasts." She paused for dramatic effect, or maybe to catch her breath. "And it did. For a while at least. Long enough to remove them from the island and bring them to the mainland. You can imagine the rest."

Silence fell and enveloped them as a restrictive gag. Their own people were responsible for the world's demise. And for what? A super-soldier? What the hell did they need a super-soldier for? Wars had not been fought in decades. The world was not perfect, but it was at least the most peaceful it had been in centuries. There was no need for extra soldiers. The thought that Central had given gas masks only to the Blessed told another terrible story; the chemical they had produced to control the beasts was meant to be a double-edged sword. Had Central been preparing for a thorough ethnic cleansing? Had they planned to loose the creatures on the lower castes and then take care of the survivors with the lethal gas?

"What we need to win this war is water." Cees' voice startled them all off their trance. "Lots of it. We need to evacuate what survivors there are and take everybody to an island. Then wait it out. The Predators won't have anything to eat and will turn on each other until there are none left."

Alfons laughed. It was a bitter, almost manic laugh. "It sounds very simple. All we have to do is run around the whole world trying not to be eaten alive and collect every survivor we can find to take them to an island somewhere. Are we going to swim there?"

Jia looked up, her eyes hard as stones. "It's the best chance we have. We won't save everyone, and we may die in the process, but it's the only way."

They all stared at her as if she had two heads. Lieven was not crazy about this *Gezegenden* girl, but she was proving to be extremely useful and determined. Cees was a great judge of character with his weird ability to see people's auras. He should trust him like he had always done and not allow petty jealousy to stand in his way.

"Jia's right." Lieven stood up and walked to the center of the circle. "It's better than what we had this morning. It's a chance at survival. It's hope. Something we did not have a few hours ago. We should rejoice."

Cees joined him in the center. "I'm with Jia and Lieven. Now, we need a plan. Are you guys going to just sit here and moan and groan about how ridiculously hard this is going to be, or join heads to come up with something that will work?"

It didn't take long for all the others, including Alfons, to join them. They talked until late at night, eating and drinking. The mood was the most positive it had been since their whole misadventure begun. Even Jia seemed a bit more animated, joining in conversation with some of the other women. She didn't talk to Cees, though. What could have possibly happened between those two?

"It's good to see the men this excited again." Lieven approached Cees, who was standing to the side, cradling a mug of beer in his hand. "With hope in their eyes."

His friend turned his head to look at him and smiled. "Yes, even a tiny kernel of hope can produce miracles," Cees brought the mug to his lips. "Want a beer? Good quality, not the junk we normally drink. There are lots of perks to being a *Gezegenden*, it seems." He laughed at his own joke and took a long sip.

Lieven noticed a thick foam mustache on his friend's upper lip and, reaching out, wiped it with his finger. Cees flinched. "What's wrong?" Lieven asked, surprised by his reaction. "What's going on with you? You've been acting really weird today."

Cees grabbed him by an arm and gently pulled him away from the others and into a separate room. "Lieven, I wanted you to know..." He licked his lips and looked around him as if checking to see if they were alone. "Hell, this shouldn't be so hard."

Confused, Lieven shook his head. "What are you talking about?"

"I love you, you know that. You're my best friend, my brother. I couldn't love you more if you were my real brother. But I don't—"

Lieven realized what his friend was trying to say. He had no clue how Cees had figured it out, but it was obvious now that he knew.

"Stop! You don't have to say anything else. I know." Lieven nodded and sighed deeply. "I might as well admit it; I feel a lot more than a brotherly love for you, Cees. I never told you because I was scared I would lose your friendship. Above all else, I need you in my life, one way or another."

Lieven looked pleadingly at his friend. He was so scared of losing the connection with the one person in this world he felt closer to than anybody else. "Tell me you are not going to feel all weird about this and keep your distance. I don't think I could handle that."

Cees' face opened into one of his amazing smiles. When he smiled like that, it was as if the sun had come down to shine upon everything and everyone. It filled Lieven's heart with a song of joy and a wave of relief washed over him.

"Of course, I won't keep my distance," Cees said. "I was just afraid I was going to hurt your feelings. You're my only family. I don't want to lose you."

They sealed their conversation with a hug and their usual exchange of playful punches.

"What about Jia? What's going on with the two of you?" Lieven finally asked.

"She's afraid of letting anyone in. She's fighting it, but I will climb that wall." He sounded so sure of himself, Lieven had no trouble believing him. No doubt Cees would break through the *Gezegenden*'s defenses sooner or later. After all, hadn't he been the one breaking through Lieven's?

Cees

The flames from the fireplace danced their strange, slow dance and drowned the room in a soft glow. It was not a real fireplace. The flames were fake and let out no smoke or smell. The heavy curtains in the apartment were shut, and there was no danger of it being detected from the outside. However the artificial flames did indeed warm up the chilly air just enough to make it comfortable and cozy. Jia's cold mood was not as easy to dispel. She had been sitting by herself on a small armchair, barefoot and with her knees pulled up to her face. Cees, sitting cross-legged on the carpet in front of the fireplace, stole a glance in her direction. Jia was like a statue. He was not sure she had even blinked for the past hour since they had been alone in the house.

Cees was surprised she did not argue when Alfons had announced she would be sharing his room for the night. The squad leader felt it was important that Cees and Jia worked out their differences and had rather forcibly thrown the two together again. But she hadn't said a word yet. Stubborn as hell, she was. And beautiful. Cees couldn't take her out of his mind any more than he could stop breathing. Like it or not, she was an integral part of him, even if she wouldn't hear of it. He shivered.

Exhaustion was getting the best of him, so he stood up, grabbed a blanket from the bed and crossed the small space to where Jia was sitting. He stood there for a moment, looking at her unmoving body, and then gently layered the blanket over her to keep the chill out.

"I know you're mad at me." He kept his voice just above a whisper. "But I'm here if you want me. Any time." She was surrounded by a wavering aura of red. Still angry at him. Or maybe herself for allowing her vulnerability to show for a moment. He wanted to wrap her in his arms and sing her to sleep. He wanted her to trust him and lean on him for comfort. But he was willing to wait.

With an audible yawn, Cees walked back to the bed and crawled on top of it. His body felt drained of life and heavy as if his limbs had been replaced by rocks. When his head hit the pillow, he felt his consciousness slip away and his eyes immediately closed.

The sound woke him up. Confused at first, he rubbed his eyes and looked around in the semi-darkness. The fireplace was still going, but Jia was not on her seat anymore. He belatedly realized she was the source of the soft rhythmic sound he heard. She was lying in bed with her back turned to him, curled in a fetal position. Cees could tell by the subtle movement of her shoulders and her whimpering that she was crying. Turning on his side, he watched her in silence, trying to decide what to do next. All he wanted was to pull her to him and hug her, but he knew she would probably bristle against it. He didn't want to make her uncomfortable or suspicious in any way. He wanted her to feel wanted and protected but not smothered.

"Jia," he whispered, a hand on her shoulder blade. "Are you okay?" She didn't answer, but he noticed she hadn't recoiled from him either. Drawing encouragement from that he scooted closer until his body lined along hers and his arm went all the way around her, wrapping around her waist. "I'll go away if you want me to. I can sleep in the other room."

Just as he was getting ready to let her go of his embrace, her hand came to rest on top of his. "No, stay. Please," she begged.

He did. His chin resting in the crook of her neck, Cees whispered, "Can I do anything to make you feel better?"

Cees felt her hesitate, but it only lasted a few seconds. Jia turned around to face him. Tears streaked her face, her eyes red and swollen. She brought a hand to his face in a caress.

"I'm sorry, Cees." She buried her fingers in his hair. "I was taught never to let anyone see me cry."

"It's okay. I understand." Cees rubbed her arm.

"No, you don't understand." Her hand was now curled behind his neck. "Being Blessed has not protected me from being hurt."

"What do you mean?" Cees lifted his head, surprised by her words.

There were new tears in her eyes. "I was popular with the guys." Her voice choked. Jia hid her face on his shirt.

"Did they beat you?" he asked, lifting her face to him. "Did they...did they rape you? Did they force themselves on you?"

Her aura had turned almost black. "It's not rape if you let them do it to you." She cried, her sobs strangling her voice.

Cees was livid and not sure of what to do or say. Everything he had thought about the *Gezegenden* and his own people's beliefs and traditions had just been rewritten. How was it possible that a caste which received special treatment from Central could be so barbaric? The *Zuiver* may have a lot of flaws as a caste, but women were treated as equals—respected and even revered as the carriers of new genera-tions.

He swallowed his anger for fear of scaring her with it and allowed himself a moment to cool off before speaking again. Jia had hidden her face in his shirt once more. He could feel the wetness of her tears soaking through the thin fabric into his skin. Her tears burned him. Not in a painful, unpleasant way, but rather in welcomed heat, as if she was branding him hers, baptizing him with her own DNA.

"You will never, ever receive that kind of treatment from me or any of the *Zuiver* men, I promise you," he said finally, cradling her neck with his hand and planting a kiss on the top of her head. "Never."

For a while there was silence, her soft whimpering the only sound. Gradually even that faded and her breathing became regular against him. Jia had fallen asleep. Cees knew he should also sleep. They were leaving in the morning and the next town was at least a couple days' walk from there. They couldn't risk using the abandoned transports in town for fear of alerting the creatures. The group would walk. It was comforting to know they had enough supplies to keep them fed and semi-comfortable for the journey, but winter was coming, and the skies had turned a strange grayish hue. The weather would be yet another obstacle in their path sooner or later.

He couldn't sleep. With Jia nestled in his arms, Cees felt at home. It was both exciting and unsettling to feel so strongly about someone he had just met. A woman from another caste, one who would not give him the time of day in different circumstances. But these were the circumstances now, and there was no point in dwelling on what might have been. Whatever that was, it was no more. The important thing was to enjoy what they had at that moment, for the next might never be.

Jia stirred in his arms. "It's not morning yet," he whispered, pressing her against him. "Sleep."

Her face surfaced, and her tear-swollen eyes drifted up to his. "Cees?" He was not sure if she was checking to make sure he was still there or if she was calling him. "I'm sorry."

"What are you sorry for?" He tilted his head to better look in her eyes. Was she talking in her sleep?

"For fighting you." Her hand came up to spoon his cheek. "I'm scared. I'm terrified of my feelings for you. You're a *Zuiver*. We were brainwashed into believing your caste was dangerous, inferior. I trained myself not to feel much other than passing lust for anyone that crossed my path. It was my mother's recipe against getting hurt. The truth is, I have been hurt so many times I've lost count. I'm afraid you will hurt me more than anyone else."

Cees propped himself up on the pillows. "I would never hurt you." His voice sounded louder than what he had planned. "Never. How can you even think that after what we have been through together?"

"Not on purpose." Her voice wavered. "But when you feel so strongly about another human being, you're bound to get hurt."

Cees' eyebrows curved upward. "You feel strongly about me?" A little smile danced on his lips.

Jia laughed and slapped him playfully on the shoulder. "You're so annoying." Her smile bellied her words. "Yes, I do feel strongly about you, but don't let that go to your head; I also feel strongly about the Predators."

Her aura was now a beautiful shade of pink. She did have strong feelings about him, he realized with a jolt of joy. Pulling her closer, he reached down and brushed his lips on hers gently. "I feel strongly about you too." His smile matched hers. "In a very different way from what I feel for the Predators, though."

With a chuckle, she crossed her arms behind his neck and pulled his face to hers until their lips were joined again. Her tongue caressed the sensitive skin just inside his mouth, and the fire that had been slow burning inside of him all night exploded. A glint of red sparkled through her pink aura. Cees smiled above her lips. She was on fire as well.

Jia wiggled herself up and straddled him, her fingers spread wide across his chest. "Let's make a deal." A mischievous sparkle lit up her eyes. "You will not mention the words *vulnerable* or *scared* during this make-out session and we may just be okay."

Smoldering under her, Cees lifted an eyebrow. "What's a make-out session?"

Jia laughed. "Man, they really kept you in the dark, didn't they?" Cees was not sure who *they* were, but the flames in his core didn't really care at that point. "I will show you what it is then."

Her fingers were sure and steady while ridding him of his shirt. His, not so much. Suddenly aware of how inexperienced he was in these matters of the heart, his hands shook like leaves on a tree branch during a storm. Try as he may, his fingers wouldn't latch on to the edges of her shirt.

Jia giggled. "I'll do it."

For a very brief moment he wondered whether it was common practice among the *Gezegenden* women not to wear anything under their shirts, but the sight of her bare skin quickly removed any question he may have otherwise voiced. He was hungry for her. His trembling hands yearned to touch her. The rest of his body was yelling out for more contact.

After descending on his lips one more time, Jia slid her body along Cees' until she was sitting on his knees. She went to work on undoing his pants and sliding them down his legs, dropping them to the floor behind her. Unable to stay still, Cees helped her remove his under clothes. It was strange to be lying totally naked in front of a woman like that. As a boy, he had often stood naked in front of women and men at the institution when the children were taken to the front yard every month for the public "humbling ceremony". As soon as he was old enough, Lieven and his dad had made sure Cees did not have to suffer that humiliation anymore. Unwittingly, he made a choking sound.

"Are you okay?" Jia's aura turned into a burnt orange, her eyes worried. She was still sitting just above his knees, her beauty showing through the gloaming of the room.

Cees sat up, wiping a rogue tear from the corner of his eye. "Just a bad memory," he replied, his face now leveled with hers. His lips sought hers, and she met him half-way. "Erase those memories, Jia," he begged when their lips drifted apart.

Jia's hands explored his face, brushing over his brow, his nose, the length of his stripe, tracing his lips with infuriating slowness. "I'm not sure I can erase them." She dipped her lips on his again and again. "But I can maybe make you forget them for a while."

The couple slid along the bed until Cees' legs were hanging off the edge. Jia slipped to the floor and stood in front of him. "Undress me."

Cees held her by the waist and pulled her to him. He looked up at her as if asking for permission, and Jia guided his mouth to one of her breasts. She tasted of honey. He felt himself swell as his tongue drew a moan from Jia, and he lifted his hand to cover her other breast. The need in him was growing urgent. He pushed her away just enough to peel off her pants and under garments. In seconds, she stood gloriously naked in front of him, and his heart must have stopped because he couldn't breathe.

"You're beautiful, Jia," he managed to utter, drawing her breast into his mouth again. Was it always like this? He had disciplined himself throughout the years not to think about sex, not to want—not much point in it, for he knew being Tainted meant having very little chance at ever having a relationship of any kind, even among his fellow

Tainted ones. Now, in the arms of the gorgeous, warm Jia he couldn't believe he had lived all of his twenty-odd years without it.

Jia climbed on his lap and wrapped her legs around his waist. The feeling of her heat on his arousal made him cry out loud. Jia laughed softly and kissed him, deeply and long. "*This* is a make-out session, sweet Cees." She slipped her hand between them to caress him. Cees moaned against her neck, drowning in waves of pleasure.

Guided by instinct rather than experience, Cees lifted her up slightly and gently brought her down onto his lap again. Being inside of her was almost more than he could bear. He felt out of control as his muscles contracted at the contact. "Jia, I don't know how long..."

In a slow, sensual dance, Jia moved on top of him, back and forth like the moon tides. Helpless against the overwhelming feelings taking over him, Cees felt as if something inside of him was screaming to get out. He held onto her even tighter and joined her in the dance. The waves of pleasure intensified, grew taller and more demanding until he couldn't hold it any more. He yelled out as his body reached a climax. Jia was holding onto him, her hands entwined behind his back, her face buried on the side of his neck, whimpering sounds of a different nature from earlier that night escaping her lips. Had she felt the same as him? Gods, he hoped so. He wanted her to feel what he felt, to give her what she had just given him. He wanted Jia to have him whole.

"You're okay?" he asked, a nervousness growing in his heart. He was still inside of her, her legs crossed behind his back, her head buried on the crook of his neck. He moved to let her go.

"No!" Her head snapped up. He stopped. "Don't move. Not yet. I like having you inside of me."

They remained still for a while, holding each other; body against body, keeping each other warm against the chill of the night and the horrors of their reality.

Jia

If she didn't know any better, she could almost believe everything was well with the world. The silence, broken only by the crackling of the fireplace and Cees' quiet breathing, enveloped them in an elusive cocoon of peace and safety. Jia ran her fingers softly over Cees' bare chest, not wanting to wake him up but itching to touch him. The young *Zuiver* was a balm to her aching eyes and heart. She was having trouble fully believing that he was there. Jia had caught herself checking to make sure he was truly material and not just a figment of her imagination.

Showing herself, vulnerable and open, was not an easy feat for Jia. Her mother had trained her well. *Keep it inside. Don't show your true self. Never allow them to see beneath your shell.* For some that might sound harsh, but to Jia and her mother it was a necessity. When her father had disappeared after being called to Central, he had condemned them to a life without status, without a male protector. The Blessed was a male-centered caste. Females had the same rights and were treated equally as long as they had a male protector; a father, a husband, even a life-partner. Those who were not so fortunate had to build their own status.

Jia shivered, partly from the chill that lingered in the air and from the unpleasant memories that assailed her. She didn't want to think about the years that proceeded her father's vanishing act. Memories of that time made her skin crawl and her stomach clench to the point of nausea. She wanted to focus on the vessel of beauty and love who lay by her, pure of heart despite everything he undoubtedly had gone through as a pariah of his own people. Her fingers drew small circles on his powerful chest, his hard abdomen, his narrow hips and strong thighs. Cees slept like a baby, his breathing calm and quiet, face relaxed and at peace with the world. His peace spilled over to her, like a river running through the meadows, refreshing the earth, quenching the thirsty plants, feeding the green and creating life.

"I love you," she whispered, knowing he couldn't hear her. Despite her trust in him, Jia was not ready to let him know that. One day maybe, but not yet. For now, he must be satisfied with knowing she wanted him as badly as he wanted her, that she trusted him like she trusted no one else.

Being an abandoned Blessed woman had not been easy on her mother, but it had been exponentially harder on Jia; a young woman with no male to protect her. Proving her toughness and willingness to "take it like a man" to her world had not been a walk in the park. Ever since she was a child, Jia's life had been a never ending succession of attempts at proving herself. "You got to be tough like a man, Jia," her mom told her daily. "Suffer in silence and harden your heart."

Young Jia had cried in her sleep, muffling her sobs with the pillow and often wishing the same pillow would steal her breath away once and for all. But life kept going. Harder and crueler with each year that passed. As soon as her body had grown curves, she chopped off her hair. Short like the warriors of her people, an exterior sign that she was tough. She could take it. She did take it. Over and over again, her pillow the only witness to her pain. Even her mother was not privy to her aches and pains—physical and emotional.

Jia squeezed her eyes shut in an attempt to keep those memories out, but they kept coming. The first time she had watched the puddle of blood around her feet after the doctors had "cleaned" her, the Blessed word for an abortion. The feeling of numbness, disbelief this was really her on that stretcher, a child's life spilling out of her... Her child, her flesh and bone. Then a second time, and a third... But the men wouldn't stop seeking her out. *A beauty. Tough as nails.* With a shattered heart inside. Nobody knew, nobody cared.

A sob rose from the bottom of her lungs and escaped her lips. Cees stirred beside her. "Jia?" His hand sought hers, his eyes still closed, weighed down by sleep and exhaustion. "Are you crying?"

"No," she said, choked up and shaking her head. "Go back to sleep." It would still be a couple of hours before sunrise.

For a moment it seemed like he had fallen back asleep, but with a pivot, he turned to face her. His long, strong legs wrapped around hers, and a sense of serenity washed over her. Cees was the only one who had ever been able to do that; erase her growing panic, assuage her fears. Jia opened her lips and melded them to his. She could feel his heart drumming against her breasts and his body quickly responding to her. It would have been so easy to lose herself again in his arms, but they had to be able to walk for miles the next day and both needed their rest.

"I want you," Cees whispered, his lips moving on hers. She inhaled the hope and promise in his kiss like precious oxygen.

"We have to rest," she said, her hands drawing him closer against her. A wave of heat flowed through her, threatening to make her lose control. "Oh gods, I want you, too."

Lost in the sensations that Cees was able to conjure with a simple touch, Jia forgot her woes for a while and surrendered to the delight of his lovemaking.

Morning found them half asleep, still entangled in each other and the bed coverings. Jia didn't want to leave the comfort of Cees' embrace, but they had to move on before the beasts got a whiff of them. Cees rolled out of bed and stood, his hand stretched to her, beckoning. He pulled her off the bed and they both stood facing one another, drinking each other with their eyes, a smile playing in the corners of their mouths.

"We could stay and hope for the best." Her hand was pressed flat on his chest. She giggled, knowing all too well how fanciful a thought that was.

Cees brought an arm around her and, pulling her to him, kissed the top of her head. "Maybe one day. One day we will be able to linger in bed, naked together, making love for days on end." She laughed. "You don't believe me?"

"Something to look forward to." She reluctantly let go of him and picked up her clothes from the floor. "But for now, we have to get going."

Most of the squad was already gathered in the restaurant on the ground floor, eating a small breakfast and packed to go. Lieven threw them a glance, and Jia's heart clenched. There was such hurt in his eyes, the soldier with the gentle heart and an infinite love for her Cees. Because he was hers, now and forever. No one was going to take him away from her. Not unless they killed her first. Now that she knew what being wanted felt like, she was never going back to what her life was like before. Instinctively, she sought Cees' hand and weaved her fingers through his. A few of the soldiers looked at them surprised. Lieven lowered his eyes and his mouth tightened into a thin line.

"Good of you to join us," Alfons greeted them. "Slept well, I trust?" Their clothes were even more rumpled than the day before, their hair was disheveled and the redness in Cees' eyes did not leave anyone any doubt as to their lack of rest.

"We slept well enough." Cees grabbed a biscuit from the plate on the table and handed it to Jia. "We're ready when you are."

Jia took a bite of her biscuit and peered around her. She and Cees may not have had any sleep, but the others didn't look like they were in any better shape. The whole squad held a haunted look in their eyes and a tightness around their lips. Guilt filled her heart. Cees had given her hope, something to hold on to. He had made her smile. What did the others have?

Alfons gathered all of them around a table to study a giant map they had collected from the library. Jia hadn't looked at a map of the continent of *Oostzee* in a long time. It felt foreign now. A big star marked Central, the capital of their world, and smaller, more faded stars the cities of the Blessed. The map was written in the old language, the language the *Zuivers* still used. She understood it—they all learned it in school—even though it was a dead language in the civilized world. She chided herself. How could she still be thinking of the non-Blessed world as uncivilized? The teachings of her people were so deeply ingrained in her brain, even now she thought of the *Zuiver* and the other castes of *Oostzee* as inferior.

"We should aim at the coast," she said, surprising herself. All eyes lifted up to her. "If the beasts are unable to cross a body of water, then we should head to an island." She pointed to the map where the blue shade of the sea started. "There are many islands off the coast. Some inhabited, some not. We should focus on getting to one of them."

The leader nodded his head. "I agree." He pointed at a couple small island groups just off the coast. "The *eilanden* closest to the coast are our best bet. They will be easier for us to reach; they are inhabited and have an infrastructure already in place, but still too far off into the ocean for the Predators to follow us."

A crescendo of chatter replaced the quietness of the morning. They all seemed to concur.

"Jia showed me how to contact surviving cities through the computer," Cees said. "We have warned as many people as we could. Unfortunately, the *gemeden*—non-Blessed—are not as easy to reach." Jia heard a sliver of bitterness in his voice. She didn't blame him.

"We will rescue whoever we find in our path," Lieven spoke for the first time that morning. His voice was hoarse, and his eyes swollen and red. Jia's stomach churned with guilt. "That's not much, but it's something."

"Our goal is to reach the next city, *Volgende Stad*, as quickly as we can and hopefully renew our supplies." Alfons pointed at a faded star on the map. "It will be a good two days walk there."

"Winter is upon us," Lieven said. "Make sure you have blankets and warm clothing with you. I know it feels wrong to steal from the dead, but we must."

Alfons looked at all of them and raised his hand in front of him. "Let's pray."

Jia watched as all the *Zuiver*, including Cees, bowed their heads and clasped their hands together.

"*De Heer is mijn herder, mij zal niets ontbreken.*" Jia recognized the words. An ancient prayer, long forgotten by the Blessed, only remembered by academia and the naturally curious. *The Lord is my shepherd, I shall not want.* Although she had never prayed or was taught to believe in a higher power, she bowed her head in respect.

With an *amen,* they all lifted their heads again. "Go and find what you need," Alfons told them. "Come back here in half an hour and be ready to go."

Lieven turned his back to walk away. Still feeling guilty that she was the cause of all the pain she could guess in his eyes, Jia stopped him. "Come with us, Lieven. It will be quicker if we work together." Cees looked up at her, surprised.

"I don't want be in the way," Lieven said with a wave of his hand.

"Don't be daft." Cees pushed him playfully. "Why would you be in the way? You're not as big as you fancy yourself to be."

Lieven laughed. "I'm bigger than you," he said, returning the push.

Jia rolled her eyes and turned around to leave. "When you guys are done comparing sizes just meet me upstairs."

The two men followed her up the stairs, still throwing friendly barbs at each other. Jia, walking ahead of them, smiled. It was good to hear them laugh. She didn't want to steal their easy friendship. Cees was hers, but he had been Lieven's first.

CHAPTER SIX
THE BEREJONG

Lieven

The temperature had dropped significantly, and their breath came out in great white puffs as they walked through the thick bush of the forest. The evening was slowly insinuating itself around them, and the forest took on an eerie tone. Cees walked in front of Lieven, his arm protectively over Jia, who looked tiny and immaterial next to him. Lieven's heart bled, but he was not going to let anyone know. He couldn't make Cees love him the way he wished he did. Being his best friend had to be enough. Lieven would find a way to accept the fact and live with the pain that knowledge caused him. Until then, he tried to avoid noticing how Cees looked at Jia when he thought she wasn't looking.

Ahead of them, Alfons had picked up his pace and, just as suddenly, he stopped, his hand raised up in the air. "Listen." He placed a finger in front of his lips. They all stopped and stood still. What were they listening to? Lieven couldn't hear any sound other than the icy wind blowing through the branches of the evergreens.

"I hear it." Cees pointed to the left. "It's coming from over there." They quieted down again, perking their ears.

Lieven heard it this time; a faded mumbling mixed with the crackling of branches. Was there someone hiding in there somewhere? Then he took the lead, walking fast in the direction of the sound, looking behind bushes and rocks. The sound stopped and then resumed; chattering teeth? In front of him there was an entrance of sorts, maybe the opening to a cave half-covered in branches. He moved them out of the way and couldn't believe what he saw behind it.

"What is it, Liev?" Cees asked, approaching.

"Not sure," Lieven said, trying to decide on what to do next. Inside the cave there was a human being. Not a *Gezegenden* or a *Zuiver*, but a human nevertheless. He was dressed in torn clothes that could not possibly protect him from the cold and sat curled in a corner shivering, his teeth chattering together. His thick white hair stood up in spikes on the top of his head and a tattoo of a bear peeked from the side of his exposed neck. Not sure if he was conscious, Lieven reached out to him cautiously and touched his shoulder. The man flinched at the touch but didn't move otherwise.

"He's not well," Lieven yelled at the rest of the group. Cees and Jia ran forward and crouched by the entrance. "We need to get him out of here. He's half-naked and probably hypothermic."

Lieven and Cees crawled inside of the cave and grabbed the unconscious man by the arms and legs to pull him out. Jia was waiting outside with a blanket at the ready. The man mumbled but didn't fight them as they wrapped him in the warm cloth and started rubbing his arms and legs to bring some heat back to his body.

Jia dug in her backpack and removed a small bag that she began shaking vigorously. "Heating pad," she explained, folding the bag in half until they heard a small pop. "Put it between his legs. The heat will spread to the rest of his body."

"What is he?" Lieven asked, turning to Alfons. The leader shrugged his shoulders just as puzzled as he was.

"He's a *Berenjong,*" Jia said. They all stared at her, surprised. "One of the *gemeden* castes. See the tattoo on his neck? A bear, the symbol for his caste."

Every eye was diverted to the unconscious man. He looked frail, thin, and emaciated. His clothes were so shredded they barely covered his body, and his breathing came out choppy and labored.

"We might as well camp here for the night," said Alfons, taking a quick look around them. "We will be in tight quarters, but so much the better to keep us all warm through the night."

"He needs new clothes." Jia gently examined the *Berenjong.* "Anyone have something he can wear?" They had all brought at least one change of clothes from their last stop. One of the men donated a pair of pants, another a shirt, and Cees gave up a warm sweater he had brought with him. Shoes were more complicated, for none of them had brought extras. "We'll have to wrap his feet in cloth stuffed with leaves for warmth and cushioning."

"How do you know all of that?" Lieven was suspicious but he also begrudgingly admired her creativity.

"I guess I paid better attention in my survival classes than the more academic ones." She shrugged her shoulders.

With the help of Aleid, the *Gezegenden* girl changed the unconscious man's clothes and wrapped him tightly with the blanket before dragging him inside the cave again.

"Do you think he's dangerous?" Cees asked Lieven as they sat down in a tight circle just outside the cave to share some food.

"Why don't you ask your girlfriend?" Lieven was unable to keep the bitterness from his voice. "She seems to know a lot more than me."

Cees glanced up at him, a question in his eyes. "Why can't you trust her?"

Lieven licked his lips before taking a bite of the tough bread in his hands. "I trust her," he lied, keeping his eyes down.

"Don't lie to me," Cees said. "I know you too well. You just don't like her. Is it because she's a *Gezegenden*?"

Lieven looked at him in disbelief. "You really have to ask?" He thought that now that Cees knew about the true nature of his feelings, he would have figured out why he had such trouble accepting Jia's presence among them. How could he not? He tilted his head like a bird and opened his mouth to say something but decided against it. "Never mind."

Jia came to sit next to them. "He's comfortable now." She nodded her head toward the cave. "We managed to get some liquids in him."

Cees threw Lieven another glance before turning to Jia. "Is he dangerous? Never heard of his caste."

With a sigh, Jia reached out to grab a bottle of water. "Not many have. It's a pretty small group. Wild, a bit like animals... also gifted."

Lieven's head snapped up. "Gifted? How?"

"I only know what they told me." Jia shrugged her shoulders and took a long sip from the bottle. "Remember they were the same people that told me the *Zuiver* were unstable and dangerous."

Both men looked appropriately contrite. "Still, what do you know?" Lieven asked.

"They have some of the bear's gifts. A sharp sense of smell and the ability to climb things easily."

Lieven was a little disappointed. Not sure how those gifts would help them, he took another bite of the bread. The world was obviously a lot bigger than he ever thought it was in terms of diversity. *Zuivers* were so isolated, other than the *Gezegenden* they really were not aware of any other races. He now wondered if the people from Central—who were still a major mystery for all of them—were themselves part of a different breed of humans altogether.

Jia dipped her head onto Cees' shoulder. Lieven's heart lurched as he watched Cees turn his head slightly and kiss the top of hers. Was there no end to this subtle torture?

Once the darkness had deepened enough that it was hard to see, they all retired into the cave. There was no room to lay down, so they all leaned against the walls, settling close to each other and arranging their legs and feet around each other's. It was warm in the cave, and most were asleep before long. Lieven couldn't sleep. His eyes had taken a life of their own and they kept escaping in the direction of his friend and Jia. In the dim light of the small luminescent sticks they had activated, the two had cuddled in each other's arms, Jia's head laying against Cees' chest and his chin tucked into her black hair. He wanted to be happy for his friend. He really did, but it was not easy when his heart was so full of want, so full of need.

A small movement to the side of the couple caught his eye. The *Berenjong* was waking up, his transparent eyes darting this way and that, taking in the surrounding humans. Soon, his eyes met Lieven's, who was the only other human in that space still awake. There seemed to be a question in the strange eyes of the creature—what color were they?

His lips suddenly moved, and Lieven realized he was talking to him. The young man was using some language Lieven did not understand. Liven shook his head and lifted his hands to let him know that. The stranger fell silent for a moment, thinking.

"*Spreekt u de oude taal?*" the man finally said in a whisper carried to Lieven by the silence of the cave.

Lieven recognized the words. "No, I only speak words in the old language...*Begrijp je dat*? Do you understand?" he asked, speaking as softly as he could.

The man nodded. "You speak the language of Central." His voice was hoarse and scratchy. Lieven had never thought of their everyday language as the same language they used at Central, but he supposed that was a fair assessment. "My name is Daan. What's yours?"

Lieven was a little surprised that he would ask that. After all, he didn't know who any of them were, and it must have been startling to come to among all these strangers. He had expected the *Berenjong* to ask who they all were instead. "Lieven," he said, feeling he should breach the short distance over all those bodies and shake his hand but unable to.

The other man smiled a crooked, thin smile that lit up his face. "Nice to meet you. You're a *Zuiver*." It was a statement of fact, not a question. Once again surprised, Lieven nodded. "You're all *Zuivers*." Daan scanned the cave. "Except the *Gezegenden* girl. *Roofdieren?*"

Lieven recognized the old word for Predators. "Yes, we're all survivors of two attacks." Daan tilted his head to the side like a bird. "You?"

"Yes. I knew they were coming and managed to run before they got to my village. Thank you for this." He pointed at the blanket and the clothes.

"We didn't have any shoes," Lieven said apologetically.

"No matter, I'm used to running barefoot." Another crooked smile erupted on Daan's lips. "You should sleep."

"Can't." Lieven's eyes unconsciously went back to Cees and Jia, sleeping very close to the *Berenjong*.

"Ik begrijp het." The man's eyes followed Lieven's. "Love is cruel sometimes." Unaware—or not caring—of Lieven's shock at hearing his words, the young man curled up upon himself like a cat or a bear and went to sleep.

How could he possibly know that? Was one of his so-called gifts that of telepathy? Lieven had heard of such things but had never been sure they were a real thing or just myths. Deciding he would not stress too much on something he couldn't figure just then, Lieven crossed his arms, tied the blanket tighter around his shoulders, and closed his eyes. He would ask him the next morning.

Morning dawned, frigid and snowy. Big, fat snowflakes greeted them as they moved out of the cave, stretching their aching legs and arms. Their muscles and joints had joined in complaint about the long hours of restricted movement, but they were at least well rested. When the *Berenjong* emerged from the cave, everyone stopped and stared. Lieven was already outside debating the risks of making a fire to warm everybody up.

Daan was a striking human being. Not handsome or pretty, but different. He was very tall, towering over both Cees and Lieven by almost a foot, and slim. Now that he had had water and some warmth to bring him back to the land of the living, he did not seem as pale and frail as the night before. In fact, despite his slender frame, he seemed strong and solid, a short stubble of hair covering his chin and face. The spikes of his snow-white hair still stuck up every which way, denying the theory that they were a cosmetic fancy of some kind. His most startling feature, though, was his eyes—of an almost transparent icy green nestled in wide, almond-shaped eyes that closed to a near slit when he smiled. And he was smiling! A full and generous smile that stretched from ear to ear and into his eyes.

"*Goedemorgen*," he said, loud and clear. "Thank you for saving my skinny butt from this cold."

A couple of the men laughed. Lieven stretched out his hand in greeting. "We were not properly introduced last night." He shook Daan's hand. "Welcome."

Cees and Jia were nowhere to be seen, and Lieven preferred not to imagine where or what they may be doing, so he dove into conversation with this fascinating new addition to their group. Daan's voice was a bit smoother this morning, but it still showed obvious effects of prolonged exposure to cold. Lieven offered him a honey stick, which he accepted enthusiastically.

"What happened to the others in your village?" Lieven asked, as they sat down, sharing a bite to eat.

"Probably dead," Daan said simply. "Not many have the gift like me."

"What exactly is your gift?" Lieven was curious. Daan was attacking a piece of bread with gusto.

"I have a super-sensitive sense of smell." Daan's mouth was full and cheeks puffed up. "I can smell from miles away. I was hunting outside my village when I smelled the *Roofdieren* and was able to run the other way. I'm sure the others weren't so lucky."

He didn't seem particularly upset about the fact that his village had all perished in the attack. "Anyone you loved?" Lieven asked, stealing a sideways glance.

"Nuh." He took another giant bite off the stale bread. "I lived on my own just outside the village ever since my parents died years ago. I only went to the village if I needed something. Having my gifts didn't exactly endear the villagers to me."

Lieven swallowed a mouthful. "I thought you all had gifts," he said, remembering what Jia had told them the night before.

"No way." He opened his eyes wide, displaying two startling eyes the color of lakes. "Maybe a long time ago, but the gifts have been vanishing from my people. I believe I was the only one in my village. Before me, my father had the gifts, but he is long gone."

Afraid of asking what the other gifts were and feeling very self-conscious of every thought going through his head at the moment, Lieven sat silently.

"Where's your *liefje?*" Lieven's head lifted suddenly. "Your loved one? The one with the face stripe?"

Lieven waved his hand as to ask him to quiet down and looked around him. Cees and Jia were nowhere. "Why do you say that?"

"It's obvious." Daan shrugged. "It's all over the way you look at him. I was watching you watch him as he put his arms around the girl. There was jealously and love in your eyes."

"Well, you're wrong," Lieven lied. "I am just concerned he is falling in love with a *Gezegenden,* that's all."

Daan laughed heartily, throwing his head back and spitting out the pieces of bread he still had in his mouth. *"Leugenaar,* liar! Did I mention I also have the gift of mind-reading?"

Lieven's eyes opened wide and his whole body went rigid. "You do?"

The *Berenjong* laughed again. "Don't be daft." He slapped Lieven across the back playfully. "That doesn't exist. I'm just really good at interpreting face expressions. From a lifetime of watching people from afar." His laugh was so contagious, Lieven found himself laughing along with him.

Jia and Cees appeared from behind the trees, side by side with smiles that belied their less-than-desirable situation. "What's going on?" Cees asked as they sat next to the others. "Did we miss a joke?"

Daan's feline eyes shone in the crisp morning light. "We are just commenting on how good some lovers are at disappearing," he said, a mischievous smile on his lips.

Lieven choked on the piece of bread he was munching on, and Jia's white skin became furiously red. Cees was the only one who laughed, blissfully unaware of the uneasiness the others were feeling. "We just wanted some privacy," he explained unnecessarily.

Lieven coughed to clear his throat and handed some bread to both of them. "Daan was telling me a little about him and his people." He departed on a brief retelling of what the enigmatic man had told him. "We'll get you shoes in the next town." Lieven pointed at Daan's bare feet.

Daan stretched one of his very long legs and shook a foot in front of them. "No urgent need. These babies are tough as nails." They couldn't help but stare at the soles of his feet; they closely resembled the paws of an animal. Both the bottom of the heel and the ball of his foot were covered in thick, callused, brownish skin. "We are not called the Bear people for nothing." He laughed again, his chuckles floating up in the air like bubbles.

Alfons called from the edge of their small campsite. It was time to move on. Lieven stood up and held out his hand to Daan. "Are you up to the long walk?" he asked, helping him up.

"I'm good as new." Daan stood, steady and tall. His unusual, cord-like hair made him look even taller than he really was, and his hand was callused where Lieven's was soft. A strange tingling went through Lieven's hand into his arm. "Felt that too, did you?" Daan winked at him with his unnerving green eyes and turned to follow the others.

"He's strange," Aleid said as she went by.

Lieven couldn't argue. Daan was indeed odd in more ways that he could count, from his physical appearance to the way he acted. He was not sure whether he liked Daan or not. Then again, Lieven was not sure of much anymore. With a sigh, he took his place behind Cees and began walking.

Cees

Dark clouds had rolled over the band of survivors, turning the previously blue sky into an ominous ocean of gray and black that seemed to chase them as they hurried through the brush. The group's hopes of getting to *Volgendestad* were beginning to dwindle along with the light of the day. It looked like they would have to spend another night outdoors. Cees took a deep breath and tried to ignore the pain in his cramping muscles. Slightly ahead of him, Jia walked steadily, her face locked in a serious and determined expression that denounced no discomfort, no difficulties. Yet, Cees was sure she had to be in at least as much pain as he was. Not for the first time, he felt his heart swell with pride. He had never met anyone as brave as she was; at least not anybody below five-feet-ten.

The new "recruit" seemed impervious to the hardships of their trek, walking with a spring in his step, his nose held up high as if constantly sniffing the air. Daan was an odd sort with his weird white hair, his towering frame, bare feet, and feline eyes. He often seemed more animal than human, stopping once in a while to climb on trees with the ease of a bear and coming down with strange nuts in his hands which he had gathered upon the high branches.

"What do you think he's doing with his nose stuck up like that in the air?" Cees asked Jia, who had slowed her pace down just enough to walk near him.

Jia smiled. "Who knows? I half expect him to take off hunting some little animal for dinner."

Daan was walking next to Lieven now, talking and waving his arms. Once in a while, he would circle the gentle soldier, chatting all the while. Lieven's step would stagger, uncertain of whether to move forward or stop, his eyes staring at the *Berenjong* in confusion. Cees stifled a chuckle behind his hand. Lieven looked a little lost.

"Do you think we should rescue Liev?" he wondered, nodding in his direction.

Jia laughed. "He's a big boy. He can handle it."

Cees looped his arm through hers and pulled her closer to him. She resisted at first, but quickly yielded against him. "I'm not so sure," he said, kissing her cheek. Then, he lowered his voice to a whisper. "You smell good."

"Liar," she teased. "I haven't had a bath in... forever. I'm not sure I remember what a bath looks or feels like."

A bath sounded heavenly. Neither of them smelled too sweet. They had tried to freshen up a little, using the snow for a quick, unsatisfying, and freezing wash, but it was no use. The stench of fear and sweat was well-absorbed and settled into their skin, and even the clean clothes they were all wearing were not able to change that. By the looks of the sky above, they would have to wait a bit longer for a well-deserved bath.

A cold, thick flake fell on Jia's nose, and he watched her, mesmerized as she stuck her tongue out and licked it off. His stomach tightened. Another flake replaced the first and this time, Cees twisted around her just in time to lick it off her nose himself. A soft moan left Jia's mouth as she melted in his arms, her mouth just beneath his. His body quickly reacted to her and suddenly he was not cold anymore.

"Cees," she whispered, her lips touching his chin. "The others…"

He looked around, suddenly aware they were not alone. With Jia it was so easy to shut out the rest of the world, to travel to their own private safe haven where only the two existed and mattered. Reality was not as kind. Several pairs of eyes were looking at them as if they had suddenly grown an extra head. He shrugged at them, dismissing their surprise.

"Damn!" He turned to Jia again. "I guess we should be going." They both giggled and resumed the walk, a little closer to each other this time, their fingertips touching and a new spring to their step. Stolen glances would have to be enough for now.

The snow was accumulating on the ground beneath their feet, and the possibility that they wouldn't reach their destination became a certainty. Alfons had just sent a couple scouts to find a good shelter for the night when Daan, still walking ahead of the group, stopped and lifted his hand. His nose up in the air, the tall man circled slowly with his eyes closed. They all stopped, watching him.

"Call your scouts back now," he finally spoke, his eyes popping open. "*Roofdieren* ahead. Predators."

Cees' heart leapt in his chest and he instinctively pulled Jia closer to him.

"How do you know?" Lieven's eyebrow arched as it always did when he was suspicious.

"I can smell them," Daan said simply. "Call your men now. We need to head the other way."

Alfons didn't argue. He immediately sent two more men to stop the others before they got too far ahead. "But if we head the other way, we'll be walking away from our destination," he said, a worried frown on his face.

"By just a few miles," the *Berenjong* said. "We walk back just enough to put some distance between us. The wind is in our favor, and they are moving away from where we're going. Show me a map."

Cees was impressed with the young man's assertive attitude. *He may still be a great asset for the group after all.* Lieven pulled a small map from his bag and unrolled it on the white, cold ground. Daan crouched by him and studied the map for a few moments. Then, he traced a line on the paper with his finger.

"Here." He pointed at a spot on the map. "We back up to here. There is an old road that crosses it. We can follow the road up to this spot." He pointed at the map again. He seemed to see things in the map no one else could. "Then we are on track again. That will take us away from the beasts enough they won't sense us."

Lieven looked at the white-haired man with a bemused expression. "How do you know all this?" he asked, rolling the map up again.

"I'm talented that way," said Daan, a mischievous smile playing in the corner of his mouth. Lieven looked at him and frowned. "You are a tough audience." Daan chuckled. "You learn a lot when you have nothing else to do. Being alone has its advantages. I studied, I listened when everybody thought I was not paying attention, I observed... And I have an amazing memory."

Lieven chortled. "And you are obviously very humble."

"Obviously." Daan winked.

The scouts returned, and they all backtracked a couple miles, their heavy hearts reflected on their faces. The very idea that the Predators were near made Cees' blood curdle in his veins. Even though none of them wanted to go back the way they had just come from, it was a much better option than what lay ahead.

The night was upon them, and their noses were hurting from the cold. Daan scouted ahead and found them a small but sheltered area by a creek. There were several spots where they could lay underneath rock outcrops for the night, semi-protected from the falling snow. But there would be no protection from the cold. It was going to be a long, uncomfortable night.

Cees crawled under some rocks with Jia, their backs to the wall, and wrapped both of them the best he could with the blankets they had brought. For a moment, he considered inviting Lieven into their small human-heated cocoon, but he realized it would be awkward for both his friend and Jia. He followed the young soldier with his eyes, worried that he would end up freezing during the night with no one to share body heat.

"Lieven," Daan called from the narrow space he had taken shelter in. "Come and sit with me. I'm a great heater." He laughed at his own joke.

Lieven looked at him, surprised first and then obviously conflicted. As a soldier, Lieven was sure to know that was the right thing to do to survive, but Daan was a stranger to them.

"Come on, soldier." Daan patted the spot next to him. "I promise I won't bite. You guys saved me, just returning the favor."

Lieven had another moment of hesitation before giving in and crawling next to the *Berenjong*. Cees watched half-amused as Daan—in an almost motherly fashion—tucked the blankets around his obviously ill-at-ease friend.

"If we ever make it out alive, I will have so much to tease Lieven about," Cees whispered to Jia. She laughed and scooted closer under the blankets. His blood warmed up inside his veins and he felt comfortable and happy despite everything. It didn't take long for Jia to fall asleep. The sound of her soft breath caressed his cold ears as she cuddled against him, her head over his chest, her arm crossed over his middle in a half-hug. A little slice of heaven in the midst of chaos.

Cees woke up sometime during the night, panic in his heart. It took him a few minutes to realize he was still leaning against those cold rocks, cloaked in Jia's arms, her ear to his crazed heart. The sound of voices, soft and quiet, wafted to his ears with the snow in the freezing breeze. With a quick scan of the surrounding area, he saw Lieven and the *Berenjong* in conversation. Daan was speaking in his characteristic exuberant way, ignoring the cold and waving his arms along with his words. Lieven's voice was much quieter, almost inaudible.

"How long has this been going on?" Daan asked, uncovering the two of them as he spoke.

Lieven pulled the blanket back up to his chin. "Since we were teens." He said something else, but Cees couldn't hear it.

"You never told him?" Surprise was obvious in his voice. Maybe even a little shock. "Why wouldn't you tell him?"

"I couldn't be sure he loved me that way," Lieven said. "I didn't want to lose his friendship."

"And now he has the *Gezegenden* girl. And you still won't tell him?"

"He knows now," Lieven said, a tremor in his voice.

Cees' heart contracted. So focused on their flight from the Predators and his overwhelming feelings for Jia, he had not given much thought to what Lieven was feeling. As hard as it still was for him to accept that his friend's feelings for him had been much deeper than brotherly love, he now felt guilt gnaw on him. He had made very little effort to hide his feelings for Jia. All those displays of affection must be killing Lieven. How would he feel if he had to watch someone kiss and look at Jia the way he did?

"So, what are you going to do?" Daan asked, stopping Cees' musings.

"What can I do?" Lieven asked. "Go on. There is not much choice for me. I will have to go on."

Cees had never suspected Lieven's feelings for him. Not once. They had grown up so close, the thought had never crossed his mind. Causing his best friend that much pain was an unsettling feeling. It filled him with an irrational sense of guilt, as if he had somehow encouraged, and then dismissed his love. The wind had picked up and changed directions enough that their conversation was now inaudible to Cees. Resigned, Cees closed his eyes and willed himself to fall asleep.

CHAPTER SEVEN

PREDATOR

Jia

Half of what he was saying sounded like gibberish to her. Jia had never met anyone quite like Daan. He was by far the most exuberant, strangely charismatic human being she had ever set eyes on. In his defense, he was very entertaining to watch and listen to, but the man could talk your ear off and be totally oblivious to the fact you had stopped listening to him a while back.

As she and Cees walked behind the *Berenjong* and poor Lieven, who seemed to have found a friend—however unwanted—in the strange creature, she couldn't help but laugh softly under her breath at his chatter and effusive body language. To be truthful, she was grateful to Daan for offering her—and the others—a welcome distraction from their predicament. On the other hand, Cees didn't seem as thrilled with their new companion as she thought he would be. Jia had thought that now that he knew about Lieven's true feelings for him, he would welcome anything that would distract his friend from dwelling on it. However, that was not the case. Her beautiful *Zuiver* was sullen and at times outright cranky, his eyes throwing poisoned darts at Daan for most of their march.

"What's wrong with you?" Jia looped her arm through his and pulled him backwards just enough to make some space between them and Lieven.

"What do you mean?" He lowered his eyes to the ground. "There's nothing wrong."

"Well, you could have fooled me." She looked up at him, rolling her lips between her teeth. "You won't even look me in the eye."

As if to prove her wrong, Cees lifted his deep blue eyes to hers. There was pain behind those beautiful orbs. "See? Nothing wrong," he said in a childishly petulant voice.

"Don't lie to me." Jia lowered her voice to a mere whisper. "I can see it in your eyes. You're hurting."

Cees blinked and licked his lips. "You're imagining things, Jia. You don't know me as well as you think you do."

His words burnt a hole in her heart. Blinking away tears, Jia felt as if her throat had suddenly constricted to the point she couldn't get any air in. She dropped the hand that held on to him and backed up a step or two.

Cees stopped and stared at her, his eyebrows gathering in and his hands falling along his sides. "Shit, Jia. I didn't mean it that way," he said, his voice trailing off. "I'm sorry. I'm..."

"You're what?" Jia's voice was still low but pregnant with anger. "Are you jealous of Daan? Is that what it is?"

Cees stepped back a few inches and shook his head. "Jealous? Why would I be jealous?"

Jia felt she wasn't in control of her words anymore. "Maybe you're in love with Lieven after all. Maybe you just don't want to accept it."

As soon as the words were out of her mouth, she wanted to take them right back. Now, who was the jealous one?

"I'm not in love with Liev." Cees was careful to speak low enough so the others couldn't hear it. "I love him as my brother, that's all." Strangely enough, Cees didn't sound angry. He reached out to her.

"Then what's wrong?" Jia ignored his hand, but her voice was not angry anymore.

"I feel guilty," Cees said, his eyes clouding over. "I feel like I let him down by not returning his feelings."

She lifted her hand to his face. "No one can tell your heart who to love or hate. It just happens. You should not feel guilty. I'm sure Lieven himself does not blame you for it."

Cees' lips quivered a little. "Maybe." His voice broke. "But I still feel guilty. And now he's kind of stuck with the *Berenjong...*"

Jia looped her arm through his again and resumed the walk. Lieven and Daan were already at some distance from them, still deep in conversation, never once noticing they had stopped. She laughed. "I don't think he minds." She nodded toward the two men ahead. Daan was still waving his hands above his head and Lieven was roaring with laughter.

Cees tilted the corner of his lip up in a half-smile. "You might be right."

The snow had stopped sometime during the night, and the air was crispy cold. A cloud of visible breath rose above them as they made their trek through the woods. Alfons and Aleid walked in the front and expected the two scouts sent ahead to come back to them at any moment. They were all freezing and exhausted. The thought of a warm shelter, warm food, and maybe even a bath was strong in her heart. Jia couldn't remember the last time she had gone that long without thoroughly cleaning herself. Despite her low-status in the

Blessed society, she had all the human comforts any other citizen was entitled to: a nice home, good food, running hot water... The fact that she had to "prove" herself to the society males on a frequent basis to keep those comforts was irrelevant now. Jia felt she would kill for a long, hot bath.

When the scouts appeared around a corner, Jia's heart jumped. After a short, animated conversation with the leader, one of the scouts turned to the rest of the group and waved them on.

"Less than a mile," Alfons announced before continuing the march.

Jia looked at Cees with a big smile. An unusual sense of excitement swelled in her chest and she tightened her hold on Cees' arm. Soon they would be able to rest for a while. They both sped up their step. The terrain changed abruptly, and what had been a mostly flat trail now started sloping down rather steeply. The city of *Volgendestad* rose before their eyes, nestled between several high hills as if hiding from the rest of the world.

"Do you think there is anyone there?" one of the men asked.

Daan answered, his nose sticking up in the air again. "No, there are no humans left here," he said. "But no beasts either."

It was not a big city, at least not the part that had been hidden away in that valley. Just like the other city they had visited, it looked serene and untouched, as if the inhabitants had just vaporized. Unlike the other, though, there was no trace of human blood anywhere. What had happened? Did the humans here have time to flee the atrocities happening in other parts of *Oostzee?* Maybe they had been one of the few who had received their radio warning. Whatever the reason, the place had been abandoned with no trace of life.

Once they started exploring the buildings, they also realized that the people here had taken quite a lot with them: food supplies, clothing, weapons. They had left some behind, but it was obvious the supplies had been raided.

"It looks like they saw it coming and ran," Alfons said after they had finished their survey of the place. The group had gathered in the lobby of a hotel. Some had found food supplies and were eating, while others were satisfying their cravings for a hot drink. The electric fireplace had been turned on, and the air was now comfortably warm. Divested of her thick coat, hat, and gloves, Jia felt a hundred pounds lighter. She had found hot cocoa in the hotel kitchen and had prepared some for her and Cees.

"That's good news, right?" Lieven asked. Daan was nowhere to be seen.

"I hope so," Alfons took a sip of a steaming mug. "Hopefully they were able to get themselves to safety in time."

It was such a luxury for them to all sit together, semi-relaxed in quiet conversation, that she didn't hear Daan come back. Jia saw him first. He was obviously agitated, his face pale and transparent eyes haunted by some invisible danger.

"They're coming."

Everyone looked at him, confused.

"The *Roofdieren* are coming this way." The terror in his voice left no doubt in anyone's minds as to what he was talking about. "We have two, three hours tops before they get here."

Despite their shock, they all gathered their wits pretty quickly, and the planning started. Alfons sent several scouts in search of safe places to hide, while a few others did an inventory of how much Stank they had left. The rest gathered food, drink, and clothing from nearby houses. When the scouts came back with the news of a few bunker-style places not too far from where they were, they wasted no time.

Jia didn't have time to feel scared. Holding on to precious food and clothing, she followed the others into the building the scouts had found. She recognized it for what it was. Similar buildings existed in almost all Blessed cities; a high security prison.

"We keep the dangerous criminals in these places," she told Cees. "What if some were left behind?"

There was no one within its walls. Apparently in their flight from the Predators the citizens of *Volgendestad* had also let the criminals go. Doors hung ajar in almost every cell.

"Which are the safest cells?" Lieven asked.

"Downstairs." Jia pointed at a door. "Isolation cells. They don't open from the inside, though."

They looked at each other as realization dawned; someone had to stay outside the cells if they were ever to be able to get out again.

"I'll do it," Lieven said. Cees turned his head so fast, Jia could have sworn she heard the vertebrae clicking in his neck. "I'll sit guard, and I will open the doors for you after they are gone."

Cees stepped forward and grabbed his friend's arm. "No way! You'll be a dead man."

Lieven shook his head. "No, I will cover myself in stank and hide well. They won't find me."

"Like hell you will." Cees hissed the words, his jaws clenched tight.

Eyes hard as rocks, Lieven spoke in a quiet tone. "You can't tell me what to do. I'm a soldier, and my job is to protect other soldiers and civilians." Ignoring the pleading glares from his friend, Lieven turned to Alfons. "I volunteer for the job, Alfons."

Alfons swallowed hard before shaking his hand. "Agreed."

"No!" A guttural scream escaped Cees' mouth. "If he does this I will stay with him. It makes sense for two in case something happens to one of us."

Jia felt a surge of panic in her chest, a flurry of bee-like wings buzzing in her ears. "If you stay out, I will stay out too." She was not going to lose him now. He ran in her veins like her own blood, and she was not sure she would survive without him.

"Let's all keep calm," Daan said, taking a wide step forward. "I owe you people my life. I will stand with Lieven." Cees was about to protest. "I will make sure he survives."

Somberly, they went about with the job of making the basement of the prison as secure as they could. They closed and locked the double-barred gates, locked the metal enclosure doors behind them, and divided into small groups. Jia, Cees, and a couple other soldiers were ordered into one of the isolation cells. Once inside they wouldn't have any control over what happened.

At the last moment, Cees took a few steps forward and drew Lieven into a hug. "You better survive this, Liev." He buried his face in his friend's neck.

"Or what?" Lieven asked, a sad smile on his lips.

"Or I will kill you myself. I love you, brother. Don't you go dying on me now."

Released from the hug, Lieven laughed. "I promise to do everything in my power not be eaten."

When the cell door closed, Cees stood staring at it for a long time. Jia laid a hand on his back to let him know she was there for him and felt his quick breathing and the loud beating of his heart.

Jia prayed for the first time. Not sure what she believed, she sent prayers to all the deities she knew. *Please protect my friends, Lieven and Daan. Please allow the Predators to pass through without detecting them.* The realization that she did indeed think of Lieven as a friend now hit her full force. She thought of all of them as her friends now. How had that happened? Not certain about how to feel about it, Jia laid her head against Cees' strong arm and prayed a little more. It was going to be a long, hard night.

May the gods protect us all.

Lieven

The door closed too fast, leaving him and Daan alone in the enclosed yet vulnerable space. Even after the door shut, Lieven could still see his friend's face, eyes shiny with unshed tears and an expression of both sorrow and terror. He hoped it wouldn't be the last time he saw those beloved blue eyes. For the first time, he was thankful Jia was there, holding Cees, loving him and offering him a shoulder to cry on. Cees wouldn't be alone, and that somehow was a relief, a weight removed from his heart and soul. If he died that night, he could die in peace knowing Cees would be well taken care of and never, ever left alone.

Daan was opening the container of stank, crouched by the metal doors that separated them from the outside. From behind, he looked a little like a real bear. A thin bear, granted, but a bear nevertheless. He had elected to wear this bulky fur coat he had found in one of the houses they searched, and he had finally found some footwear that felt comfortable enough for his unused-to-confinement feet. The fur that covered the huge boots—far too large even for his big feet—completed the ursine look. His white, corded hair in stern contrast with the gray and black of the coat gave the illusion of snow. All in all, it was such a wild look, Lieven almost laughed.

"Why are you standing there staring at me?" the bear man asked, his white eyebrows arching furiously. "Come and cover yourself with this horrible mess... What did you call it?"

Lieven crossed the distance separating them and crouched by the container. "Stank, we call it stank."

Daan shook his head and grunted. "I would have called it *stront* instead, because that's exactly what it smells like." That brought a smile to Lieven's lips. *Yes, it does smell like shit.* "Why do you *Zuiver* don't call things what they are?" Daan seemed genuinely puzzled.

"So you call sugar *sweetness* or lemons *tartness*?" Taking a handful of the awfully odorous material, Lieven started to slather it along his arms, neck, and over his clothes. *Stront* indeed.

"No, but those words have been around forever." Scooping some stank gingerly with his fingers, Daan lifted it up to his nose and flinched. "Gah! This *stront* is criminal. What is this anyway?"

Lieven told him the story of how they had discovered the smelly product and how it had protected them on their way here. They sat companionably, leaning against the wall that backed into the isolation cell where their friends were, chatting as if a band of monsters was not closing in on them.

Daan kept sniffing his coat and wrinkling his nose as if he didn't like the smell it carried. "It has a familiar smell, but I can't put my finger on it," he had told Lieven earlier. "I know I've smelled this before."

Lieven laughed and asked him why he was wearing it then, if the smell offended him.

"It's not offensive," the *Berenjong* replied. "It annoys me because I can't name it."

Hours may have passed before they heard the first tale-tell sound of something moving outside the walls. Those walls were thick and obviously built to keep the world out, but the sounds still reached their ears. Lieven's heart skipped a beat. On the very edge of his hearing, there was a faint scratching. Daan placed a finger across his lips. The Predators were just outside the doors.

Minutes, unlike their hearts, dragged on like molasses. The scratching noises were replaced by the clear sound of claws scraping against metal. Lieven could almost see them, sticking their razor-sharp claws through the narrow spaces between the iron bars outside that door, trying to breach the first obstacle between them and the humans. Could the Predators smell them? They must sense something; otherwise, why would they be interested in that place?

Lieven scooped more stank from the container and daubed some alongside the edges of the door from top to bottom, hoping to create a stench barrier between the creatures and them. As he sat back down beside Daan, he realized with some shock he was shaking. His whole body, from head to toe, trembled as if an earthquake was making its way through him. The *Berenjong*'s hand came to lay on top of his, his callused thumb rubbing the top of Lieven's hand and wrist in a strangely comforting way. Even more astonishing was the way that simple, unexpected touch managed to ground him. Suddenly, he could breathe normal again, and the tremors that assailed him just seconds before were now gone. A great and welcomed peace washed over him like a cleansing wave. Lieven exchanged a grateful look with the bear man. He was ready for whatever was about to happen.

He couldn't be sure how much time had passed as they sat, deriving comfort and courage from each other's hands. The Predators slammed against the door in even-spaced intervals as if they had a plan. The knowledge that they had already bridged the metal bars was unwelcome but not surprising. These were not only extremely strong animals, but there seemed to be a trace of intelligence behind their moves. When the door suddenly buckled in, Daan squeezed his hand tighter. They were coming in. Shocked into action, both men bounced to their feet and pulled their guns in front of them. They wouldn't go without a fight.

A frightful hairy limb edged in the sharpest claws Lieven had ever seen broke its way through the metal, and when it yanked back, it managed to take away a big chunk of the door with it. A gaping hole, the size of a man had replaced part of the door and the only thing that separated them from their doom. The creature didn't waste time. In a nanosecond, it had squeezed through the opening and was now facing them. Lieven couldn't help but stare at the creature in some wonder. Easily over seven feet tall, it stood on its hind legs, two powerful limbs that could easily and by themselves destroy Daan and him. The other two equally strong limbs were stretched in front of the creature at the ready for an attack. The Predator was covered from head to toe in a blackish-gray fur that seemed oddly familiar to Lieven, its pointy ears turning this way and that, tuned in to every sound. But it was the creature's eyes that terrified Lieven the most. There was human cunning behind those wild and cruel eyes as the Predator snarled and bared its needle-sharp fangs at them. There was intelligence behind those eyes.

Taking advantage of the temporary surprise, the monster pounced at them. Lieven's gun went off, but the creature was too fast. The bullet missed it, and Lieven felt the sharp pain of claws being buried into his arm. Instinct kicked in, and he drew up a leg and hit the Predator hard with a knee. The pain on contact was excruciating. The monster's corded muscles were like rocks. Lieven's kick seemed to have absolutely no effect. The creature bent down and aimed his lethal fangs at Lieven's neck. Liven had just enough time to duck out of the way. He had planned to circumvent the beast and shoot it from behind, but its claws were still buried in his arm and as he moved, he felt and heard his own flesh tear apart. Blood spurted from the wound, and Lieven experienced a momentary moment of panic as his sight blurred and he felt the strings of oblivion pulling strongly at him. The creature was fast and, sensing Lieven's sudden weakness, leaped forward and sunk its fangs into his left shoulder. A scream escaped Lieven's mouth as the full agony of the mauling reached his senses. The fight went off him like a shrugged-off coat, and he could feel his life force slipping away. His blurred vision focused on the creature's head, which had come up for air and was coming down on him for another attack. Lieven closed his eyes and accepted his fate.

The pain never came. A loud thud made him open his eyes to see the beast turned away from him, all four legs on the floor, preparing to pounce on Daan, who was on the other side, his gun up and ready.

"Come and get me, you *stinkend haarbal*," the *Berenjong* yelled, legs braced firmly on the floor.

The Predator sniffed the air as if something pleased it. It suddenly hit him. Lieven knew now why the creature's coloring felt so familiar—Daan's coat! The bear man was wearing a coat made of Predator's fur. Which, of course, made no sense at all. Maybe the loss of blood was making him hallucinate.

Sobered by the sudden knowledge that Daan was about to be mauled by the beast, Lieven reached out for his gun, discarded not too far from where he was lying. The predator had lost its interest in Lieven and was now inching closer to Daan, sniffing and making strange, guttural sounds. He lifted the weapon and, without any further delay, shot several rounds into the beast's back. Time froze, and all he could hear and feel was the sound and the vibration coming from the barrel of the powerful weapon he had never used before. The Predator's body shook and convulsed for a few long seconds before dropping to the ground, unmoving. Daan stared at the fallen beast with his mouth wide open and unblinking eyes. He looked so bizarre, Lieven chuckled weakly and dropped the gun to the floor. He had no strength left in him.

"I think that *stinkend haarbal* had a thing for me." Daan approached the fallen soldier. "Shit. You're bleeding bad."

"Is he dead?" Lieven asked, unable to keep his heavy eyelids open. Consciousness was slipping away like a morning mist over the waters.

"Yes, very dead," he heard Daan say. "He was alone. No furry buddies with him. Thank be the Guardians."

"I'm..." Lieven couldn't speak anymore, his lips refusing to form the words he wanted to say. *Tell Cees I've always loved him. Tell Jia to take care of him.*

"Lieven, Lieven." Daan's voice seemed to be coming from far away, as if transmitting through a long tunnel. "Stay with me. I don't like to lose what I just found. Stay with me."

Hands were working on his wounded shoulder, but Lieven couldn't tell exactly what they were doing. The good news was he felt no pain. The bad news was he couldn't feel anything at all. His body had gone all tingly and heavy as if he was lying under a sheet of lead. Sounds reached his ears, but he couldn't tell them apart anymore or make much sense of what he was hearing.

"Liev, please open your eyes." The voice was not Daan's. It was a voice he would recognize anywhere, under any circumstances. Even under the fog that had rolled over his brain. Cees! With a super-human effort, Lieven tried to open his eyes. He wanted to look into Cees' eyes one last time, but his eyes wouldn't open. "Stay with us, Liev. Please, stay with me."

The faint light coming through his closed eyelids was fading and the voices farther and farther away until there was nothing but void. The warmth of something moist on his lips momentarily brought him back. His chest contracted and expanded under the pressure of something hard and strong. Lieven felt precious, reviving air being blown into his mouth and insistent pressure over his heart. Slowly and painfully, he began feeling again. First his extremities, then his arms and legs... He wanted to scream. The pain on his chest and on his arm was growing in agonizing waves, yet the scream wouldn't leave his chest.

"Fight it, Liev," he heard Cees' voice plead. "Fight it."

The pressure on his lips eased for a moment. "Come on, *liefje*, breathe..." Lieven hadn't realized he wasn't breathing on his own anymore. As soon as that life-saving air stopped being pushed into his mouth, the lights started fading again. "Shit! He's going under again."

The air was back after a brief period of darkness. Again, he felt his chest expand and burn. "Come on, Liev," a female voice said.

An overwhelming urge to cough overcame him, and he realized he was now breathing on his own—however painful it was, he was inhaling and exhaling in great bouts of hacking cough. Someone rolled him on his side, and he threw up. His mouth tasted of metal and bile as he emptied his stomach on the floor beside him.

"He's fine." Was that Daan's hand flat against his back, supporting him while he vomited his insides out?

Lieven's head was swirling; he was dizzy and confused. When he finally managed to open his eyes, the first face he saw was so close to his, he couldn't identify it. As his eyes gradually regained focus, the strangely welcoming face of Daan came into view. He had a big, goofy smile on his lips, and his eyes were scanning Lieven's for some kind of assurance that he was indeed *fine*. Lieven licked his lips and immediately regretted it. The sour taste of bile in his tongue almost made him heave again.

"Someone get him some water," Daan ordered, looking around him.

After swirling around some water in his mouth and spitting it out, he felt better. His chest and his arm were on fire, but he was happy to be alive. Lieven scanned the room, looking for Cees, and he found him, crouching at a corner, his haunted eyes reminiscent of the animal-like creature he was when Lieven first met him. Jia was crouching beside him, her arm protectively over his shoulder, whispering something in his ear.

"Daan." Lieven's voice scratched his burned throat with the ferocity of a shard of glass. Daan lowered his head down to him to better hear what he was saying. "Tell Cees I will be all right. He looks..."

"Destroyed," Daan finished for him. That was the exact word Lieven was looking for; destroyed just like he had been all those years ago at the hands of his so-called institute guardians. "I will, don't worry."

The *Berenjong* moved to leave, but Lieven held his arm. "Wait. Are you aware you are wearing a coat made of Predator's fur?"

The stunned and yet withering look on Daan's face confirmed he did not know. How was that even possible? The bear man could smell a Predator from miles away. Why couldn't he smell the fur on his own body?

"That's not possible." Daan shook his head. "I would have known."

"Look at the dead monster." Lieven's voice was flowing a bit easier now. "Look at his fur. The same markings, the same color. Different sizes, but same animal."

Daan turned his head around, looking toward the dead beast a few yards away. His shoulders slumped so deeply, it was like looking at the body of an old man. When he turned back around, there were tears dancing in his eyes and anger in the setting of his mouth.

"I messed up." Daan's lips curled into a grimace. "Because of my stupidity you almost got killed. Hell, we all almost got killed."

"It wasn't your fault." The man seemed so distraught by the realization, Lieven was scared of what he might do. "But how come you didn't recognize the scent?"

Daan dropped to his knees beside Lieven, his shoulders slumping even deeper. "I don't understand. It does not smell like the other Predators. There is something familiar about it, but it's a totally different scent."

Lieven closed his eyes for a moment, trying to clear his mind. *Think, Lieven, think. There has to be something.* The size difference! While the Predator lying not far from him was well above seven feet tall, the one that had once been inside the fur Daan was wearing couldn't have been taller than five feet. Was it possible the fur belonged to a young Predator?

"The Predator," Lieven said, his eyes popping open. "Is it female or male?"

Daan looked confused. "What does it matter?"

"Female or male?" Lieven's voice did not leave any doubt as to the seriousness of his intent to find out.

"Female," Daan answered. "Why?"

His mind was percolating with an idea. Lieven was not sure it was possible or if it made any sense, but... "That fur you're wearing is from the Predator's young, a nursling most likely." It made sense. The beasts were mammals, and if their young were being nursed, they wouldn't emit the same odor. They would leave a totally different scent trail, wouldn't they?

Daan blinked his eyes. "That would explain me not being able to identify the smell," he said. A smile appeared on his lips just as his shoulders rose to their normal height. The youthful *Berenjong* was back. "Thanks be the Guardians! I couldn't tell…"

"It also explains why there was only one Predator," Lieven continued. "The female must have picked up the scent of her lost young and broke from the pack to come and get it."

The tall *Berenjong* stood up, shrugged the coat off his back, and threw it on top of the dead beast. "The *Roofdieren* can have it. I'd rather freeze." Then, dropping to his knees again and bending forward, he hugged Lieven. "I'm so happy you're okay."

Lieven groaned in pain. "You may still kill me if you don't let go." A little chuckle escaped his lips despite the pain.

As Daan backed up with a quick apology, Lieven's eyes came to rest on Cees again. He was still crouching in the corner, but his expression was not of fear or sadness any longer. His lips had furled, and his eyes were burning with anger. Jia seemed to be trying to calm him down with very little success.

In a liquid move, Cees jumped to his feet and strode to where they were, clenched his hand on Daan's shoulder and pulled him roughly backwards. Under the unexpected attack, Daan fell on his back with a thump. "You stupid, irresponsible idiot!" Cees growled rather than talked. "You almost killed Lieven." Without delay, the *Zuiver* threw himself of top of the fallen man, punching him mercilessly with his fists.

"Stop, Cees!" Lieven yelled, trying to lift himself from the floor and causing a gush of blood to spring from his chest wound. With a shriek of pain, darkness fell upon him once again and all was quiet.

Chapter Eight

LOVE AND CONFUSION

Cees

With a mighty blow, Cees' hand came down on Daan's face. Blood splattered up in the air, tiny little fluid drops flying in every direction like rain falling the wrong way. He vaguely recognized the voices telling him to stop as his vision had turned red with anger. This odd creature was to blame for Lieven's near-death. Cees noticed the man's aura had turned a bright shade of green instead of red, the color of fear. For some reason this angered Cees even more. How dare Daan feel peaceful and balanced when he had caused his friend's brush with mortality.

Hand up in the air, he braced himself to bring it down once again, but someone had grabbed his wrist and was pulling it backward.

"Stop, Cees." It was Jia, her tiny frame and arms proving to be a mask for her real strength. Her hand had wrapped itself around his wrist and held it in place with the power of a metal vice. "It was not his fault. Stop it."

Fighting her hold would mean hurting her, something that, despite his wrath, he was not willing to do. He dropped his arm alongside his body and flopped to the ground beside the *Berenjong*. Cees turned to face his friend, his chest rising and falling rapidly to the frantic rhythm of his heart and lungs. Lieven was unconscious again. In a panic, Cees scooted on his knees all the way to his side and flattened his hands on his friend's blood-drenched shirt and chest.

"Liev, please Liev, say something..." The Tainted man's choked voice mingled with a sob. His hands moved from one spot to another, afraid to cause more bleeding, afraid they would find no heartbeat among the ocean of blood. "Wake up, Liev. Wake up!"

It was Jia again who came to pull him away, gently this time, her hands on each of his shoulders, comforting despite his pain. "He passed out," she said, her quiet voice a balm for his nerves. "He's okay... He'll be okay. Let me take care of him."

Cees allowed her to steer him away from his friend and guide him to a corner of the room where he sat, his heart still beating way too fast, and his eyes trained on his *Gezegenden* girl as she knelt beside Lieven's mangled body and began examining his wounds.

Daan had sat up, his nose bleeding profusely and dripping down his mouth and chin. His aura was still strangely green as if being beaten up did not bother him, as if he was at peace with being blamed for Lieven's near demise. Maybe he was. Cees couldn't help but notice the quick and unlikely bond that had developed between the two men, as different as two humans could be. Yet something connected them, something clicked. Hadn't the same thing happened with him all those years ago? Cees' personality and life experiences laid totally opposite of Lieven's, yet they had such a strong connection, such a strong friendship. Why not between his friend and this towering, odd creature?

Someone—was that Alfons?—handed Daan a small towel, and the man joined Jia on the floor. "I have some medical experience," he said, wiping his bloody nose with the terry cloth. "My father and I lived in isolation. We had to learn how to deal with medical emergencies."

Cees watched with a sense of fascination as the two of them went about removing Lieven's shirt, cleaning the massive wound on his upper chest and on his arm without as much as a hint of hesitation. Cees was woozy just watching it. Lieven had a gaping hole almost by his shoulder and the flesh on his arm seemed to have gone through a shredder. Daan and Jia pulled out the medical kits they had salvaged from their last stop, and soon Lieven was all bandaged up. Two of the other soldiers carried him carefully out of the cells after Daan's confirmation that no scent of Predator—other than the one lying dead on the floor—was around. They were going to take him to a comfortable bed and wait on him until he came to again. Most of the others filed out of the cell, throwing weary glances at the dead creature and the discarded fur. Jia half crawled to Cees' side, wiping her hands clean of blood on a piece of cloth.

"Are you doing okay?" she asked him, her voice still low and gentle.

He nodded, grabbing his lower lip between his teeth. His heart had finally settled down, and he was breathing normally now. He was not so sure he would ever be okay again. When he thought he had lost Lieven to the Predators back home, it was painful, but rather an abstract idea. He hadn't seen it. He couldn't be sure it had actually happened. This was different. He had seen him lying there, bleeding and gasping for air, slowly losing the grip on his life force. Cees had seen the rainbow of color as Lieven's aura wafted away with his life, a beautiful, frightening sight that would forever haunt him. No, he was not okay...

Jia, her body encircled by an orange aura, slid her arms around his neck and pulled it to her shoulder. Her hand lay flat on his face, her thumb gently caressing the edges of his cheek bones. "He will be fine. The wound is big, but it didn't hit any vital organs or arteries. We managed to stop the bleeding and pack the wound. It will heal."

A sob gurgled up his throat, and tears quickly followed. He couldn't remember the last time he had cried. Growing up, even when he was hurt—physically or otherwise—he had Lieven, and somehow that made everything bearable. Tears always dried before they emerged, and sad thoughts flew out of his mind at the sight of his soldier friend's face, the sound of his comforting voice. Lieven had always been there for him, the one grounding element in his life. The thought of losing him was....

"Daan had no way of knowing that coat was from a Predator's offspring," Jia said, her fingers now working on wiping some of his tears away. "He cares for Lieven, you know? He was shaken to see him hurt like that."

Anger still gnawed at the edges of his soul, but it was fading fast. "I know." He wiped his face with the palm of his hand and lifted his head off Jia's shoulder. "I know."

"Let's get out of here, Cees." Jia looked briefly at the bloodied corpse in the room. "This room is giving me the creeps."

They walked together in the darkness to the hotel where the group was hiding. The night was very cold, and they huddled together in each other's arms, trying to keep the chill and the jitters out. By the time they arrived at the hotel, the others all had already retired to their rooms, too exhausted to worry about eating. Their stomachs couldn't handle food either, so they went up one floor to the room they had picked on arrival. It was a small, modest room with a comfortable bed piled high with blankets but little more. The electric fireplace was crackling softly in the corner, and the whole space was dipped in its cozy, sleepy light.

Cees shed his coat on the floor and dropped on the bed, his legs hanging off the bottom edge. "I don't think I could walk another step." He threw his arm over his eyes.

Jia crawled on the bed beside him and stretched out like a cat, yawning. "Every muscle in my body hurts," she said, laying on her side and brushing her hand up and down his arm. "Are you feeling better?"

With a flip, Cees turned around to face her, bringing his legs up on the bed. "I always feel better when I'm with you." A smile peeked in the curl of his lip. "I forget everything else when we're alone together."

It was true. Her very presence obliterated all else; every bad thought, every anxiety, every fear. Her beautiful gray eyes performed magic. They brightened his soul. And her touch... Her touch made him feel new, made him feel whole. Every time she touched him, he grew wings and flew.

Jia moved closer, her hands slipping under his shirt to spread on his chest like fans. The warmth of her fingers on his cold skin made him shiver in pleasure. Holding the edge of her shirt, he pulled it up and over her head until it was flying across the room. Jia giggled and did the same with his. As his bare chest touched hers, a quake of emotions and sensations rolled through him from head to toe. He was suddenly taken over by an overwhelming need to make her his again.

Urgency colored their kiss, fast and furious. Passionate.Thei r tongues danced together, and their legs entwined. Cees didn't understand his feelings for this petite woman. Why did he lose all control when she was in his arms? Why did he feel like he wanted to squeeze her so tight, no one could tell them apart? Was this what love was? And did she love him back? They had known each other for such a short time, but it felt like forever.

The rest of their clothes removed, Jia straddled him, her eyes shining in the semi-darkness like two rare gems. Cees could feel his body responding to her, quickly and intensely as his hands went up to caress her breasts. She moaned and rubbed herself against him. A wave of desire ran through him with the power of fire. Fearful of losing control too soon, Cees held her on both sides of her waist, lifted her up slightly, and brought her down over his arousal. They both moaned this time. Their bodies fit together like two pieces of a puzzle, beautifully and perfectly. It was like they had been made for each other.

Jia moved on top of him, gyrating and bringing him quickly to the edge. With his arms around her middle, Cees sat up, his lips closing around one of her breasts. Jia arched against him, shuddering and whimpering in pleasure. He brought his arms lower on her back and pulled her closer until there was no space between them. They were one.

Jia

It had been so long since she had been able to stay put in one place for more than a couple days, she didn't know what to do with herself. Jia felt jittery and restless, as if something inside her wanted to crawl out. Cees had been giving her strange looks for the last few days, surprised with this new side of her. She could hardly recognize herself as well, and she wondered whether this need to move sprung from fear rather than a real wish to move. In the back of her mind, and deep down in her heart, she was scared to death the Predators would close in on them as they sat in *Volgendestad* waiting for Lieven to grow strong enough to travel with the group.

As it had become her habit, she knocked at the door of the ground floor room in a silly pattern that had somehow become their private joke. The door was ajar, and she stepped inside hesitantly. "Lieven, can I come in?"

The blond man was sitting on his bed, propped by a mountain of pillows, his bandaged chest visible under his shirt. "Come in, Jia," he said, a generous smile spreading across his lips as he waved her in.

Jia closed the door behind her and approached the bed. She came every day to change his bandages and check on his wounds. He was a fast healer, and the wound on his chest was closing a lot quicker than she thought possible. Maybe being a *Zuiver* had its benefits after all. The wound in his arm was more complicated. Even though it was healing as quickly, the flesh had been so torn and twisted, he would forever have an ugly and giant scar marring his muscular arm.

"How do you feel today?" Jia faithfully kept to the usual script. She still felt a bit awkward around him, as if she had stolen something precious from him. Lieven didn't seem to resent her anymore, however. It was as if the Predator attack had given him a new perspective on life.

"I feel better now that my nurse is here," he said with a chuckle. "I'm feeling a lot stronger. I think I will be ready to travel very soon."

Jia sat on the edge of the bed and began removing his shirt. "Do you *Zuiver* heal faster than others? I have never seen anyone heal this fast."

Lieven twisted a little to help her with the shirt. "I never thought about it." He shook the shirt sleeve off. "We all heal like this."

"Trust me." Jia laughed. "You guys heal fast."

Jia uncovered the wounds, cleaned them, and dressed them with fresh bandages. While she helped him into his shirt, Daan came in, stepping gingerly into the room as if afraid to wake someone up. "I'm not asleep, you fool," Lieven said with a frown. "Stop walking on your tip-toes. You look like a freakish pixie."

There was no doubt as to the strangeness of the way the *Berenjong* looked, all height and whiteness, spikes and edges. Despite all that, there was a rare beauty to the way he moved and the way his almost-transparent eyes glowed every time they landed on Lieven. Jia smiled, noticing his bruised face where Cees had punched him the day of the attack. *Berenjongs* obviously didn't not have the *Zuiver's* power of healing.

"Do you need meds for that bruise?" Jia asked him as he came to sit next to Lieven.

"I'm fine," he replied dismissively. "It will heal. How is he doing?" Daan nodded toward the other man.

She threw the dirty bandages into the trash bag. "He is healing incredibly fast," she said, unable to keep the awe out of her voice. "Hell, I wish I could do that. A simple little scratch takes me weeks to heal"

"How's Cees?" Lieven suddenly asked. "He hasn't come to see me in the last couple days. Is he okay?"

Jia was surprised. She thought Cees had come to see him every day. "He hasn't?"

"He's probably avoiding me." Daan had a self-deprecating smile on his lips.

"He's not mad at you anymore." Jia shook her head. "If anything, he blames himself for having allowed Lieven to face the beast alone.

He feels responsible for his friend—his brother," she added, sneaking a glance at the soldier.

Daan didn't let Lieven talk. "It was my fault." His chin tipped to his chest. "I was so stupid."

Lieven's hand cocooned the *Berenjong*'s. "It was *not* your fault," he said, lowering his voice. "Gods, Daan, how many times do I have to tell you that? Stop blaming yourself. Why are both my friends so quick to blame themselves for what happened to me? It was no one's fault. No one but the Predators and the idiots that thought it would be a good idea to create a super-beast."

Jia's eyes locked on the two men's linked hands. It was an intimate gesture. Jia wondered whether Lieven was even aware of that. Daan's transparent eyes lifted to Lieven's blues and glowed. A smile crept up to her lips. She recognized that look of adoration, of total awe.

"I should go," she said. "You need your rest." The truth was, she wanted to give them some privacy, some time to get to know each other better.

"Can you tell Cees I miss him and wish he would come to see me?" Lieven asked, his hand still covering the *Berenjong*'s.

"Of course." She moved toward the door. "Daan, make sure he rests. He's healing really fast, but he still needs time."

Daan smiled at her. "I won't let him move an inch." He chuckled. She believed him.

The hotel was quiet today. Most of the soldiers were doing their rounds, scavenging for supplies and exploring the surrounding area. Alfons had been studying maps with her and Cees, trying to figure out what to do once Lieven was well enough to travel. Where to go and how to get there. There were functioning transports in town, and they had been considering the risks of using them to go forth. On one hand, they would travel faster, and it wouldn't put as much stress on the weakened Lieven. But transports could be noisy at times and emitted a certain smell. None of them could be sure the Predators wouldn't be attracted by the scent. It was truly a conundrum. They still didn't know enough about these beasts to be able to plan effectively. The only certain thing in their minds was that they must reach the coast in order to flee to an island where they could finally breathe in peace.

Jia searched for Cees and found him sitting on an armchair in a corner of their room, sketching furiously in the notebook she had seen before. She watched him for a moment. It had been a while since she had seen him drawing. Her memory took her to the first time she had seen him doing that exact same thing. It felt like a lifetime since they were in that bunker. She had been so scared, so lost. Suspicious of the young *Zuiver*, she had reluctantly at first chosen to extend a certain measure of trust to this stranger, a member of a caste with the reputation for instability.

That day—or maybe it was night; it was impossible to tell in the bunker—when she set eyes on the sketch he had made of her was when she had finally accepted he was not her enemy. It was hard to believe anyone could see her like that, beautiful, pure, and full of life. Inside she felt broken, full of darkness. The hollowed spaces carved by the men who had used her, by the babies the doctors killed, by the death of her mother, were filled with self-loathing and blackness. Cees had seen her in a very different light. That drawing still made her eyes sting with tears. Not of sadness or anger, but of joy, of wonder that someone saw her in color.

Cees moved, uncrossing his legs and planting his unshod feet on the floor. Jia released the sigh she had been holding for fear of breaking the spell and he heard her. "Jia, what are you doing there?" he asked. He dropped the notebook gently on the floor beside the chair and came to meet her by the door.

Tears, finally freed from the constraints of her unwillingness to show weakness, rolled down her face as she ran to Cees. Her arms enveloped him in a tight embrace, and she felt his arms wrapping around her, hands flattening on her back and pressing her against him. He didn't ask, and she did not offer an explanation. Jia cried within the protection of his long, muscled arms and into the hardness of his chest. She cried all her pain and loneliness of the past few years, all of the emotions she, like a miser hoarding coin, had held behind her facade of strength and indifference. Inside that wall of bravado, there had always been a young girl screaming for help. Cees was the first one to hear it.

"Sorry." She whimpered, reluctant to move away from him. His arms, his generous chest... This was home.

His hand came up to sweep through her hair in a gentle caress. "Why are you apologizing?" His lips touched the top of her head. "You needed a good cry. I've been there. There's no shame in it."

With all the strength she had left, Jia pulled apart from him just enough to look into his blue eyes. "Thank you, Cees," she whispered.

The generous smile she had come to love appeared on his lips again and quickly spread to his eyes, the black band making them shine. "For what? A hug?"

Jia grinned. Her heart felt so light as she stood in the small room with this amazing man she wouldn't have looked at twice before the Predators came. "You make my heart sing, you beautiful *Zuiver*." Her hand rose to touch his face.

The smile died in his lips and was replaced by something else. Something deeper and intense that made his eyes burst and pour warmth into hers. He bent down slightly and covered her trembling lips with his, gently prying her mouth open with his tongue and drinking her in. Jia met his thirst with her own and lost herself in his kiss.

When his mouth pulled away from hers, she groaned in disappointment. He didn't go far. She could feel the warmth of his breath on her lips as he whispered, "*Ik hou van je, liefje.* I love you, Jia. "

Lieven

A soft knock stirred Lieven from a light sleep. He lifted his head up from the pillow and looked in the direction of the door as if hoping he could see through its heavy wood. He cleared his throat and told whoever it was to come in.

The door opened timidly, and a familiar dark-haired head popped through the opening. "Can I come in, Liev?" Cees asked, blinking a few times.

"Since when do you have to ask?" Lieven said, slightly irritated. It had been several days since Cees had come to see him, and he couldn't figure out why. Was Cees put out because of Lieven's feelings for him? "Long time, no see. What's going on, Cees?"

The tall artist stepped into the room, arms awkwardly crossed in front of him. Lieven was reminded of earlier times in their relationship when Cees was still not at ease with him or his dad. "Sorry Liev." Cees' voice was quiet and his glance on the floor. "I've been busy."

Lieven's stomach churned with frustration. They were friends, first and foremost. Cees knew that. What was he playing at? "Busy doing what? Too busy making love to Jia?" Lieven regretted the words as soon as they were out of his mouth. Cees' head shot up and his ocean-blue eyes searched Lieven's in confusion. "Sorry. That was un-called for. I am just frustrated with the way you have been acting around me."

Cees tugged on his ear and licked his lips. "What do y-you mean?" he stuttered.

Lieven rubbed the back of his neck with a frantic hand and bit his lower lip. "Ever since I told you how I felt about you, you've been acting like..." He searched for the right words. "Like you don't even know me. As if I'm a stranger whom you are always afraid to bother or offend with the wrong word."

Cees opened his mouth to protest, but then his shoulders slumped, and his eyes softened. "I..."

"Shit, Cees. We have been best friends since we were kids." Lieven's arms moved in front of him. "No matter how deep my feelings run for you, I'm still—and always will be—your friend first."

"I know, me too, but..."

"But what?" Lieven had lifted his body from the pillow and sat cross-legged on the bed that shook every time he moved his agitated hands. "We are friends. Forever. Period. I get it, Cees. You don't love me the way I love you. I do. I get it. But you are my friend—at least, I hope you still are—and your friendship means the world to me. You're the only family I have." Lieven's eyes were suspiciously moist.

Cees swallowed hard, his Adam's apple bobbing up and down. "You are my only family too, Liev." His eyes clouded a bit. "Your friendship means a lot to me. I don't care about anything else between us. That's not why I've been acting weird."

Lieven stopped moving and stared at his tall friend, furrowing his eyebrows. "Then what?"

Cees took a few steps forward and sat on the edge of the bed, his eyes never leaving Lieven's. "I'm scared." Cees lowered his voice to a mere whisper. "I was so scared I had lost you in that cell. My heart was crushed, and my world collapsed when I came out of the locked cell and found you bleeding to death. I thought I lost you, Liev."

The soldier's eyes opened wide and he moved his lips as if to say something, but no sound left his mouth. Was that all it was? Cees had been so scared by what had happened he couldn't bring himself to look him in the eye?

"I have been avoiding you because every time I see you lying there with all those bandages, I'm taken back to that cell and that horrifying moment when I first saw you after the attack. The memory hurts just as bad as the real thing. I'm not strong like you, Liev. I can't handle the thought of losing you any more than I can losing a vital organ."

Despite the pain he still felt every time he moved, Lieven leaned forward to envelop Cees in his arms. "I'm still here, Cees," he whispered into Cees' neck. "Like it or not, you're stuck with me." He felt his friend's body shake in a mixture of laughter and tears, and he squeezed him tighter. "Friends until the end, fool."

A faint cough made them move slightly apart. Daan was standing by the door, obviously uncomfortable, staring at the two of them bound in their embrace. "I didn't mean to interrupt." He twisted his hands. "I'll leave."

It was Lieven who spoke first as the towering giant turned to leave. "No, Daan, don't leave. Come and join us. We were just sharing a moment."

Cees laughed at the choice of words and wiped a few stray tears rolling down his cheeks. "Yes, that's what we were having; a *moment*.

You always had a way with words, Liev." Just like that, the awkwardness was gone, and their easy-flowing interaction had returned.

"I had to have some stern words with Cees about the fact he has not come to see me in a few days," Lieven explained as the *Berenjong* hesitantly turned back and approached the two men. "Cees often forgets who the boss is in this relationship."

Cees chuckled. "Right, keep believing that."

"Daan thinks you're still blaming him for my attack," Lieven said unexpectedly, fixing his gaze first on Daan and then on his friend. "Are you?"

Cees turned his eyes to the odd man, noting his wild, spiked-up white hair and his liquid eyes. "I did at first. I was scared, and I needed to have someone to blame. You were just in the right place at the right time, Daan. I don't think that anymore."

Cees extended his hand in a peace, offering and Daan took it between his in a shake. "Thank you, Cees. The truth is, I was to blame. I should have figured out that fur was Predator's. It just smelled so different..."

With a wave of the hand, Cees offered Daan a seat next to him on the bed. "We've talked about that, Jia, Alfons, and I." They had spent hours pouring over documents in the library and on the machines Jia called computers trying to figure out why that was. "We think that, as most mammals, Predators' offspring are brought up on a diet of mother's milk and therefore have a different body odor. Human infants are like that too. They have a distinct sweet and sour smell that is so different from the adults. You couldn't tell it was Predator's fur because of that."

Daan shook his head, his hands beside him as he braced himself on the bed. "I still think I should have known," he said stubbornly.

"There was something familiar about it, and I should have connected it to the beasts. It was an unforgivable mistake."

Cees had jumped to his feet and looked at the *Berenjong* with sympathy. "Don't be too hard on yourself. No one else blames you. Now we know, and we will be more careful moving forward." He patted the tall man on the back. "I will leave now. I told Jia I would join her scavenging for berries. She has been craving those berries we saw on our way here and hasn't shut up about it yet."

The other two men laughed and watched Cees leave the room with a wave. Silence descended on them and Lieven sighed. It was good he had cleared things with his friend. The awkwardness between them was weighing heavily on his heart, and he now felt lighter and freer. Lieven smiled.

"You seem happy." Daan's lips stretched into a grin. "It's nice to see your face light up like that."

Lieven didn't say anything and watched the strange-looking man busy himself with straightening his sheets and clearing the bedside table of dirty dishes. Lieven had grown accustomed to Daan's strangeness. He was like an exotic animal, both odd and beautiful. Lieven found it increasingly more difficult to take his eyes away from him as he moved about the room, fussing and cleaning like a mother hen. He muttered to himself all the while as if he was having a conversation with an invisible creature in the room.

"Why do you do that?" Lieven asked, his head tilted to the side.

Daan stopped and turned to him. "Do what?"

"Talk under your breath when you're doing something?"

Daan laughed and resumed his cleaning. "Force of habit. When you grow up in almost total isolation, you either talk to yourself or you go insane. I chose the former."

"Will you stop fussing and come and sit with me?" Lieven patted a spot next to him on the bed. "I'm here. You don't have to talk to yourself. I'll be glad to be your sounding board."

It was Daan's turn to tilt his head in question. "What's a sounding board?" Lieven chuckled and patted the bed again, sending a little puff of dust up into the air. "Your bed is covered in dust. Let me change the sheets."

Daan came around and reached for the edge of the sheets, but Lieven had closed his hand around his wrist. "Stop, for the gods' sakes. You're making me dizzy. Just sit down already."

With obvious reluctance, Daan obeyed and sat facing Lieven. "You know, dust is very bad for your health," he said, still fiddling with the sheets.

Lieven pulled his hand and made him sit closer still. "Stop talking." His voice had gone down an octave, insistent and assertive, not leaving room for discussion. Daan lifted his amethyst eyes to his, and Lieven's heart leaped in his chest. Those eyes were so transparent, Lieven could see all the way into his soul. It was a beautiful soul, one he would very much like to get to know better.

Daan had gone obediently silent, and the smile dancing in his lips just a few moments before had been replaced by an expression of longing. He scooped closer yet, until their knees were touching, and Lieven could feel the warmth of Daan's accelerated breath on his face. Lieven's head tilted forward at the same time as Daan's, and their lips met in the middle. Daan's lips were dry, cracked from the icy winds yet soft and yielding beneath his.

Lieven's heart was beating faster than it should be possible, and, as their bodies drew nearer to each other, he could feel Daan's heart beating the same frenzied song. With his tongue, Lieven's opened the *Berenjong*'s lips and breathed in his scent. Daan tasted of wild woods and bitter berries, sweet and tart, maddeningly exotic and exciting. He could drown himself in that feeling and never come up for air.

As their lips pulled apart, their eyes met again. Lieven expected to see hunger in his eyes, but there was something much deeper, much more complicated. Taken aback by what he read in the other man's eyes, Lieven backed away from him, not sure how *he* felt. He loved Cees. Didn't he? So, how could he feel whatever he was feeling for Daan? The contradiction was making his head hurt. He closed his eyes.

"Are you okay?" The worried voice of Daan shook him to the core.

No, he was not okay. On top of being injured, he was now also totally confused. Lieven shook his head, trying to clear it, but the feeling was still there—the strong magnetic pull toward Daan, the desire burning in his gut. What did it all mean?

"You look pale." Daan's face twisted into a frown of worry. His hands went up to Lieven's shoulders to push him gently into the pillows, but Lieven stopped him. "What is it? Did I hurt you?"

In spite of his confusion and contradictory feelings, Lieven laughed. "You are something else, Daan." His hand was still clenched over the other man's wrist. "Of course, you didn't hurt me. I was just... taken by surprise."

The *Berenjong* smiled, his lip curling up in the corner. "You started it." It was not an accusation. Rather, a playful statement. "I just went along for the ride."

Lieven tugged on Daan's wrist, pulling the towering man closer to him again. "I'm not sure what *this* is," he said in a whisper. Daan's lips hovered just above his, their heat singeing and intoxicating Lieven all at once. The urge to cover those lips with his and breathe in this strange man's scent and taste was overwhelming. His body shook, a mixture of desire and bewilderment going through him. "Hell, Daan. What is this?"

The bear man licked his lips, his fluid green eyes locking on Lieven's mouth. "Why don't we try to find out?"

After a moment of hesitation, Lieven touched his lips to Daan's. Gently at first, timidly. But the fire that had started inside him was running wild now, and the kiss quickly deepened. His hands slipped around Daan and pulled hard, crushing him against his own beating heart. Lieven moaned into Daan's mouth as the other man slipped his hands under the shirt to caress his sensitive bare skin.

Daan stopped suddenly and pulled away, leaving Lieven panting in frustration. "You are not well for all of *this*," the *Berenjong* said with a comical wave along his own body. "I will leave you now so you can rest."

Lieven opened his mouth to protest, but the other man was already walking toward the door in long strides. With a loud sigh, Lieven dropped on the pillows lifting another small cloud of dust.

"In the meantime, you can dream about what it will be like once you are healed," Daan teased, turning momentarily around and winking at Lieven. "Sweet dreams, *liefje.*"

Still confused and now also burning in frustrated desire, Lieven surprised himself by laughing quietly under his breath. Daan was an odd, odd man, and Lieven was in so much trouble.

CHAPTER NINE

OF MONSTERS

Cees

Restlessness had taken over him. Not even painting could calm him down. Cees stared at the canvas and realized his state of mind was splashed across it. A whirlwind of reds and yellows reflected his overflow of nervous energy; dots and dashes, sprays and swirls... He dropped the brush inside the cleaning container and left the room, wiping his hands on the paint-stained shirt he was wearing.

Jia was with some of the other soldiers, learning about the weapons they now all carried. Cees had been amused by her enthusiasm about learning how to ignite the very old-school grenades they had found in the city's armory. Since most modern weaponry was DNA imprinted, they had to rely mostly on ancient weapons and hope they would be just as effective.

Maybe a brisk walk would help relieve the antsy-feeling in his legs. The evergreens were covered in an icy sheen that made them look almost magical, and the ground crunched under his feet as he jogged through the streets of town. Cees suddenly realized that he was heading towards the outskirts of the city, the exterior edges of the once heavily-populated area, the place where outcasts like him lived and hid. Every caste had their outcasts, no matter how enlightened they claimed to be. With the help of Jia, he had been exploring history books and computer-based data banks, ethnographic accounts, and anthropological studies of the world they lived in. Surprise didn't even begin to describe what he felt when reading all those accounts. It seemed as if there was no perfect society, no perfect caste. The only caste not featured in any of these studies was Central itself, which seemed to be destined to remain a mystery, even as the world came to an end.

He ran slowly through the trails that wound around the city, hoping to find some sign of... He was not even sure exactly what he was hoping to find; maybe a thread of connection with the world of the *Gezegenden*, a sign that they all came from the same seed of humankind. A sign that he was not as different as people always made him believe he was. At least, not in an inferior way.

In front of him, there was an abrupt turn that curved around some giant evergreens and a short wall made of rocks. He slowed down in order to maneuver around its narrow path and crashed head-on with something tall and hard. The impact made him stumble backwards a few steps before he could look ahead and focus on what he had crashed against. When his eyes made their way up from the ground, he was faced with two strange men. *Gezegenden* by the looks of them. They both had guns pointed at him, and their scowls reflected their feelings—fear or hate, he was not sure which.

Cees lifted his hands above his head in a gesture of peace. "Lower your guns. I'm no foe."

The taller and the burlier of the two men waved the gun at him but did not put it down. "How can we be sure?" he asked, his voice thick with tension. "You're a Tainted *Zuiver*. You may be dangerous."

With a sigh, Cees took a step forward. The men stiffened their holds on the guns. "Look, I'm here with a group of survivors. Both *Zuiver* and *Gezegenden*. We're just trying to stay alive."

The two men stole glances at each other but still didn't lower their guns. "Where is the rest of your group?" the same man asked.

"In town." Cees nodded in the direction of the city proper. "I can take you there if you promise to calm down."

After a short conference, the two waved their guns at Cees, directing him to lead them on. He could feel the eyes of the two *Gezegenden* burning holes in the back of his head and their suspicion tainting the air with a poisonous scent. The men's auras oscillated between a sinister black to an equally ominous purple, two colors Cees was not comfortable with. For a moment, he considered taking them in the wrong direction, away from the rest of the group. But they were humans like him and running the very real risk of being hunted and killed by the Predators. He had to help them.

As soon as they walked into the city proper, voices reached his ears. The voice he now considered part of his own was yelling out in excitement. Jia and the other soldiers must be close, doing their drills. The two men following him stopped for a moment, their heads tilted, eyes trained somewhere Cees couldn't see. They seemed to be deep in thought rather than listening. Despite the oddness of their postures, smiles crept to their lips. A strange shiver ran through Cees like an omen of some kind.

"Jia," he called out. "We have visitors."

The voices subsided, and soon several faces appeared around the corner of a building. The two strange men lifted their guns in anticipation. "No need for guns, I assure you." Cees waved a hand in front of them. "These are all my friends."

The group, about four or five soldiers and Jia, cautiously approached them, staring wearily at the pointed guns. "What's going on?" Jia asked, her eyes scanning the two men from top to bottom. "Blessed... Where did they come from?"

The Blessed who seemed to be the one in charge lowered his gun, quickly followed by his mate. "We survived an attack on our city, up north from here." The man had a strong accent, so pronounced that some of the other soldiers seemed to be having trouble following him. "Haaksbergen. We were out hunting when they attacked, so we were able to escape."

Gezegenden hunted? Cees had always thought the Blessed to be far too advanced to resort to more primitive activities such as hunting or fishing. They bought their meat and their fish from lesser castes living in the outer boundaries of each city. "You're welcomed to share our food, and there is plenty of room," Cees said. "We should take you to our leader, Alfons."

"My name is Faas, and this is my companion Gillis," the leader said, pointing at the other man. He was staring at Jia in a way that made Cees very uncomfortable, his eyes studying her every move, roaming up and down her body and lingering far too long on her breasts before moving up to her face again. The smirk on his face did not endear him to Cees, neither did the incredibly brackish aura he was displaying. "Who's this Alfons?"

"He is—was the commander of a *Zuiver* squad that escaped the Predators," Jia explained, reaching out to touch Cees' arm.

"Another *Zuiver*?" The men didn't look happy about the fact there were more *Zuivers* than *Gezegenden* in the group.

"Be glad they are." Jia wrapped her arms around Cees'. "If it wasn't for them we would all be dead."

Cees walked in the front, his arms still entwined in Jia's, his feet dragging on the dirt road, weighed down by a sense of foreboding he couldn't explain. "I don't like them," he whispered to Jia, chancing a quick look behind him. The two men were flanked by the soldiers, looking none too happy to be in such company. "I don't like the looks the one called Faas gave you."

Jia leaned her head toward him until it touched the top of his arm. "He's a Blessed. He just recognized me." Her voice was so quiet he had to strain to hear it.

Cees snapped his head toward her. "What do you mean, he recognized you?" He stopped on his tracks.

"Keep walking, keep walking," Jia said, coaxing him into movement again. "Not recognize me like knowing who I am exactly. They recognized me for what I am."

"A *Gezegenden*?" He had thought that much was obvious to everyone.

There was a short hesitation before Jia spoke again. "Yes, a Blessed one. Don't worry, it will be fine." But she didn't sound too convinced herself. Her aura had turned the color of lilacs, wavering around her like a sad, apprehensive halo, and he wondered why she felt that way. He had half-expected her to be happy that two of her own caste had joined them.

Alfons met with the two men in a small room at the hotel where they all had taken shelter. Cees had thought of asking to stay, but he hadn't seen Lieven yet today, so he decided to go to his friend's room for a visit instead. Somber and unusually quiet, Jia followed him, hanging on from his arm as if to a lifeline.

Lieven, who was feeling a lot better these days, was sitting on an overstuffed arm chair, a blanket over his legs and being fussed over by the vertiginous tall bear man.

"Stop fussing over me, Daan." Lieven's smile belying the tone of his voice. "I'm not an invalid, and I can get around just fine." Seeing Cees and Jia walking in, he waved at them. "Please, tell this man to stop treating me like a baby."

Jia laughed, and Cees sighed in relief. It was good to hear her laugh. They both sat at the edge of the bed, watching as Daan cleaned and organized things around the room. "I wish I had someone to clean up my stuff like that." Jia winked at him.

"He just won't stop," Lieven said with a dramatic sigh. "What have you guys been up to?"

Cees told him about the two men he had come across in the outskirts of town and how strangely they had acted once they had seen Jia. She had nothing to add to the conversation, looking happy to sit and listen. Cees knew better though, for her aura had turned the color of grapes at the beginning of Fall, a sure sign she didn't have a good feeling about these two strangers.

"It was almost as if they knew Jia." Cees sneaked a glance in her direction. She flinched but said nothing. "Don't you find that strange, Liev?"

Lieven stared at his friend, trying to read the expression in his eyes. They had known each other for so long, at times Cees had the feeling they could read each other's minds. "Maybe he was just happy to see another of his own caste," Lieven offered with a quick rise and fall of his eyebrows.

Cees nodded toward Jia who was sitting beside him, looking into space almost as if in a trance. "I doubt if that's the case," he said, opening his eyes wide in warning. "Jia seemed rather upset about it." No reaction. She was not even listening. Cees' heart began a fast drumming in his chest. Something was going on. "Jia, are you okay?"

Jia raised her gray eyes to him, finally aware he was speaking to her. "Sorry. I was just thinking. Do you think there is a way of removing my implant?"

Both Cees and Lieven startled at the question. "Where is it?" Lieven asked, sitting straighter on the chair.

"On my shoulder." She pointed at where her neck met her shoulder. "Do you think I could take it out?"

"Wouldn't it break your connection with your weapon?" Cees asked, intrigued and rather worried.

"Yes, but we have other weapons now." Jia's eyes looked feverish. "I don't need it anymore."

What was this sudden urgency to remove an implant she had had for a long time and which had never even once come up in conversation before? Did it have something to do with the presence of the other two *Gezegenden* among them?

Jia stretched her neck toward him, pulling the collar of her jacket so he could see the whiteness of her silky skin beneath. "Can you see it? It looks a little like a tiny scar."

Cees pressed the skin of her shoulder with his fingers, and she shivered beneath his touch. He did find a small, reddish bump that he assumed was the location for the implant. "Yes, I see it." He bent down and placed a light kiss on it. "Why this sudden need to remove it? Does it hurt?"

Jia smiled feebly at him. "No, I just don't like that I am still attached to something that sets me apart from you. We are all in this together now as equals, and the implant just seems...divisive. Do you think it could be removed?"

Cees was still examining it when Daan approached and, bending down from his never-ending height, joined him. "It shouldn't be too complicated, but you may end up with a much bigger scar."

"Can you do it now?" Jia asked, her eyes glittering. Cees opened his eyes wide in surprise. "Well, can you, Daan?"

Daan glanced at Cees before returning his gaze to her. "I have to collect the surgical tools first," he said cautiously. "And some kind of anesthetic. It's going to hurt."

"I can handle it." Jia jerked her head upwards and almost hit Cees, who was still bent over her shoulder. "Go get the tools."

With his hand, Cees pulled the collar of her jacket over the scar and, grabbing her by her shoulders, turned her to him. "Not sure what the urgency is but you need to slow down." He looked her in the eye. The look he got in return was so gut-wrenchingly sad, he felt it within his own heart. "Jia, what's going on? What's this all about?"

The other two men in the room were looking at them with curiosity. Daan had stepped back and was leaning on a dresser. "I will remove it as soon as I can gather the right supplies, Jia," he said, his voice low and sympathetic. "I promise."

"Maybe you should talk in private," Lieven suggested. "Daan and I can leave..."

Cees waved his hand and shook his head, his dark hair moving along with it. "You are not well enough," he said. "We'll go...Jia?" With a pleading look, Cees offered his hand to a cowering Jia. Something was going on, and he needed to find out exactly what. What had rattled her so much she was willing to go through surgery without an anesthetic?

Meekly and quietly, Jia accepted his hand and followed him out of the room. They didn't have to go very far. The room next door was unoccupied. Jia walked in first, soon followed by Cees, who closed the door behind him. They stood in the center of the room staring at each other in silence. Cees didn't want to press her for the information he so much wanted, and she seemed hesitant to willingly provide it.

At an impasse, Cees made the first move and drew her into his arms. If he couldn't make Jia confide in him, he could at least try to console her from whatever was hurting or scaring her. "It hurts me to see you like this," he whispered in her ear, his arms crossed behind her back, eliminating any space between them. He could feel her heart beating hard against her chest, a mad banging that echoed through his body with the strength of a stormy sea. "What's wrong? Why won't you tell me?"

Jia had her face buried in his chest, and he felt her quiver and hiccup. She was crying. His hand went automatically to her head in a caress he hoped would be enough to quiet the voices that must be screaming inside her head at that moment. The voices or memories that were making her hurt and weep. Her fingers grasped the back of his shirt as if she was holding on to life itself.

They stood rooted in that spot for what felt like a long time, Cees holding her for fear she would dissolve along with her desperate tears, and Jia not willing or able to voice the reason for her pain. When she finally looked up at him her face was moist with tears and her eyes pleading. "I just can't..." she uttered, lips shaking.

Cees studied her beautiful gray eyes and decided she would tell him when she was able. Whatever triggered this reaction must have been so painful she couldn't get herself to say it out loud. He knew how that felt. Memories of the indignities he had to endure as a Tainted child in the institution were not something he would ever be able to easily voice, even to those he loved more than life itself. Even with Lieven, who had witnessed more than one of those incidents... There were things better left unsaid, locked behind the doors of his mind.

"It's okay," he whispered, caressing her cheeks with his hand. "You don't have to tell me. But remember, you're not alone…"

On her tiptoes, Jia reached out with her arms around his neck and pulled him to her until their lips were connected. Cees' body, still cold from the walk outside, warmed instantly, the flames of desire licking his skin from his toes to the top of his head. "I want to tell you, but I can't," she whispered, her lips just above his, their breaths mingling. "Not yet."

Cees nibbled on her lower lip, tasting the saltiness of her tears and the taste that was exclusively Jia's. She intoxicated him. Every time they touched, he felt light-headed and excited like a child opening gifts. It never got old, no matter how familiar it was now. Her aura was turning a soft pink hue, and he knew she felt the same. The ugly grape-colored aura was gone, and her heart still beat fast, but somehow the rhythm had changed—not frantic, anxious any longer. Both their hearts beat in unison, punctuating a song of joy, the feeling that took them over every time they were together.

Jia

Sleep hadn't come easy that night, and even when she had finally managed to drift away, her dreams made her toss and turn as if she was running for her life. Cees had pulled her into the protective shelter of his arms and cooed her to sleep, his lips trailing kisses on her face. It always felt so safe in his arms, but this time the fear was coming from inside. The heaviness of overwhelming shame.

The two Blessed men who had arrived in town the day before knew. As soon as they laid eyes on her, they had known. Her implant had given them all the information they needed to know exactly who she was. Jia had not missed the lascivious look Faas had given her. It was just a matter of time. They would both come for her. What would she do then? She just couldn't tell Cees. Not now, maybe never. The fail-safe protocols of her gun wouldn't allow her to use it against them, and even though she was a lot stronger than she had been at the beginning of this journey, she was no match for the two burly men.

Oh gods! She needed Cees' protection. He would do it without asking any questions, she knew. But was that fair? The Blessed were well-armed. Could she ask him to risk his life without telling him why?

One more toss brought her face-to-face with Cees, asleep beside her, his dark stripe giving a whole other meaning to the word *darkness*. There was no darkness in the Tainted man, not even a little stain. She had never met anyone as pure of heart and soul as her Cees. Yes, hers! Jia didn't deny it anymore. He was hers, no matter whatever else may happen; even if they were set asunder, he would always be hers. Cees was not just someone she loved. He was now part of her, so integral to her existence, she was not sure she would survive without him. The beautiful *Zuiver* gave without expecting anything back. He loved unconditionally and deeply. His very presence filled her with a sense of worth and wholesomeness she had never experienced before. It was a good feeling. A safe haven after the storm that had been her life before him. A light of hope in the distance. A reason to want to survive.

Unable to resist, she kissed him. A gentle, barely-there touch that sent ripples of pleasure and emotion through her. Cees stirred, his lips welcoming hers into a deeper kiss, his tongue feeling its way along her lips, asking for permission to dance with hers. Jia sighed. A deep, audible sigh before she abandoned herself to his embrace. She wanted to linger here. Forget the monsters; both animal and human. Jia wanted to drown herself in him and never come up for air. She would breathe through him. She would be safe and sound within his arms, inside his heart...

Too soon, they had to come down to reality. There was much to be done now that Lieven was quickly healing and almost ready for the journey ahead. It was tempting to think they could stay, but they knew that, sooner or later, the Predators would run out of food and would backtrack to pick up the leftovers. They needed to reach the coast as soon as they could and find a way to cross to an island where they would be truly safe.

The group was all in the main lobby of the hotel, some eating breakfast, others just chatting quietly. Alfons sat with the two newcomers, deep in conversation. Jia's heart stopped for a moment, her hand gripping Cees' tighter. Faas looked up at them, his eyes sliding off Cees' imposing figure to come and rest on her. He licked his lips, his tongue slithering slowly and obscenely over his cracked lips as his eyes trailed from hers down to her chest and up again. Jia's heart shattered, and her body convulsed with tremors.

"Jia, are you okay?" Cees asked, stopping and turning around to face her. Was he purposely providing a wall between Faas' unsettling glance and her? Jia looked up into his glowing eyes with gratitude. "You don't have to tell me if you don't want to," he spoke for her ears only. "But I am here for you no matter what. Lean on me. Let me carry some of your burdens. I'm stronger than I look."

Despite the fear crawling and knotting its vine-like arms around her whole being, Jia smiled. "You look pretty strong to me." The smile died on her lips. "Thank you, Cees. I do need you," she confessed in a shaky voice. "Can't tell you why yet, but I need you."

In reply, Cees bent down and kissed her. Even though it was no secret they were together, they had largely abstained from public shows of affection. Jia knew that in his own unique, loving way, Cees was telling everyone in that room she was his and he was hers. Overwhelming, warm love mixed with and displaced the fear in her heart, and she was able to breathe well again. His love made her brave, made her strong.

The lewd expression on Faas' face was replaced with an unpleasant grimace as Jia and Cees approached them. "Morning," Cees said, his hand around Jia's shoulders. "I hope you slept well."

Gillis stood up, looking surprised. "Why are you talking to us?" he snarled, a frown settling across his lips. He was not as tall as his companion, but he made up for the difference in muscle. He was built with wide shoulders and trunk-thick arms that looked capable of killing in a single swipe.

Alfons stood up, and Jia could sense Cees tensing up next to her. "What do you mean?" the *Zuiver* leader asked. "Why wouldn't he talk to you?"

"We will make concessions to talking to *Zuivers* due to the circumstances, but a Tainted one should never address us," Gillis said. Faas nodded in agreement. "An inferior being like him should be kept aside from all of us. I'm surprised you allow him free range."

Jia's body shook from head to toe, anger starting in her belly as a hot rumble and exploding through her body a raging fire. "Cees is not inferior to anyone, much less to you," she yelled out. Cees' hold on her shoulder was the only thing preventing her from attacking the man. "How dare you talk to him like that? The world we lived in is over. Do you hear me? It's over! You're the tainted ones, labeling others as inferior to make yourselves feel like more than you really are. You make me sick." The last words came out of her mouth as a hiss, her anger and fear all rolled into those four words.

Faas stood then, a smirk on his face. "I will require your services tonight," he said simply.

Alfons' eyes opened wide, his eyebrows arching all the way to his hairline. Cees' hold on her shoulder tightened, but she could feel the tremors of anger going through him.

"What do you mean you require Jia's services?" Alfons asked before Cees could.

Jia had lowered her eyes to the ground and her face burnt as if a fire had been lit and fanned over her skin. Oh gods! This was it. This was the moment she would lose all the respect she had earned from this band of survivors. This was the moment she would lose Cees and his love.

"She is a *Vaderloos*," the man said as if that explained everything.

Cees would recognize the word, if not the full meaning. It meant fatherless. It was no secret. Jia had told Cees her father had left his family to go to Central when she was a little girl and never came back. But he had no way of knowing why that had anything to do with the *Gezegenden*'s request.

"So, she doesn't have a father," Alfons said, a scowl on his face. "How's that a problem?"

Jia leaned against Cees as if she was trying to hide inside of him. It was safe and warm inside his heart. She wanted to be there instead of where she was, about to be exposed and shamed.

"*Vaderloos* are wards of the patriarchal collective." The man's eyes were hard and mocking. "The collective pays for her keep. In return, she does as she is told."

With her courage shredded to bits, Jia's legs gave out beneath her and slid to the floor. Cees' hands quickly reacted and grabbed her before she would slide all the way down. "Jia!" He held her close to his chest. "Are you all right?"

She didn't respond. Her head felt fuzzy, and all strength had gone from her limbs. Jia could hear what was going on around her, but she couldn't speak. Cees scooped her up into his arms and carried her off.

When she opened her eyes again, she realized she was in Lieven's room. All seven feet of Daan hovered over her, a worried cloud over his eyes. "She's coming to," he said, tilting his head. "Hey girl, you scared us half to death."

Jia groaned and tried to sit up, but her head was still whirling. "Stay put." Cees' familiar voice immediately warmed her heart, and a smile appeared on her lips. "Glad you're feeling better." He sat on the edge of the couch as Daan moved away. "What happened? Can you tell me?"

No, she was not ready to tell him. She may never be. How do you tell the man you love you're a *Vaderloos?* A woman who, because of her lack of paternal protection, is in more ways than one property of the male population? How could she explain that, in order to survive, she had to obey the law and be at the ready any time a male required her sexual services? How could she tell him that, in her city, among her own people, she was nothing—less than nothing? She was a walking-talking thing, to be used and abused by the patriarchs of her civilization. A pretty shell to give men pleasure and be disposed afterward. Jia had been empty for most of her adult life, but she felt whole now that she had Cees on her side. She didn't want to lose that. No, she was not ready.

Cees threw a meaningful glance at Lieven and Daan. "We'll be next door," Lieven said, holding on to Daan's arm. They both left the room and closed the door behind them. They were alone, the sudden silence pressing down on her like a vise.

"Can I tell you a story?" Cees brushed his hand gently across her face. She nodded. "I grew up believing I was less than everybody else. I heard it so many times I eventually believed it. I believed that I deserved all the beatings, indignities, abuse... I wanted to die and hated myself for being who and what I was."

Jia shivered, her hand unconsciously seeking his. "You're not—" He placed his finger across her lips, and she stopped talking.

"I never tried to defend myself and protest against the daily brutalities the Institution bestowed upon my young body and mind," he continued, his hand brushing against hers as their fingers entwined. "Until Lieven and his family. I suddenly saw myself through their eyes and realized I had been tricked into believing I deserved whatever treatment I had been getting. My shame turned to anger, but Lieven taught me how to use all that pain to make me stronger and be proud of who I was. Lieven gave me the strength by just being there for me. By believing in me and loving me."

She realized she was nodding while holding to his hand so tight her knuckles were turning white. "I believe in you, too," she whispered.

Cees smiled. "I know. And I believe in you. I love you. I don't care what you did in your life before this because that life doesn't exist anymore beyond your memory. I love you now. I need you now. Let me help you."

Jia licked her dry lips, looked into his infinite eyes, and burst out crying. The tears came flowing freely and copiously, as if the dam holding all her fears, doubts, and guilt had suddenly ruptured. Her *Zuiver* held her in silence, rocking her gently in his arms, his lips resting on the top of her head. He was not going to rush her. Cees had an inexhaustible amount of patience, a quality she was not too familiar with. It was a source of peace for her to be with someone who never seemed to be in a hurry, who just believed it would all be all right. Like the tattoo on his neck proclaimed, he believed...

"The implant identifies me a ward of the patriarchs," Jia explained, her face still buried in the folds of his shirt. "When my father left us, both my mother and I were suddenly without our patriarch. We became communal property." She felt Cees stiffen under her face. "In order to be fed and housed, we had to do whatever the men told us to do. We were given jobs, and I was allowed to go to school like every other Blessed. If I was to find myself a husband, I would no longer be *bewaard,* kept. But until such time, I was to be on-call. If I was walking down the street and a male just happened to require my services, I was bound by law to comply."

"These services... What exactly do you mean by that?" Cees asked, his body shaking against her.

"Anything really," she said, tears still falling and soaking into the cotton fabric of his shirt. "Cooking, cleaning... but mostly sex." The sobs rose up her throat and choked her. Funny how she had never said this out loud, not even to herself. Hearing it made it all so much more real, so much more shameful. "I'm not who you think I am, Cees. I'm worthless..."

Cees pulled her away from him, and she quivered at the thought of finding disgust reflected in his eyes. But instead, his summer-sky eyes were soft, wet with unshed tears. "Don't ever say that." It was a mere whisper, but it felt like a caress. "Don't ever say you're worthless. You're everything to me. You have earned the respect of our group. Even Lieven cares for you now. You're not worthless. You're Jia, a smart, resourceful, and resilient woman whom I love more than anything else in this world."

She lifted her hand and brought it up to his cheek. "But I allowed those men to do things to me." The sobs were back, shaking her and strangling her voice. "I allowed them to kill my babies as if they were nothing."

Startled by her last words, Cees tilted her chin up with his finger, making her look him in the eye. "What do you mean, babies?"

"As a *Vaderloos* I'm not allowed contraceptives, and the men who have used me don't bother." Visceral bitterness coated her words. "I had four pregnancies and was not allowed to keep my babies. They took me to their clinics and cut them out of me. The same clinics that removed warts and boils from the perfect bodies of the Blessed, removed my children from me. Cheaper than giving me a way to prevent them." Her voice caught in a hiccup as more tears made their way down her cheeks. All these years, she had never told this to anyone. Not even her mother. She had kept it inside, hidden from even herself, afraid of what acknowledging it would do to her heart. "Not all Blessed are truly blessed..."

CHAPTER TEN

OF MEN

Lieven

The hotel buzzed with activity as everyone in the band prepared for the big move the next day. Lieven was finally well enough to endure the arduous walk toward the coast, and there was much to be done before departure. Daan had disappeared somewhere outside the building, and Jia was making herself scarce since the arrival of the two strangers. More than once, Lieven had heard the one called Faas ask about her, and just as often, he had heard evasive answers from everyone in the squad. Even though none other than Cees knew exactly what this man wanted from her, they all had decided by unspoken agreement that Jia was one of them now and would not be handed over to the murky-acting *Gezegenden.*

"Is Jia okay?" Lieven asked Cees who, beside him, was collecting food items from the hotel pantry into their backpacks. Even though there was still quite a bit of fresh foods available, for this trip they were bringing mostly shelf-stable items. The cold of the snow outside would allow them some fresher items, but even with the icy weather it was too risky not to bring something they would knew would last.

Cees stole a glance around him. "She's fine," he whispered. "Trying to keep her away from those two." He nodded toward the *Gezegenden,* who were the only two people lounging around, doing nothing, as if they expected the others to supply their bags for them. Lieven chuckled quietly. They were in for a very nasty surprise.

"Have you seen Daan?" Lieven wrapped a long, sharp knife into a towel and stuffed it into an increasingly filling bag. They had become experts at packing a lot into a small space.

"I saw him going out about a half an hour ago." Cees shrugged and returned his attention to the packing.

"I bet he's collecting herbs and rocks to make his weird medicinal potions." Lieven smiled at the image that formed in his head. Daan's quirkiness had rapidly grown on him.

With a sideways glance, Cees's lip curled at the corner. "You guys have become quite inseparable."

Lieven laughed a bit uncomfortably. It was still difficult for him to explain or accept these new feelings for the *Berenjong.* It confused and delighted him all at the same time. Ever since they had kissed in the room over a week ago, neither Daan nor Lieven had brought it up again. Life went on as if nothing had happened, and Lieven found himself wondering whether he had just imagined it.

"Do you like him?" Cees' lips were still curled into that silly smile he had since they were kids. Kneeling on the floor next to him, the Tainted man reminded Lieven of when they were young boys, sharing secrets and teasing each other.

A sudden rush of heat climbed up his neck and spread like wildfire over his face. "What are we? School children again?" he said, dismissing his friend's question and avoiding his eyes.

Cees pushed him playfully, and Lieven almost lost his balance as he crouched by the pantry. "Come on, be honest. I've seen the way you look at each other."

Despite his embarrassment, Lieven had to laugh. "Yeah, we kind of…" Why was it so hard to say it out loud? Was it because he was scared of having feelings for someone after loving his friend for most of his life? Was he scared he wouldn't have those feelings reciprocated again? Or was he just afraid of being attracted to someone he barely knew?

Cees chuckled loudly. "Kind of? What does that even mean?"

It was Lieven's turn to push his friend. "Stop it." He resumed his packing. "I don't know what I feel or don't feel. Don't want to talk about it."

The laughter stopped, and Cees looked at him, cobalt-blue eyes trained on Lieven's. "You're my best friend and I love you," he spoke quietly. "You deserve someone that you can love and love you in return. It's not like we can expect to live for very long anymore. If you have feelings for him, don't delay. Enjoy it while you can. Be happy. We may not be alive tomorrow."

The truth in Cees' words hit him with the weight of lead. He was right. What reason was there for confusion? Tomorrow may never come. He had been the soldier for so long, ever-ready, ever-cautious. It was hard to let go of that, to accept that while caution was definitely still a must in almost everything they did, it did not apply to affairs of the heart anymore. Who knew whether there would be a time in the future when they could speak of ever-lasting love again? These protective shields he had built around himself all his life were useless right now. He must learn to let go, to allow himself to just flow like a river or blow like the wind in whatever direction it took him.

"Thanks Cees," he whispered back. "I sometimes forget things are very different now."

By midday, everybody seemed satisfied with their packing, and they were able to finally relax. Some went out for a walk, others lingered in the hotel lobby playing games and talking, and a few retreated to their rooms for the rest they knew they wouldn't be able to get in the perceivable future. Cees vanished into the sanctity of the room he shared with Jia. Lieven was not sure what to do. He had spent so much time in his room because of his injuries it seemed anticlimactic to go back there. He opted for a walk instead. His legs were stiff from lack of use, and his soldier muscles were begging for some exercise. He grabbed his jacket and stumbled into the icy air outside.

It hadn't snowed in over a week, but there was still a thin white covering over everything. Lieven had always liked the snow. There was nothing like walking out the door into a snow-covered street. He could never quite explain why, but the snow enveloped everything in a magical peace. The chaos of everyday life vanished as soon as the frigid flakes began to drop from the skies. As a teenager, he had often climbed to the roof of his own house and sat there, his behind sometimes frozen beyond feeling and his ears full of silence. Of course, this city was quiet anyway, denuded from its inhabitants and their everyday bustle. The snow still rendered its magic, and Lieven strolled around, watching his breath come out in small, puffy clouds and listening to the peaceful stillness of nature.

"You're going to freeze that cute butt of yours." Daan had materialized out of nowhere, his long body almost fading into the snow. He was wearing an array of white clothes which gave him the look of a lanky snowman. Lieven smiled. "Why aren't you resting for tomorrow?"

"I got enough rest for the past weeks," he said as the *Berenjong* came closer. "I needed to stretch my legs."

Daan had a full bag that he now looped into his arms and hung from his back. "Still, you shouldn't push it."

They walked aimlessly together for a while, enjoying the quiet of the afternoon, protected by their heavy jackets. Lieven had forgotten his gloves, and his fingers were quickly becoming numb from the cold. He rubbed them together in front of his mouth, warming them with his breath. "I may lose a finger or two before we're done today," he said, laughing.

Daan's large, alabaster hands that never seemed to get cold were suddenly wrapped around Lieven's. Heat began crawling through the skin of his palms and into the rest of his body. "How come you don't get as cold as we do?" he asked, grateful for the borrowed heat.

Daan roared, throwing his head and his odd hair backwards. "Genes, I'm guessing. *Berenjong* folk don't get cold that easy." His extremely pale eyes rose up to meet Lieven's. "I can be there to warm you anytime you need me." His voice had gone lower and deeper, threading a line of shivers through Lieven's body.

With a soft yank, Lieven pulled his hands away from Daan's, heat climbing up to his cheeks in a tidal wave. "Maybe we should go back." His eyes locked stubbornly on the snowy ground before him.

Without realizing, they had walked closer to the buildings and off the road. The sidewalk had a thicker layer of snow, buildup from snow falling from the edges of the roofs. Daan grasped Lieven's arm and pulled him closer. "We haven't talked about that kiss," he murmured, his warm breath caressing the soldier's face.

Lieven looked up into the almost-transparent green eyes, and something inside of him shattered. Waves of yearning flowed freely through his body, and the air became thick and hard to breathe.

"What's there to talk about?" His voice caught in his throat. Daan's lips were so close, their heat beckoning him.

Daan gave him a lazy, wicked smile as he bent down to Lieven's height. "I won't take offense," he breathed into the other man's ear, his lips brushing on its skin. "But I think you liked it." His lips went down into Lieven's cold neck in a ghost of a kiss.

With his heart racing inside his chest, and the rest of him threatening to burst into flames, Lieven got a hold on Daan's collar, pulled their bodies together, and kissed him. Daan's hands found their way around to Lieven's back, and his fingers knotted themselves on the thick, soft material of his jacket. The kiss deepened and became frantic, their tongues exploring each other's mouths and their hands desperate to find a way to eliminate whatever space there was between them. In their feverish dance, the two men crashed into a nearby building, Lieven's back to its icy wall. Daan closed the little space left between them, his palms lying flat on the wall to both sides of Lieven's head, his lips refusing to quit their exploration of the young soldier's.

Breathing hard and hungry for more, Lieven flipped positions with the *Berenjong* and, temporarily separated from his lips, looked around for a shelter of some kind. The building they were leaning into was a home. Reaching behind Daan, he tried the doorknob, and the door opened with a soft click. "Let's go inside," he said in a throaty voice, his ears throbbing with the flood of blood his heart was rushing to his whole body.

The door somehow closed behind them as they made their way down the narrow corridor, removing each other's jackets between kisses. With his long fingers, Daan unbuttoned Lieven's shirt and pulled it off him, finding a T-shirt beneath it. The *Berenjong,* living up to his name, growled. "Too many layers," he grunted, his hands fumbling to pull the offensive shirt off Lieven and over his head.

With their shirts now a pile on the floor, the two men stopped for a moment, absorbing each other, their hearts accelerating with anticipation. Lieven was past thinking. The overwhelming desire for this odd creature eclipsed all else from his mind. The all-encompassing longing that burned through his veins made every muscle in his body clench and tighten. Beneath that thick fog, he guessed at feelings that went far beyond the physical pleasure. But those would have to wait. His body craved release. Daan was lean, but every muscle in his chest and arms were well-defined and hard as rocks. Lieven reached out to brush his fingers slowly over each ripple and valley, reaping a moan of pleasure from the bear man. He slid his hands down until they reached the hard edge of Daan's pants, slipping his fingers between them and the hard muscle beneath. Daan arched against his palm, begging for more.

The world around them had ceased to exist. Gone were their fellow survivors, the monsters, the suspicious strangers. There was only the two of them, entwined in this intimate embrace, struggling to undress each other, to feel each other whole. Daan pushed Lieven's naked body on top of the bed and studied him from underneath half-closed lids. Lieven shivered under the scrutiny of the *Berenjong*'s translucent eyes, which seemed to have the same power to give him pleasure as his touch. It was a sweet and cruel torture, every inch of his skin alive with electricity, wanting and yearning.

Daan crawled over Lieven, their bare skins sliding against each other, an overwhelming wave of pleasure washing over him. He heard someone's moan and realized it was his own. His body couldn't take much more. He flipped Daan over and stretched himself along his back, his hands reaching around the *Berenjong* to touch his hard abs, and then lower. Lieven eased a finger inside Daan, his soft moan encouraging him to go further. With a thrust, Lieven was inside his lover.

They both yelled at the same time, pain mixed with pleasure quaking through them as they danced together before climaxing, bodies folding on each other, spent.

Tomorrow they would leave the relative safety of that city and face who-knew-what dangers. For now, Lieven slept in peace, wrapped in his lover's arms and legs, secure and sated.

Cees

In front of him, halfway through the small convoy of people, Lieven and Daan seemed oblivious to their surroundings, enveloped in a bright aura of reds and yellows. A surreptitious brush of the hands between them, a subtle glance and a smile, a playful tug... Cees smiled, glad to see his friend happy. The irony of it all didn't escape him. The world as they knew it was coming to an end, the danger of being attacked and devoured by monsters a very tangible threat, and here they were, happier than they both had been in a long time. Love among the ashes had become sort of a theme for their expedition, their escape. One of these days, he would paint this—the feeling of elation among sadness, the surge of hope amid destruction. He brought his hand up to his neck and distractedly brushed it over his tattoo.

"Is it bothering you?" Jia was firmly holding on to his hand as if afraid he would take off without her. She had become increasingly more anxious and afraid of being caught alone with the two *Gezegen-*

den who had joined their group. Cees looked at her confused. "The tattoo," she added. "You keep touching it."

"No, it doesn't bother me," he said as he realized his hand was indeed touching it. He had that tattoo etched into his skin shortly after he had turned eighteen. Adulthood had sneaked upon him earlier than on other boys. His exposure to cruelty and unfairness could have taken him down a completely different path. Lieven's sudden appearance in his life introduced him to a whole other side of the human character, and it had swerved him off the trail of negativity and anger into that of hope and trust. He did indeed believe that inside everyone there was goodness, that there was always light at the end of the tunnel as long as you were willing to walk it long enough. "I was just thinking of how we found each other in the middle of all this."

Jia smiled up at him and nodded. Then, she looked ahead and laughed softly. "They seem to have found each other too," she said with a tilt of the head toward their friends.

The air was crisp, but the bitter cold had eased enough their teeth didn't chatter and their hands didn't go numb inside their gloves. The snow covering was thicker in the woods, the forest bed protected from the weak sun by the evergreens, but still easily negotiated. They carried heavier loads than they did before, not willing to leave things behind they may need later. It would probably slow them down, but after debating, they had decided it was a risk worth taking. The maps didn't show any viable stop between *Volgendestad* and the coast. It was possible some small villages and outcast settlements lay in between, but they couldn't be sure.

Cees felt the tug of Jia's weight, walking beside him half leaning into his side and hands tightly grasped around his arm. He hated that this fearless woman he so loved had been turned into a bundle of nerves by the presence of two unlikable and shady *Gezegenden*. The urge to march ahead and clobber the two burly bigots was, at times, overwhelmingly tempting. Cees could take them. Easily. They may have bodies of knotted iron, but he was taller, younger, and he had the motivation behind him.

They walked all day and rested at regular intervals more for Lieven's healing body's sake than a collective need. The stops didn't last long, just enough to take the weight off their backs for a few minutes, rest their legs, get a quick bite to eat, and be on their way again. Anxiety hung thickly around them, and Jia's stomach was unsettled. More than once, Cees had taken her behind a tree and supported her as she emptied her stomach of the little she had eaten.

As the day progressed into early evening, the scouts began searching for a good place to lay their heads for the night. When a relatively wide river came upon them, many of them raised their eyes to the Guardians in a silent prayer of thanks. Being around water gave them a larger sense of safety from being found by the Predators. Better news was brought by the two scouts; there was a large cave inside the river where they could spend the night totally surrounded by flowing waters.

None of them wished to fall into the frigid river, but no one complained about having to cross the short natural bridge of slippery rocks in order to reach the safety of that little haven. Daan, who never seemed to lose his balance, offered his help as a guide of sorts, allowing them all to use his long body to steady themselves all the way across. In less than half an hour they had all been led safely into the bowels of the cave and could finally relax. It was damp and cold inside, but it was large enough they could have semi-private spots to sleep. Once it got dark, the moon reflected off the surface of the water and illuminated the cave, coating everything and everyone with a surreal sheen.

Jia had picked a niche on the rocky wall where they both could fit, and Cees left her to go relieve himself outside. A commotion alerted him as he was coming back in the cave. It didn't take long for him to realize whatever was going on involved Jia. There was a small cluster of people blocking his sight, but he could tell they were all looking toward their chosen sleeping spot. He quickened his step and pushed the soldiers aside to find Faas holding an obviously frightened Jia by the arm.

"What's going on?" Cees' voice left no doubt he was not happy with what he was witnessing.

Jia's head jerked up to face him. Tears were streaking her beautiful face and something inside of him snapped. In two quick steps he was next to them, his hand on Jia's shoulder, his eyes trained on the *Gezegenden*.

"Move aside, *vlek*," Faas said, his voice a low growl. Cees recognized the derogatory term used to address him and growled back. "This is none of your business. She's a *Vaderloos*. By law, she must obey me."

Cees gave Jia's shoulder an assuring squeeze and took a step closer until their bodies were touching. He felt her relax at the contact. "What law might that be exactly?"

The man tugged at Jia's arm, but she dug her heels into the dirty ground and didn't move. "The law of the Blessed." Spittle flew out of his mouth. "The *only* law."

Cees laughed, a deep, bitter chuckle that rolled up his throat and left his lips in slow-motion. "In case you haven't noticed, the Predators are dictating the law right now. Not the Blessed, not Central... And the Predator's law is simple—run or be eaten." His eyes sought the man's and locked there. He wanted Faas to know he wasn't bluffing. "Let go of her or you will answer to *my* law."

From the corner of his eye, he saw Gillis moving closer. In a single swoop, Alfons jumped to block his progress. Cees sighed, relieved.

"She's mine," Faas said, his hand still holding on to Jia's arm. "She is communal property and she *will* service me."

Losing his patience, Cees let go of Jia's shoulder and, before the other man could react, closed his fists around Faas' shirt and shook him. "Let. Her. Go." Faas hesitated for a moment, looking around him. The other soldiers had closed ranks, forming a tight circle around them. Their faces bespoke of their displeasure at seeing one of them being mishandled and disrespected by this *Gezegenden*. "Be smart and let go." Cees' voice went down an octave and left no doubt as to the seriousness of his warning.

Alfons, having delegated his hold on Gillis to another soldier, approached and forcibly pulled Faas' hand away from Jia's arm. "You and your friend will be going your own way come morning," he said. "We will give you extra supplies but you're on your own from here on. You don't seem to understand that the old world order does not apply to this new world anymore. Here there isn't anyone who is less or more than the others. We are all just humans trying to survive."

The two men were tied together for the rest of the night so everyone else could rest. Jia was still shaking when Cees finished helping Alfons and came to lay down beside her. As soon as he slid under the covers, Jia's hands came around and pulled him to her.

"Hold me," she whispered urgently. Cees turned around to face her. He brushed a lock of her now longer hair away from her face and nibbled on her lower lip. She wiggled closer to him, still whimpering. "Do you hate me?"

The question shocked Cees into stillness. "Hate you? Haven't you been paying attention?" He tilted his head so he could look into her gray, satiny eyes. "I love you, Jia. Love. You." To add more power to his words, he lowered his face again and took her mouth with his, gently pressing his tongue in between her lips until she opened for him and met him halfway.

"I love you too," Jia said, her lips traveling to his earlobe, making him shiver with pleasure. He swelled under the covers against her arching hips. Jia giggled, rubbing herself against him, her aura a fluorescent red that infused their sleeping niche in an otherworldly hue. He groaned in frustration. "Sorry I can't do anything about that right now." There was a note of mischief in her voice as her hand traveled down his chest to the front of his pants in a suggestive caress.

"You have me undone," he whispered back, pressing himself harder against her. He nipped at her earlobe with his teeth. "Are you sure *Gezegenden* women have no magic powers?"

He was on fire, but with the whole group just feet away from them, he was going to have to grin and bear it. Jia softened against him, molding her body to his. "No, the Blessed have no magic at all." Her voice was no longer playful. "But you do, my sweet *Zuiver*. You certainly do."

CHAPTER ELEVEN

HOPE

Jia

The simple knowledge that Faas and Gillis were no longer trailing behind them made her heart lighter and her mood exponentially brighter. Jia felt a lot of her emotional strength return and the clingy, needy woman she had been since the two men stumbled upon the group at *Volgendestad* was gone. The squad had been on the move now for almost a week, and they had yet to see any sign of life. The forest had become sparser, and the weather had a warmer tone to it, but the ocean had not yet been sighted.

Cees was walking ahead, his arm draped over Lieven's shoulders, occasionally throwing his head back in laughter. She smiled. The two friends had grown closer again throughout the trek to safety, and she couldn't be happier for the two of them. Guilt had haunted her. Not only had she been the one to reveal Lieven's secret love for Cees, but she was also the probable reason it was not reciprocated. Maybe Cees would have eventually developed more romantic feelings for his friend, had she not suddenly appeared in their lives. Now with Daan,

Lieven seemed happy—as much as they could be considering their circumstances—and so did Cees, who had his friend back with no strings attached.

The evening was rolling closer, and Jia realized she hadn't eaten yet that day. She was alternatively hungry and terribly nauseated. The anxiety causing this stomach upset was gone, yet her body didn't seem to have noticed. Even when she was able to eat, she invariably couldn't keep it down for long. Cees had become an expert at foretelling her vomiting episodes. Somehow, he always seemed to know before she did that she would have to quickly run behind something and empty her often already-empty stomach. Something about her aura turning a sickly tone of yellow, he had told her. It was both worrisome and annoying.

"Have these crackers." Daan had materialized from behind her. The *Berenjong* was able to walk as quietly as a forest wildcat despite his stature. "I noticed you haven't eaten today."

Jia stared at the unappetizing-looking crackers he was holding up to her. In his other hand he had a mug. "What's that?" she asked, nodding toward the mug.

Daan raised his hand to her. "*Gemberwortel*-infused water. Good for stomach upsets."

"Where did you find ginger root?" She accepted the mug from his hand. She was not sure she would be able to stomach those ugly crackers.

"I collected a variety of herbs and roots while we were in *Volgendestad*," he explained. "What I couldn't find under the snow, I collected from their pharmacies and eateries." He looked at her as if waiting for something. "Go on. Drink it. And eat these crackers, too."

With a frown, she eyed the suspicious food. "I don't think so." She gagged. "Those look like they were made with dirt."

His laughter echoed through the air and several eyes turned to them. "You're funny, *Gezegenden* girl. Don't judge the cracker by its looks. There is good taste and health value in them. You of all people should know better." It was not an accusation. Rather, a reminder of what their civilization had been doing wrong for so long—her included.

"All right, all right," Jia said, reaching out for the offensive crackers. "This *funny girl* knows when she's licked." Realizing what she had just said, Jia looked up at Daan, who was opening his mouth to reply, and frowned. "And don't you even go there. You know what I mean."

The *Berenjong* chuckled again and watched as she gingerly bit into the crackers and took a sip of the cold infusion. "Well?"

Jia smiled and shook her head gently. "I have to admit. They don't quite taste like dirt as I thought. More like excrement-infused sand..." She grinned at the shocked expression on his face. "Okay, it does not taste too bad at all. Thank you, Daan. You are a great medical asset to our group."

The bear man reached out with his long arms and hugged her. The fur on his all-white jacket tickled her nose. "How are things with Lieven?"

He held her at arms' length, and his pale eyes glinted as two pieces of glass. "*Verbazingwekkend*! Amazing," he said, a beautiful smile lighting his face.

She hugged him again and whispered in his ear. "So happy for you. Treasure it."

In Daan's defense, Jia was able to hold the food down for the rest of the day. It seemed like the odd man knew his way around medicinal plants. The fact that her stomach was not doing somersaults inside her made for a much more pleasant walk that day.

The sun was already dipping down in the sky when the scouts came running with news. They were so excited it took them a few minutes to gather their wits before they could make any sense.

"The ocean," they both said at the same time, their voices reflecting the awe in their eyes. "The ocean is just ahead."

Jia couldn't remember later what they did exactly, but they must have run in the direction the scouts had just come from. They stopped only when they reached the top of a promontory and were faced with a view that far exceeded all their dreams of late. Spread in front of them, as far as the eye could see, was the ocean. Shiny under the light of the dying sun, it looked like a slow-moving, star-studded sky—peaceful, beautiful, and full of hope. The squad let out a collective sigh; relief and awe rolled into one feeling of happiness.

Cees came next to Jia and pulled her closer to his side. "It's beautiful." The ocean was not a stranger to him, he had told her before. He had seen in his dreams, he said. Those prophetic dreams of his.

It was Jia's first time. She had seen pictures of it, read descriptions. Never had she seen the real thing. It was awe-inspiring with its beauty and sheer size, the illusion of eternity spreading before her eyes. The promise of freedom and safety. Just like Cees' arms made her feel alive and protected, the sight of that immense flux of waters made her feel hopeful.

She felt a stirring inside of her, a flutter of something that had laid dormant but was now awake and alert. With a gasp, she brought her hand down to her belly and followed it with her eyes, her heart beating faster and her brain struggling to come to terms with the realization. Below her fingers she could feel it, moving, stretching, dancing for joy. Tears flooded her eyes as she raised them to Cees, standing beside her, blissfully unaware of the happy turmoil in her heart. She would tell him later. For now, this was hers and only hers. For the first time in her life she felt comfortable being selfish, feeling deliriously happy and alive.

The way down to the beach was arduous and slow. The cliff was steep and had few spots that could be easily hiked down. In order to achieve it in a relatively safe way was to go out of the way and circle around to where the cliff started sloping gradually all the way to the beach. The descent left them exposed, but since dusk had already covered everything in semi-darkness, the risk of being seen was minimal. Cees placed himself protectively in front of Jia and held her hand every time he could. Jia's mind was already on the beach, inside some shelter where she could curl up with her beautiful *Zuiver* and reveal to him what had just been revealed to her.

Daan, true to his nature, hiked down the rough trail as if he was walking on a city street, never once losing his footing. Lieven, his gun hanging behind his back, followed him a lot more gingerly, often losing his balance or tripping over a loose rock. Jia thought he had heard him cuss under his breath, but Daan, heedless to any one's difficulties, sauntered ahead. Jia giggled.

"What's so funny?" Cees asked, looking back at her.

"Daan," she said, avoiding a big rock in her way. "Look at him. Steady foot and oblivious." Cees stared at the *Berenjong* and laughed.

It was dark by the time they arrived at the beach. The moon shone in the clear night sky, making the ocean waters twinkle like diamonds. They soon found a place to spend the night; a large area half-hidden by a cliff overhang. The sand was cold, but the relief of being that much closer to their destination couldn't dampen their spirits. As they prepared for the night, the soldiers chatted and joked. One of them had brought a deck of cards, and a group spent a great part of the night playing while others risked short walks in the dark along the peaceful ocean.

Jia followed Cees a little way from the rest of the group, hoping to be able to talk to him alone, but soon realized they had been followed by Lieven and Daan. They all sat together in a tight circle to protect themselves from the cold, large puffs of white breath coming out from their mouths. When Lieven shivered, Daan draped his arm over his shoulders and pulled him against his body.

"Bears never get cold," Daan said. The others looked at him with their eyebrows arched. "What? It's true."

Lieven turned a little in the other man's protective embrace and looked at him. "I seem to remember a very frozen Daan not that long ago."

Daan cleared his throat. "That was a fluke." He tugged Lieven closer.

"What fluke?" Cees said, his arm also draped over Jia's shoulders. "You were frozen solid when we found you."

Daan looked at Jia as if asking for her support. "Sorry Daan." She shrugged. "You were frozen."

It was the *Berenjong*'s turn to shrug. "Well, I must have been sick or something because I never get ... too cold." His stubborn words made the others smile. Then, his eyes roamed to Lieven's face and a mischievous grin curved up his lips. "Of course, now I feel the cold even less."

Intrigued, they all looked at him. "What do you mean?" Lieven asked. "What changed exactly?"

The wicked smile was still dancing on his lips. "Now, if I start feeling cold, all I have to do is look at you and my blood runs hot."

Even in the darkness, they could see that Lieven's face had turned a bright scarlet made even deeper when Daan pulled him and kissed him on the lips.

"Maybe we should leave them alone," Cees whispered in Jia's ear as the two men lost themselves in their kiss. They stood up and walked away, giggling softly when they realized neither Daan or Lieven had noticed their departure. "I'm tired. Are you?"

Jia was exhausted. The descent had been tough on her leg muscles, and her eyes felt heavy. "Yes, can we go lay down? There is something I want to tell you."

Finally stretched on the sand, enshrouded in their blanket, Jia and Cees faced each other. "What do you want to tell me?" Cees asked.

Jia licked her lips and her heart jumped in her chest. She was glad that the light of the moon allowed her to see his face clearly. She did not want to miss a second of his reaction to what she was about to tell him. It occurred to her in passing that maybe he wouldn't be as excited about it as she was. But it was a fleeting thought. Inside, she knew.

Jia started her story, her eyes trained on his, thirsty for his reaction. He did not disappoint. His eyes opened wide, his eyebrows arching upwards, and his lips set in a thin line at first. As she continued, his forehead furrowed as his eyebrows came together. He lifted his hands to his mouth, now slightly open, and a slow smile began to emerge. He lowered his head for a moment, and when he looked at her again, tears were rolling down his face, leaving shiny tracks over the black stripe. He sought her hands and brought them up to his lips.

"Are you happy?" Her lips skimmed the top of his head as his flittered over her hands.

Cees lifted his eyes to hers. "Happy?" He wiped tears from his cheeks. "I don't think that's a good word for what I feel right now, Jia. You just gave me something I never, ever thought I would have. I'm beyond happy." His lips latched onto hers in a tear-drenched kiss. "Are you sure?"

Jia nodded. This was not her first time. She recognized the signs. Yes, she was very sure. "We're going to be parents," she whispered over his mouth. "We're going to have a baby."

Lieven

It was little more than a dot in the horizon, so tiny it might have been an illusion, a trick of the light. Lieven knew better, though. The maps had clearly shown that was the Wadden Sea Islands. Or at least, one of them. He looked at it, and a seed of hope began growing inside him.

Daan seemed to be just as at home in the ocean as he was among the trees of the forest. Lieven had woken up to a soaked *Berenjong*, proudly carrying a large fish in his hands. When he mentioned the fact that they couldn't light a fire to cook it, Daan flashed his silly smile and proceeded to skin the fish and eat it raw.

"It's good," he said, sitting crossed-legged on the sand, his mouth full of briny flesh. Lieven gagged. "Stop being so picky. Have I ever lied to you? It's good. Trust me."

Skeptical but ravenous, and oh-so fed up with the same dried goods they had been eating for the past few days, Lieven sat beside him and opened his mouth to accept the chunk of raw fish the other man was offering him. Gingerly, he chewed the cold, chewy flesh. It wasn't as bad as he had anticipated and far better tasting than the dried fruit bars and canned foods they had been surviving on.

"Well?" Daan watched Lieven's reaction. "How is it?"

Lieven's face opened in a smile, and his heart filled with gratitude for the company and friendship of the odd *Berenjong*. Rolling into his knees, he tilted forward and kissed Daan's lips. "It's delicious," he said, his lips right above the other man's. Daan's eyes glittered in the morning sun, and he felt the stirrings of desire deep down inside.

The *Berenjong* brushed his hand across Lieven's face and then beamed. "Not as tasty as you." He winked and burst out laughing when Lieven blushed violently. "Come on, eat some more."

The scouts had gone out early that morning under the cover of dawn and had come back with good news. Just a mile or so down the beach, there was a harbor. Most of the vessels were gone, but a few had been left behind.

Everything had been gathered quickly and efficiently. None of them wanted to linger as salvation beckoned them. If it wasn't for the weight they carried, Lieven was sure they would have raced all the way to the pier, terrified of being caught by the monsters this close to salvation.

One of the boats was large enough to carry all of them. Not one member of their group had any knowledge or experience with sea vessels, but they were willing to learn fast. Jia, who had been at the helm of small boats in her city's recreational lake, had brought a manual from the library at *Volgendestad* and had been studying it every chance she had.

The trek across the sands was not long but was marred by the anxiety they all felt at walking on that exposed stretch of coast. As soon as they set their eyes on the pier with its white sea vessels, they rushed toward it. Maddeningly, the pier seemed as if stuck in some other dimension. No matter how long they walked, it still seemed to be at the same distance as when they began. Frustration began to gnaw at Lieven like a rabid animal. A strange premonition invaded his thoughts; a terrible, heavy sense of foreboding.

Lieven nearly crashed into Daan's back when the *Berenjong* stopped abruptly, his nose smelling the air around them. Lieven's heart contracted and the dark feeling in his heart swelled up. After a moment, Daan came out of the semi-trance he always seemed to go into when he was smell-tracking something and yelled out, "Run! Run! Predators!"

Panic ensued. Resorting to speed he never thought he had and scared of losing the bear man, Lieven grabbed hold of Daan's hand and ran. The thin sand made it hard to pick up speed, their feet dug into it deeper and deeper at each step as if the tiny grains of rocks were hands holding on to their ankles, pulling them back. In his mad dash, Lieven searched for his friend; Cees and Jia had been walking ahead of them and were still some steps ahead but losing speed. Jia seemed to struggle to keep up, often stumbling and staring behind her, a haunted expression in her eyes.

Lieven chanced a quick look behind and immediately wished he hadn't. Running on four limbs at speeds hard to fathom, the beasts were quickly gaining on them. They were mere seconds from those in the very back. The young soldier picked up speed, muttering a prayer under his breath. Had they come this far only to be caught anyway?

Shrill screams of terror and pain reached his ears. The Predators had claimed their first victims. Lieven scrunched his fists against his ears trying to mute the gut-wrenching sound. In front of them the pier was finally coming closer. But was it too little too late?

Alfons, who had been in the forefront, had stopped running and stood looking back at the Predators. "Alfons, run!" Lieven yelled at him as they passed him. The squad leader didn't budge. With horror,

Lieven realized what the soldier was going to do. Lieven stopped in his tracks and turned back. "Don't be a hero, Alfons. Run!"

"Aleid is in charge now, Lieven," Alfons yelled back, his hand sliding along the barrel of his gun. "Make sure they all get to the island safe. Go! It's an order."

The young soldier hesitated for a moment, glancing between Alfons and the approaching monsters. Daan came back for him and pulled him into action. He ran, his heart bleeding. Alfons had been like a father to him ever since he had joined the squad. Losing him was like losing his father all over again. Tears burned in his eyes, but he refused to look back and kept running.

As he reached the pier and climbed aboard the small vessel, he heard it. First the sound of a gun going off several times, then the mighty roar of the beasts and Alfons' agonizing scream. He closed his eyes, refusing to allow the stinging tears to roll freely. Grief had to wait.

Jia and Aleid were checking the boat's engine and were relieved to find out it had a tank-full of fuel, and everything else seemed to be in working condition. When one of the soldiers moved to remove the walking plank, Lieven stopped him. "No, Alfons is still out there."

Daan came over to him and wrapped him in his arms. "He's not coming, Lieven. Alfons is gone. We need to leave before the beasts get here. Alfons sacrificed himself to earn us a few more minutes. Don't let him down."

Lieven waved a reluctant assent to the anxious soldier, and the plank was removed while a couple other soldiers were pulling the anchor aboard. The boat was finally moving, but Lieven felt no joy, no relief. However hard it was, the soldier in him picked himself up and buried all the pain deep inside to focus on the flight to safety.

After the initial confusion, the sea vessel was underway. Those who were not in charge of the navigation stood on the deck, the cold maritime breeze blowing their hair and chastising the skin of their faces, staring back at the land and the friends they were leaving behind. The Predators, finished with the body of Alfons and the other two unfortunate soldiers, now stood growling on the beach, staring at the departing vessel, a spine-chilling reminder of the end of their world.

Jia sat with a numb Lieven and the rest of the survivors to plan for the crossing. According to the maps and books they had consulted, the crossing shouldn't take longer than a day and a half. The fact that there wasn't a single experienced sailor in their group didn't dampen their spirits. The Wadden Sea was not known for its storms, even during the winter. The waters were choppy, but not dangerously so. They figured that if they could keep the boat moving forward in a straight line, they couldn't miss the islands which formed a line off the coast of the mainland of *Oostzee*. Even the loss of their leader and two more companions couldn't totally obscure the fact that they were finally on their way to a safe haven.

This had been a fishing vessel. Not a lot of luxuries but plenty of space. Underneath the deck, cabins with bunks offered more comfort than they had had since leaving the last city, and there was even running water. Some, physically and mentally exhausted, took immediate refuge in the lower deck. Others lingered outside, conflicted between feelings of relief and grief.

Lieven was suddenly stricken with the knowledge that what he had always thought of as his home was behind him now. He would never see it again. The streets where he raced with Cees, the school they both attended, the little studio where Cees painted — where he'd found refuge from the chaos of the world. All gone forever. Tears rolled down his cheeks.

An arm came to rest over his shoulders. "We will create new memories," Daan whispered in his ear, wiping Lieven's tears with a finger. "We'll build a new, better world."

Lieven leaned into Daan, grateful for the heat and the comfort of his body. Funny how as the world crumbled around them, a new hope emerged. He watched Cees protectively hover over Jia, who had taken her role as the only one who had ever piloted a boat of any kind very seriously. Now manning the helm, standing confidently with her hands solidly on the wheel, she braced herself against the rolling of the waves. Every so often she would bump against Cees, turn her face to his and smile. Their love for each other was so obvious, Lieven felt that conflicting pang inside his heart. He was happy for them, but even though he was falling hard for Daan, it still stung a little to see his friend so in love with someone other than him. His feelings for Cees had been so strong and ran so deep they still surfaced once in a while.

"It hurts, doesn't it?" Daan's voice blew warm air onto the side of his face, startling him. "It's okay. I didn't expect you to just forget you had loved this man for so long."

Lieven's heart clenched—in sorrow or shame, he was not sure which. "I'm not..." He wasn't going to lie to Daan. "I'm sorry. Sometimes these feelings still rattle me."

"And so they should." The *Berenjong* surprised Lieven. "If you had just forgotten about it in the short time we've been together, it would mean your feelings are shallow. The fact that you still have feelings about this means your heart is true." They had both slid down to the deck, Daan's back against the gunwale and Lieven nestled between his legs with his back against the other man's chest. "I'm a patient man, Lieven, and I'm not going anywhere."

Daan's hands reached around Lieven's chest. With a twist of the neck, Lieven turned his lips up to the *Berenjong*'s and kissed him. "Thank you. Can't tell you how much I love having you with me."

Daan laughed in his unique, funny way. "Me, too," he said, planting a kiss on Lieven's head. "It turns out the apocalypse is a pretty lonely place to be."

The passage was graced with good weather, the cotton ball clouds sprinkling the bright blue sky not posing any obstacle to the winter sun to shine through. The sea was calm, the waves slow and regular under the gentle, cold breeze. By the afternoon, Aleid, who had been watching and learning from Jia, took the helm. Jia and Cees went down to the cabins for a well-deserved rest. Lieven couldn't stop noticing the *Gezegenden* girl looked more tired and paler than ever.

"What do you think is wrong with Jia?" he asked Daan. "She's been throwing up a lot and looks like a ghost. Do you think she's sick?"

Daan snorted. "Are you kidding me? You haven't figured it out yet?"

Lieven turned around just enough to look at his mate. "What do you mean? What am I supposed to figure out?"

"Were there no women where you come from?" Daan teased, his lips curling into an amused smile. "She's with child."

If he hadn't been already sitting down and braced against Daan, Lieven would have stumbled in surprise. "What? No, that's not possible."

Another snort escaped the *Berenjong*'s lips. "You do know how babies are made, right?" he said. "The two of them have been...intimate for a while now, so how are you surprised?"

"I know that, but—pregnant? Really?" He hated that he didn't seem to be able to put a coherent sentence together. "Shit!"

"You're going to be an uncle, *Zuiver* boy," Daan said, rubbing his hand on top of Lieven's head. "Congratulations."

When the sun was so low on the horizon it seemed to be dipping its toes in the water, the island they were heading toward became more solid and visible. They were close enough now they could almost see the greenery and its white-sand beaches. Or maybe it was only their wishful thinking. The sun went down, and soon only the moon offered its light to a dark world, reflecting off the waves into a million little sparkles.

"The ocean looks a little like the fields of my commune at night." Lieven sighed. The night had taken a certain quality of silence and peace that he didn't want to disturb. "The lightening bugs would fly low over the grasses and sparkle just like that. When we were kids, Cees and I used to sit in the middle of the big fields and watch them." Lieven smiled at the memory. "We called them our own private fireworks since Cees was never allowed to come and watch real fireworks with the rest of the town."

Daan was leaning forward on the rails of the gunwale next to Lieven, looking out into the vast dark ocean. "It must have been great to grow in a town with your family and your friends."

Lieven was reminded that his lover had grown up in semi-isolation, and his heart bled for him. He couldn't imagine not having people around him. Not as a child. "Was it lonely? Growing with just your father?"

"Sometimes," Daan admitted, his eyes turned down into his own hands on the rail. "But better than being shunned by the villagers or called names. There were other outcasts. Once in a while, we talked, visited each other..."

Lieven turned around so his back was now to the rail and he could look at Daan better. "No one in town would talk to you?"

"They did when they needed something from me." Daan growled low in his throat. "I used to think they wanted to be my friends... I was very young and naive. I so wanted to belong." The last words came out as a prayer, and Lieven threw his arm over the other man's back. "I got you now..." It was a question, a doubt he obviously wanted cleared and erased from his heart.

Lieven's eyes bore into the *Berenjong*'s ghostly eyes. There was pain in them. Daan was always so independent, and easy-going, it was easy to forget his life had not been a bed of roses. There was a deep hurt in the green waters of his strangely beautiful eyes, and Lieven felt his heart fill with such an overwhelming flow of love it almost choked him. "I won't leave you," he whispered, his lips dropping on Daan's shoulder.

Daan stood up to his full height and wrapped his arms tightly around the young soldier, his head nestled in the crook of Lieven's neck. "I love you, *Zuiver* soldier." Daan's voice came out muffled but fervent. "Whatever waits for us in that island, I'll be there for you too."

The cold breeze sent shivers up Lieven's back as he brushed his long fingers gently over Daan's face, his lips seeking his lover's. Desperate, their lips crushed together, hard at first, then softening into one another, savoring, no longer frantic, no longer rushed. Whatever awaited them in the Wadden Sea islands, they would face it together.

A frantic Cees came to break them apart. His hair sticking up where he had raked his fingers through. Lieven recognized the gesture. Something was wrong. "Daan, there is something wrong with Jia," he said, wringing his hands. "Can you help her?"

They all ran down to the cabins where Jia lay in a bunk, writhing in pain. Cees sat next to her, holding her hand and looking at Daan and Lieven with such desperation in his eyes, Lieven's heart clenched in sympathy.

The *Berenjong* sat right next to Cees. "What do you feel?" he asked her, reaching to her forehead with the palm of his hand. "Are you in pain?"

Jia nodded and whimpered. "Lots of cramping. I'm not going to lose this baby, am I?" She had grasped his wrist as if holding on to hope. "I can't lose my baby."

With a frown of worry, Cees turned to his friends. "Jia is pregnant."

"We know that," Daan turned his attention back to Jia. "Are you bleeding?"

Jia's eyes dilated like balloons. "I don't know. I haven't checked."

Lieven and Daan moved away from the bed to give her some privacy. A small group of people were starting to gather in the cabin, curious and worried about what was going on. Aleid pushed through the small crowd. "Is she bleeding?" Jia's pregnancy was not much of a secret after all.

A screeching made them all run back to the bunk where Jia was sobbing hysterically. "I'm bleeding. It's happening again." Cees wrapped his arms around her, trying to comfort her. "It's happening all over again."

Aleid sat next to them and pulled the inconsolable Jia away from Cees. "Stop crying," she ordered, the authority of a lifetime as a soldier seeping through. "You haven't lost the baby yet. You may not lose the baby. But you need to relax or you will lose it for sure."

With those words Aleid seemed to have soothed Jia into peace. Her sobbing stopped, and even though she was still in tears, she was able to calm herself down. "Good," Aleid said. "Where's the pain?"

For the next few minutes Aleid and Daan performed a series of checks while asking a million questions. "Why did you say it's happening again?" the other woman asked. "Have you had a miscarriage before?"

Jia's lip and chin trembled. Her eyes, filled with tears, threatened to spill over at any time. She looked at Cees as if asking for permission before looking at Aleid again. "Abortions. I had three abortions before." Silence dropped over them, heavy and oppressive.

Aleid was the first one to snap out of the shock-induced stupor. "This is what you are going to do." She pushed Jia back down on the sheets. "You are going to rest. I mean, no moving at all unless it is to go to the bathroom. Cees, you are in charge of making sure she doesn't budge." Cees nodded his head in agreement. "There is not much we can do, but there is no point in expecting the worst. The running and the scare on the beach must have triggered it. Are you bleeding heavily?"

"No, just spotting." Jia shook her head. Hope softened her face.

"Good," Aleid said. "So, rest, relax, and I will come check on you soon. Daan, do you have one of your miracle herbs?"

Daan was already on the move, looking through his bag. "I have a root here. Somebody get some hot water."

The ensuing activity helped all of them unwind and take their minds off the crisis. Lieven ran to heat up some water, Cees helped Jia change her stained clothes, and Daan brewed his tea. Lieven watched the *Berenjong* as he meticulously cut a slice of the root, steeped it in the boiling water, and then stirred it patiently until he deemed it ready. Jia drank it slowly, the pungent tea tickling Lieven's nose and soothing his nerves. He didn't know what that tea was, but he didn't care. If nothing else, it had magically calmed everybody down.

Lieven weaved his fingers through Daan's and pulled him gently away from the bunks. "Let's go up on the deck. They need some quiet."

The night outside had turned into a mesmerizing miracle of lights and shadows, the black velvet of the sky studded with glittering diamonds and the wavy ocean waters an ombre of blues interspersed with black and white. Underneath it all, Lieven felt small and insignificant but also filled with wonder. They bent over the railing and stared into it all, their eyes and their hearts filled with a new sense of possibility. Their new life awaited.

Chapter Twelve
A New World

Cees

A group of people waited for them on the shore. They had seen the ship at a distance and were waiting for them to land. Many had questions none of them could answer; questions about their hometowns, their families. These were the fortunate ones who had either been on the island already when the Predators began running loose inland or were able to jump on a boat and flee. Cees felt their pain but couldn't find time to commiserate. Not now. Not when Jia was at risk of losing their child.

Losing the baby would hurt him more than he thought it would at first, but it was the pain it was causing Jia that made him want this baby to survive. After all she had gone through, the simple possibility of this child had given Jia a new sense of self-esteem, empowerment. She had been at the mercy of the *Gezegenden* men for so long with no control over anything, including her own body, her own decisions. This baby represented her freedom and also the hope that new life always brought with it.

Upon arrival, Jia was immediately taken to the hospital. It was a rather grandiose name for what was little more than a rectangular building with a few beds, an examination room, and a few medical supplies and tools. Normally the islands were lightly inhabited, and whenever someone got sick, they were taken to the mainland for treatment. The beds were comfortable at least. And clean. After weeks on the road, a bed with clean sheets seemed heavenly.

Jia was not in any pain anymore, but the spotting continued. Aleid, who had delivered a few babies in her lifetime, was of the opinion that bed rest was the best and only thing they could do to make sure Jia didn't miscarry. The woman who was serving as the *burgemeester* had offered the hospital as their temporary quarters, which they gladly and gratefully accepted.

With Jia asleep finally, Cees went for a walk around town. Like the hospital, town seemed to be too grand of a title for what it was really, a bigger village. The buildings had been haphazardly built around the center, where the market and a few small shops were located. The rest of the town was spread as far as he could see; small, squat structures made of brick or stone, some with thatched roofs, all with deep v-cut roof frames to keep the snow from accumulating. Their white companion for the past many weeks, the snow, was scarcer here, but its flakes still sprinkled the dark roofs and side streets. In stark contrast with the terrain they had crossed just a few days ago, the island was almost bare of trees. Instead, tall grasses danced in the wind even in the cold of winter.

"Different, no?" Lieven had caught up with him. He had on different clothes and smelled faintly of grass. "Beautiful though."

Cees had to admit there was a wild beauty to the island, with its sand dunes buffeted by the wind and protected by grasses that grew taller than him in some areas. It was peaceful, a luxury they hadn't had in a long time.

"Where's Daan?" Cees asked heading to the beach. He could smell the clean scent of the ocean and hear the cries of the gulls, their white wings dotting the clear skies above.

"Taking a long bath." Lieven shoved his hands in the pockets of his jacket and wrinkled his nose. "He was getting a little ripe." He laughed softly, stealing glances at his friend. "What do you think about him?"

A smile stretched across Cees' face. "What do you care what I think? What do you think, that's the important question."

Lieven bit his lip and kicked the dirt in the path in front of him. "I like him. A lot." He chanced a look at his friend and blushed. "I may be falling in love with him."

Cees slapped Lieven's back in a friendly gesture. "I'm so happy for you. You deserve to be happy."

Lieven brushed his hand away playfully like they had done a million times in the past. "You don't think I gave up on you too quickly, do you?"

"Liev." Cees suddenly stopped. "No matter what, I will always be your friend. And I hope you'll always be mine. We're good, me and you. No regrets." He was rewarded with the most sunlit smile in Lieven's face, which started on his lips and traveled across his whole face and into his eyes.

Despite the cold, the breeze coming from the ocean felt soothing as it blew against them. The sand under their shoes was white as snow, and the waves crashed into the shore with a soft churning sound as if afraid to bother them. The two friends dropped to the sand and sat in silence for a while, watching the ocean, the seagulls, and the seals that had crawled out of the waters to sunbathe in the sand in great piles of animated blubber. For the first time in a long while, Cees felt peace wash over him. Even with the threat of the loss of his child, there was such a promise of serenity around them. With a deep breath, Cees inhaled the salty air and exhaled all his anxieties, his fears, his pain. They were safe, finally.

Jia was awake when they returned, sitting on the bed, sipping on a steamy cup. She sounded and looked excited as she called Cees to her side. With a glance, he drank her in. His beautiful *Gezegenden* always made his heart jump for joy. Every time he looked at Jia's face, her dark hair, her clear, gray eyes, he felt his insides melt, as if muscle and sinew had suddenly liquefied. The love he felt for her was overwhelming and even scary at times, like a wildfire that couldn't be controlled. Not that he wanted to control it. For the first time ever, he liked that feeling of chaos, allowing himself to be guided by something he couldn't define, understand, or change.

"What's going on?" Cees asked Jia as he sat down beside her on the bed. She looked radiant, as if emitting a light from the inside.

She giggled and grabbed his hands excitedly. "It stopped." Cees tilted his head uncomprehending. "The bleeding. It stopped."

Cees smiled and squeezed her small hands in his. "That's good, right?" he asked, afraid of getting too hopeful. "What did Aleid say?"

"It's a good sign," Jia said, pulling him closer to her. "She says a couple more days rest and if the pain or the bleeding don't come back, I should be okay." Pulling him even closer, she covered his lips with hers in a soft, quick kiss.

"That's amazing, Jia." He kissed her again. Climbing on the bed with her, he stretched himself alongside Jia, her head on his chest. He could feel his fast-beating heart pound against the side of her face. "It's hard to believe we made a baby. Me and you. We made a life."

Jia laughed softly into his chest, her hand sliding across his belly. "Blessed and Tainted... Who would have ever thought that was even possible?"

"Boy or girl?" Cees hadn't had the chance to put too much thought into it, afraid to get too attached to the idea of being a father and then losing the child. But now those thoughts were emerging from the depths of his mind. "I never thought I would father any children. I wasn't even allowed to date. Not that anyone would date me anyway."

"Their loss," Jia said, tilting her head up and kissing his chin. "I should thank the Predators. Without them, I would have never met you."

It was true that out of something so horrible, so many wonderful things had surfaced: their relationship, Lieven and Daan, the breakdown of the unfair and irrational caste system. Silver linings had always been his thing. As an artist, Cees tended to see color in everything, even when black and doom seemed to be the only available hue. As they lie side by side, Jia was surrounded by an intense, happy yellow, and he allowed himself to relax in her arms and fade into sleep.

That night, the hospital was a festive place. All the squad members, now rested and clean, came to visit and celebrate not only their arrival at their promised land but also the creation of new life, a new future they thought was gone for good. Several islanders joined in the party with offers of fruit and sweet wine.

Cees watched with a light heart as Lieven sat next to Daan, their hands joined and their eyes full of what he knew was the exhilaration that came with feeling loved and loving in return. He noticed the features of all the other companions relax from the mask of fear and doubt they had been locked into. There were a lot of smiles, even grins. Jokes were told, and they were graced with music for the first time since the attack as two of the islanders played the guitar and sang.

Aleid stood up, glass of wine held up high. "A toast—ladies and gentlemen, soldiers." She folded comically into a curtsy of sorts. "First, thank you Wadden Sea islanders for welcoming us into your community." She raised her glass in their direction. "Thank you to my squad of exceptional soldiers who just proved what I already knew about them; you are amazing soldiers and great people. You're my family now. We are all family now."

There was a moment of silence as they were all recalled of the fact they had all lost their leader and many family members.

"But this is not a moment for sadness. It is indeed an occasion to celebrate life and hope. Thank you, Daan, my *Berenjong* friend. Your presence amongst us has enriched each one of us... especially my young friend, Lieven." Aleid winked at Lieven, who was quickly turning scarlet. Daan raised their entwined hands into the air and laughed.

"And thank you, Jia." Aleid had turned to Jia, still reclined on her bed, Cees sitting next to her. "Thank you for showing us that not everything is what it seems and that we never really know what's going on below the surface." Totally out of character, Aleid stepped forward, bent over the bed, and gave Jia a hug and a kiss. "Alfons would want me to thank you for him," she quietly told Jia.

Cees was startled to see that Aleid was now turning to him. "As for you, my Tainted One, I want to apologize for the behavior of my own people," she said, suddenly serious. "I may not have made the rules, but I followed them without question. I knew Lieven was good friends with you and not once had it occurred to me to meet you or even ask questions about you. I just accepted what my Elders and Central told me."

Cees was somber, but not sad or angry. He looked Aleid straight in the eye, listening to and absorbing every word.

"I'm sorry I wasted all these years without even trying to get to know you or the other Tainted Ones," the female soldier continued. "I am very glad you came with us and I got to know you. You are part of my family, Cees, and I do hope you'll be able to forgive me."

Aleid was enveloped in so many colors it looked like a rainbow had fallen from the skies and draped around her body. Cees smiled. "There's nothing to forgive," he said. "But thank you for asking."

"So, the only thing left to do now is to decide what we are going to name this baby..."

Cees and Jia

Through the window, the ocean spread in its blue serenity as far as the eye could see. He stopped painting for a moment and stared at the sight. A healing peace he hadn't known in so long washed through him, comforting him inside and out like a cup of hot chocolate on a cold day. It had been a long journey here, fraught with danger and fear, but also full of bliss. Cees' eyes wandered toward the bed on his right, nestled in the wooden wall, and watched Jia as she slept. Her face was serene, like that of the angels in the old paintings he had seen in books a long time ago.

It was still hard to believe that they had lived in this little slice of heaven for almost a year, safe and protected from the horrors of the mainland. A few more survivors had joined them along the way, and at times, it had been difficult to bring them to accept the idea *Zuivers*, *Gezegenden*, Tainted Ones, and *Berenjong* were all just people, and that they could all live together in harmony. Some had left for the other islands because they couldn't wrap their heads around the concept of a society without castes, but most of them came to embrace it eventually. All in all, they had a thriving, albeit sleepy, community where no one was more or less than the other.

The door of the room opened and Lieven came in carrying Cees' favorite bundle; his baby girl, Carola. His friend and Daan had nominated themselves as the baby's nannies and found all kinds of excuses to take her off her parents' hands. Jia didn't seem to mind, and Cees couldn't deny that small joy to his friend. He walked silently to them, his arms outreaching for the child.

"Did she behave?" Cees asked, cradling his daughter in his arms.

"When does she not behave?" Daan's long, white fingers brushed an imaginary curl from the baby's face. As it turns out, the gentle giant was a natural with babies even though he had never been around any. "Bear cubs, yes," he had explained once. "Human babies, no."

"Are you ready?" asked Lieven, stealing a glance toward the bed. "You need to wake her up. Aleid is already waiting by the shore."

"You go on ahead," Cees said. "We'll meet you there in a few."

With the two men gone, Cees sat on the edge of the bed, laid Carola by her mother, and kissed Jia's lips. "Sweetheart," he whispered over her mouth. "It's time to go. Carola is ready."

Jia opened her eyes slowly, and the face of her lover greeted her, blue eyes shining at her. "What a great way to wake up." Her eyes roamed to the baby next to her. "My two favorite faces in the world." She kissed the baby and then Cees.

It was a glorious day outside, the sun shining softly the way it often did in the autumn, still warm but allowing the cooler air to mix and mingle, giving the air a special quality of cool warmth. They walked together in no hurry, Cees carrying Carola, Jia hanging from his arm, happy and content. The walk to the beach was short. Nothing on the island was too far from the beach, and their house was no exception. In less than five minutes, they were standing by their friends, a small crowd by the shore, their light-colored clothes flapping around them as the breeze made itself noticed.

Lieven, ever the soldier even when no soldiering was needed or warranted, was wearing the modest uniform he had salvaged from the journey to the island. Cees had tried to argue with him and convince him to wear more relaxed clothing for the occasion, but he wouldn't hear any of it. This was an important event in all their lives, and in lack of anything more ceremonial, he would wear the uniform he had sworn into some years ago. Daan, on the other hand, did not stand for ceremony. Clad in all-white robes that floated around him like billowing clouds, he could have easily vanished into the white of the sands if it wasn't for his vertiginous height and oddly-spiked hair. The two made quite an odd couple with their blatant differences while at the same time blending and merging together seamlessly.

"It's about time you showed up," Lieven said, stretching out his arms to Cees who, without hesitation, handed him the baby. "We thought we were going to have to do this without the guest of honor."

Cees laughed. "Don't think that would work, Liev." He pulled Jia to his side. "Is everybody here?"

The small crowd comprised mostly of the same people who had journeyed there with them and a couple others who had joined their ranks since. They all held small bunches of greenery in their hands, collections of grasses from around the island, artistically bound together by Aleid and Daan. As they approached the sea, just where the waves turned into foam, they all removed their shoes and walked ankle deep into the cold waters of the Wadden Sea.

Lieven lifted Carola up in the air; she whimpered a little, startled awake by the movement. "Friends, family," Lieven said, his voice thick with emotion. "We are gathered here today to witness the baptism of Carola, daughter of Cees and Jia, first born citizen of *Gelijkheidland*." He lowered the child into the cocoon of his arms and she cooed. "The ocean saved us, so it is only fitting we choose it to welcome this little one into our midst."

The waves rolled almost reverently over their feet, soaking their pants and the edges of their dresses. Cees could have sworn he could feel the ocean's heart beating under his feet. He squeezed Jia's hand in his and felt a knot of emotion grow in his throat. A year ago, he was a nothing, an outcast invisible to all others, reluctantly accepting his fate as the invisible one doomed to a life of solitude. Now, here he was, surrounded by friends, a woman he loved more than life itself, and a child—a life he had somehow made. A living creature that carried his genes, his blood, and who encapsulated all his wildest dreams.

"Carola, may the liquid soul of the ocean cleanse you of any sadness, any fear." Lieven lowered the baby into the waters. "May it receive you, welcome, and protect you as it protected your parents." Carola started when her little body met the coldness of the salt waters, but then she relaxed, a contented smile stretching across her baby lips. She was home in the fluid arms of the sea. "Long live Carola!"

Everybody echoed Lieven's last words, and one by one, they threw the green bouquets into the ocean as a symbolic gift. Daan approached Lieven with a blanket to wrap the now-soaked child and to deliver her to her parents' arms.

Cees touched his lips to the baby's forehead as the *Berenjong* gently handed the child to him. Jia watched as tears welled up in Cees' eyes.

Eyes the same color as the ocean their daughter had just been immersed in. Her heart skipped a beat as she realized that the ocean that had saved them all was the same color as the eyes of the man who had saved her. She felt an overwhelming surge of love rush through her veins and fill her heart. On impulse, she stepped forward and wrapped her arms around Cees and her daughter.

"I love you both so much," she whispered, looking at her love's ocean-deep eyes. There were tears dancing in them, a few leaving streaks against his stripe as they rolled down his cheeks. She knew them to be happy tears. Her beloved *Zuiver* had no guile, no secrets. His heart was an open book that she never tired of reading.

"I can't believe how far we came," he said to her ears only. "I was a Tainted One, cursed to be mostly alone for life. And now..." The words caught in his throat.

Jia kissed him, Carola between their bodies sleeping blissfully unaware of her parents' emotional state. When their lips separated, Jia brushed her hand across his face. The dear face she loved and couldn't get enough of.

"You are not alone, *liefje*," she said, echoing his words from long ago "You are not alone anymore."

MANY THANKS

When I first published this book I was beginning to think this story would never see the light of day. Just like its characters, it's been through a lot and suffered many setbacks. But like them, it has risen against adversity and fought for its day in the spotlight and here we are with this beautiful second edition.

I'd like to thank my friends who originally read parts of it and provided me with much needed feedback: Nicole, Janna, Jenn, Guinevere, and Tammie.

Thank you to all the fantasy and sci-fi writers I've been inspired, entertained, and awed by my whole life.

For those who stand against any kind of bigotry and prejudice, I thank you. The world is a better place because of you.

For my writing groups and writer friends who both inspire and support me. You guys are awesome.

Adrijana Cernic, I am so jealous of your talent and wish I had enough money to buy ALL your cover art and enough time to write stories for all of them.

My family, here and abroad, I couldn't do it without you. Love you all.

And of course, thank you wonderful readers. Without you none of this would be possible. Keep reading. Keep dreaming.

ALSO BY

If you liked **Heart's Prey** you might want to check out Natalina Reis's other books.

Romantic Comedy:

We Will Always Have the Closet

Loved You Always

Blind Magic

Her Real Man

Fictional-ish

Dating the Intern

MM Paranormal Romance:

Lavender Fields

Infinite Blue

Of Magic & Scales

Of Scales & Fire

Of Fire & Bone

Of Tails & Mistletoe

Foxy Tails

Sleeping Love

FM Paranormal Romance/Romantasy:

Dark Feathers

Kiss of the Swan

Desert Jewel

Snow Jewel

Rebel Jewel

House of Blood and Whispers

Queen of Hearts

About the Author

Natalina Reis is an international bestseller who wrote her first romance at the age of thirteen. Since then she has published many romances that defy the boundaries of her genre. She enjoys writing all kinds of rebels and outcasts into her stories and she always roots for the underdog.

Natalina doesn't believe you can have too many books or too much coffee. Chinese historical fantasy dramas are her (not so) guilty pleasure and she is pretty sure she could survive on lobster and bananas alone.

When she is not writing or stressing over lesson plans, she shares her life with her husband and two adult sons.

To keep up to date with Natalina's news and books, follow her on the Web:

Facebook: @authornatalinareis
Website/Blog: www.natalinareis.com

GoodReads: @natalina_reis

BookBub : @natalinareis

Instagram: @reisnatalina

Enter

the magical world of

International bestselling author

NATALINA REIS

Writing romance for the rebels, the outcasts,
and the lovers unafraid to run against the grain

9 781737 441342